Better Than Nun

The Giulia Driscoll Mystery Series
by Alice Loweecey

Novels

NUN TOO SOON (#1)
SECOND TO NUN (#2)
NUN BUT THE BRAVE (#3)
THE CLOCK STRIKES NUN (#4)
NUN AFTER THE OTHER (#5)
BETTER THAN NUN (#6)

Short Stories

CHANGING HABITS
(prequel to NUN TOO SOON)

Better Than Nun

A
GIULIA DRISCOLL
MYSTERY

Alice Loweecey

HENERY PRESS

Copyright

BETTER THAN NUN
A Giulia Driscoll Mystery
Part of the Henery Press Mystery Collection

First Edition | May 2019

Henery Press
www.henerypress.com

Trade Paperback ISBN-13: 978-1-63511-479-9
Digital epub ISBN-13: 978-1-63511-480-5
Kindle ISBN-13: 978-1-63511-481-2
Hardcover ISBN-13: 978-1-63511-482-9

Printed in the United States of America

To all Giulia's fans: Thank you.

ACKNOWLEDGMENTS

First and foremost: The biggest thank you goes to Diane, who gave me the idea for the haunted drawing toy. We met over breakfast at Malice Domestic 28.

Thanks also to Shelagh, who instructed me in the ways of superpower-level online searches and Annette Dashofy, for her eternal patience with my Pittsburgh-area questions. And last but never least, *Better than Nun*'s guest stars: Dru Ann Love and Sue Ann Jaffarian.

Throwe no gyft at the giuers head
For better is halfe a lofe then no bread.

This is the original of the familiar saying "Half a loaf is better than none." In 1546, John Heywood collected all the sayings he could find in his *A dialogue conteinyng the nomber in effect of all the prouerbes in the englishe tongue.*

Eight Days to Mardi Gras

"The house doesn't look haunted." A young woman in overalls hesitated on the bottom step.

The white-haired paralegal turned to the cleaning crew with an infectious smile. "According to our records, it isn't."

"But what about all the rumors?" A second woman held a mop and bucket like a shield. "I heard the owner was murdered in his bed."

A third woman with startling blue hair stepped in front of the other two. "I heard a poltergeist frayed the wires in his bedside lamp and electrocuted him."

The paralegal's smile brightened. "The owner was somewhat eccentric. When you see his collection, you'll understand. The news outlets ran with the haunting story because it made good copy."

She unlocked the front door of the sprawling rose brick mansion and flipped on the lights.

The youngest cleaner screamed.

One

Giulia Driscoll—formerly Sister Mary Regina Coelis—shadowed the giggling creeper through the craft store. She kept out of sight without a problem now that she'd returned to her pre-pregnancy weight. The creeper was intent on the goth sixteen-year-old and never changed his laser-like focus.

Each breathy giggle added a layer of goose bumps to Giulia's skin. This guy was worse than the last ghost she'd encountered.

Wouldn't that make her assistant laugh. Sidney would probably beg to deal with the creeper instead of a ghost, but Giulia would never send her staff into danger rather than face it herself. Besides, she could take down this scarecrow in a tan raincoat in three simple moves.

The pervert, whoever he was, didn't realize he'd chosen the wrong day to pick a new victim. Glad she'd remembered at the last minute she needed picture frames, Giulia shifted them to a more comfortable position and entered the same aisle as the teenager. The creeper lurked at the opposite end, glancing at engraving tools in between sizing up his prey.

The craft store was long and narrow, squeezed on one side by a Dahlia Dress Boutique and on the other by a yoga studio. The shelving used every millimeter of available space, with items stacked an inch above the floor to an inch below the ceiling. The drop ceiling hampered the lights, giving shoppers the effect of being trapped in a dark alley.

The teenager held a different brand of miniature soldering gun in each hand. Intent on the descriptions of each, she hadn't raised her head for a good five minutes. She blended into the gloom with her black jeans, black boots, black coat, and black hair from an obvious home-dye attempt.

Giulia put herself between the teenager and the creeper. He stepped around her. The teenager returned one blister pack to the shelf and headed for the checkout. Giulia walked faster. In line behind an old woman with fifteen skeins of American Flag dyed yarn and in front of the teenager, Giulia adjusted her messenger bag and surreptitiously scanned the front of the store. The creeper had placed himself at a display of birthday cards with a direct line of sight to the cash register. He picked up a card and giggled.

Giulia stepped up to the register and leaned across the counter. "The man at the card rack is following the girl behind me."

The cashier's eyes flicked to the girl, then to the card rack. She picked up one of Giulia's picture frames with an air of looking for the UPC sticker. With her other hand she pressed her earpiece. In a low voice matching Giulia's, she said, "Suspicious customer at card rack. Escort out."

As Giulia inserted her credit card into the reader, a young man wearing a green apron over jeans and a bright blue t-shirt approached the card display. He topped the creeper by half a foot and his biceps were bigger than Giulia's head. She turned away to sign the screen. When she looked again, the door closed on the creeper's butt.

"Thank you," she said to the cashier.

"He's not the first." Her lip curled in disgust. "Two weeks ago it was the opposite. A woman about forty trying to look twenty attached herself to this cute thirteen-year-old boy buying model car kits." The curl became a grin. "I escorted her to the sidewalk and didn't offer to help when she tripped on her stilettos."

Giulia waited outside for the teenager to exit. Lord, she even wore black eye shadow. Giulia tried to remember her own years of embarrassing makeup choices, but all she could come up with was freshman year in high school when every girl in her class slathered on baby blue eyeshadow in the girls' bathroom before homeroom and the nuns made them all troop back to the bathroom to wash it off before first period.

"Excuse me."

The teenager started, then made a wide detour around Giulia.

"Excuse me." Giulia followed her.

"Get away from me. I have mace and I don't want to find Jesus or give money to charity."

"That's not what I—"

"Get lost, creep." She ran. The craft store bag bounced against her thigh until she stuffed it in a coat pocket. The high-pitched *meep* of a car unlocking and blinking headlights followed. A minute later, a well-used Ford Escort—charcoal gray—pulled away from the curb.

Two

An excited young voice greeted Giulia as she opened the door to Driscoll Investigations. Her staff—both of them—hovered at one computer monitor.

"Giulia, you have to see this." Sidney, the all-natural Earth Mother of the office, caught Giulia's sleeve and dragged her around to the monitor.

"Ms. D., *The Scoop* has leveled up." Zane, the gaming geek genius—literally—admin, offered her his chair.

"Do I want to know?" She sat. "You're watching a kid."

Sidney bounced in place. "It's *The Scoop*'s next generation. Ken Kanning's son has his own YouTube channel."

Giulia buried her face in her hands. "You people are obsessed."

"Ms. D., anything Kanning is the pinnacle of entertainment."

Giulia pushed back the chair. "Talk to me when you end up on one of his *TMZ*-wannabe shows."

"That would be so cool," Sidney said.

"My girlfriend would be thrilled," Zane said.

Giulia groaned. "I shall await my one-thirty appointment in the solitude of my office," she opened her door, "which will not have *The Scoop* or its spawn on the monitor."

She categorized emails and wrote up case reports for twenty-five minutes, then called Sidney's mother.

"Gabrielle, how's everything going with Finn?"

"He is a little trickster." Her voice was a clone of her daughter's, perkiness and all. "I fed him and he reached up like he wanted to hold my finger and instead he *booped* my nose."

Giulia's voice hitched. "I wish I could've seen it."

"Now, honey, don't get all postpartum weepy on yourself. You'll see him in a few hours and he'll give you all the *boops* you can handle." A toddler's cry came through the phone. "Uh-oh. I took my eye off my granddaughter for ten seconds. Talk to you later."

Giulia hung up and buzzed Sidney. "Have I told you your mother is the best day care person on the planet?"

"At least once a day. You should worry about Jessamine. She thinks your Finn is better than any of her dolls and she'll probably want to marry him."

"I see no problems with our children forming a lifelong bond."

"You will if the evils of processed sugar come between them."

"Sidney, you do realize your passion for all-natural ingredients means Jessamine will most likely become a Hostess Cupcake addict."

Sidney's voice dropped. "If your clients hadn't just opened the door, my response would get me an official reprimand."

Giulia laughed in her ear and hung up. Zane buzzed an instant later. "Ms. D., your one thirty is here."

One half of Giulia's one thirty was a prematurely old man who once must have been tall but was now hunched with arthritis. A neat white fringe ringed his egg-bald head. His faded brown eyes matched the faded brown suit hanging loosely on his frame. He might have been the jolly uncle at family gatherings if his frown ever lifted.

The other half was a tiny, much older woman whose long gray dress was also too big for her. From its many repairs, Giulia figured it was a favorite garment. She herself had a bright red sweater in her closet with half a dozen mends. The woman's faded blue eyes blended well with the gray dress. Despite her colorless face, she looked like a walnut with a gray wig and thin lips.

Giulia rose. "Good afternoon Ms. Burd, Mr. Jevens. How can Driscoll Investigations help you?"

"It's good to see manners in the younger generation, isn't it, Owen?" The old woman *humphed* and sat in the chair near the window.

"Get over it, Blossom." The old man sat. "If you're going to waste our time moralizing, play *Candy Crush* on your phone while I conduct business with the detective."

"At least I have a hobby besides negotiating endless business deals."

"Which keep a roof over our heads." He wrenched his face into a less-forbidding expression. "Ms. Driscoll, I don't know if you're familiar with the upcoming Children with Cancer charity event?"

Few things made Giulia the detective happier than clients who didn't censor their personal lives in front of her. "Yes, I've been seeing ads for it on TV."

"Our family is the driving force behind this year's event. Our father—"

"Your father. My brother-in-law." Blossom's hands twitched in her lap.

"Details. My father the family tyrant had offered his unique house for this year's venue, as long as it took place on Mardi Gras. He also stipulated that it had to be a costume party."

Giulia took notes on her usual yellow legal pad. "Yes?"

"He died six months and three weeks ago."

"I'm sorry."

Blossom gave a short laugh. "Don't be. Our lives are better without the kook, even though the cops think we killed him."

"Blossom, think of the impression we're giving the detective."

"We'd give a worse one if we told her he was the salt of the earth or that children and puppies flocked around him every time he went for a walk." She transferred her pale eyes to Giulia. "The housekeeper found him on his bedroom floor with his hand still holding his antique nightstand lamp. The wires were frayed in a suspicious manner, the police said. It wouldn't have killed a younger person, but the shock was too much for Vernon. He would've been ninety-eight years old last Halloween."

Owen picked up the story. "My father was a collector. He crammed his house with hunting trophies, bizarre paintings, and ridiculous antiques he claimed were haunted. The police assumed I killed him for his money."

Blossom interrupted. "I hated him and never made a secret of it. They think I killed him because he kept trying to scare me into an early grave. I never crossed the threshold of the nonsensical house after he tricked me one night by rigging the eyes of a china doll to glow in the dark."

Owen coughed out a grating chuckle. "Best laugh I've had in my entire life. See what I mean, Ms. Driscoll, about our esteemed deceased relative? He liked to play games. Never mind if the rest of the family wanted to join in. One Christmas Eve—"

"Owen, we're here on business."

Owen showed all his teeth to Blossom in what might have been a smile. "Thank you for your timely reminder, dear aunt. Ms. Driscoll, we want to hire your firm for next Tuesday's shindig."

Giulia's pen hovered above the paper. "To guard the charity donations?"

"Certainly not. The charity organizers hired off-duty policemen to take care of the money. You'll be working for us, the family."

Years of dealing with the public enabled Giulia to pretend she hadn't heard the implied insult.

"In what capacity?"

"Getting back what belongs to us." Owen snapped open the locks on his briefcase. "Charity is a fine idea, except when it empties the pockets of your family." He removed three printouts and set them on Giulia's desk. "Ever see those old movies where a lawyer reads a will to the family a few days after the patriarch kicks off? They're hogwash. The courts took six months to prove my father's will. If his lawyer had come to our house and read that piece of toilet paper to our faces, my nephew would've led the charge over our dining room table to throttle the leech."

Giulia scanned the papers: A list of stock certificates, an investment summary, and a bank statement. "Vernon Jevens' estate was extensive."

"Was." Blossom poked the paper in Giulia's hand. "Look at the amounts he willed to the paranormal societies in Pittsburgh and Philadelphia and New York City. And the National Taxidermy Foundation. And do you see those ruinous grants to several struggling-artist foundations?"

"The only space on the 'Will of the Rich and Eccentric' bingo card he missed was a cat rescue foundation." Owen's voice dripped disgust. "Before you ask, the family lawyers told us it'd be a waste of time to contest the will. The shysters were honest enough to admit they couldn't in good conscience take money for a venture doomed to fail."

"Mr. Jevens, if you could give me details of what exactly you hope DI can do for you?" Giulia was on the cusp of escorting them out.

More extracts from the briefcase. "Look at these pictures. I took them last week when we were allowed to enter my father's house again."

Giulia raised her eyebrows. While she was still trying to craft a neutral remark, Owen saved her the trouble.

"You don't have to be polite. The place looks like all three days of the Cottonwood art festival vomited all over the house."

A photo in each hand, Giulia identified a dozen papier-mâché sculptures attached to floors, walls, and even ceilings, another dozen framed paintings of varying skills and styles, and what looked like life-size china dolls posed with equally tall Cabbage Patch-style creations. The combined effect made her dizzy.

"My brother-in-law was raised by pack rats." Blossom plucked one photo from Giulia's hands. "My mother's side of the family wasn't. When my sensibilities became accustomed to the shambles, I saw a houseful of opportunities to squirrel items away."

"She convinced me," Owen said. "We knew our family would have neither the time nor the manpower—"

"And womanpower," Blossom murmured.

"Manpower," Owen repeated. Blossom made a face at him. At least Giulia thought she saw a few more wrinkles form around the old woman's nose.

"My point is, the fundraiser is in eight days. The house will be wall-to-wall people. If Blossom could see the danger, anyone can. We want you to watch the attendees. My father must have hidden money in the house. He loved to play games only he thought were funny."

Blossom made a sound not usually made by ladies. "He especially liked to hint about his will. I lost my temper once and dropped a stack of murder mysteries on his writing desk. In every one of those books the rich murder victim taunted their relatives about the contents of their last will. He laughed and kept dropping hints."

Giulia made some mental calculations. "How extensive is the house?"

"Here." Owen held up a third photo.

Without hesitation, Giulia said, "The project is outside the scope of our company."

Owen set the photo on the desk and slapped a banded stack of twenties on top of it. "Will this change your mind?"

The magic words "Finn's college fund" danced across Giulia's vision. But she willed them away and shook her head. "Thank you for your offer, but the project is outside the scope of Driscoll Investigations."

Rather than answering, Owen said to Blossom: "See?"

His aunt waved a withered hand. "Fine. Make it happen."

Now Owen grinned at Giulia. "That was a test. We researched you before making this appointment. Your reputation for honesty isn't exaggerated. It's essential for what we need."

Giulia knew her irritation leaked into the curve of her polite smile.

Blossom cut in. "We're also concerned my brother-in-law leaked information to one or all of the charities who stole our inheritance from us and is sending representatives to the party. We're worried they'll find our money when everyone's too busy to notice them."

Owen followed up. "We're convinced my father used his unnatural fondness for tricks on the crazy objects in his house. He hid money in there. I guarantee he thought we'd deserve it only if we could find it ourselves."

"My idiot nephew here paid good money to a psychic before we called you." Blossom brushed at the wrinkles in her dress. "I told him just because I've never seen a ghost doesn't mean they don't exist, but psychics are nothing but spiritual pickpockets."

Her nephew ignored this remark and continued to address Giulia. "We're operating on the assumption that everyone's hands are grabbing at our inheritance. Charities aren't staffed by disinterested angels. They're full of people scheming for new ways to part the rich from their riches. We need you to keep the charity siphon out of our pockets."

He set six colorful tickets on the desk. "These are for you and your staff plus one guest each. What we want is quite simple. You six come in costume like everyone else. You eat and drink and mingle. At the same time, you watch everyone, and I mean everyone. I'm not even sure I trust the cops who will be guarding the gambling money. You're detectives. You're used to being suspicious. We want you to put that suspicion to work for us."

Giulia tried another tactic. "Mr. Jevens, DI doesn't offer any guarantees."

He held up a hand. "We don't think you're God the Omniscient and Omnipresent and all those other Omnis. I'm a businessman. I understand contract limitations." He produced a charming smile. "As I said earlier, we chose your agency for several reasons."

Giulia locked her screen. "One moment, please." She opened her door and went into the main office, leaving the door open because she too trusted no one, especially after the last break-in attempt.

"Guys, conference, please."

Sidney and Zane glanced into Giulia's office then followed her to the table under the window.

Giulia kept her voice low. "You know about the big Mardi Gras charity party?"

"Sure," Zane said. "It's been in the paper and on the news for weeks."

"My one thirty wants us to attend."

"Cool," Sidney said. "Wait. Why?"

Giulia explained the proposal.

"It's bigger than our usual case." Zane's "Genius at Work" face appeared.

"We can't be everywhere at once," Sidney said. "Are we going to hire anyone?"

"No. Not even temporarily. There's no time to work someone new into our dynamic."

Zane's face returned to the mundane. "I can write an algorithm to make us as efficient as possible for the duration of the event." He met her eyes. "I can't give 100 percent assurance of effectiveness."

"Don't worry. I told them we don't guarantee results." She leaned closer. "They're offering tickets for each of us plus a guest. Are you willing to make it a working evening at overtime rates? Sidney, can your mother watch Jessamine? Zane, do you have a commitment?"

"A night out?" Sidney said. "The answer is yes, yes, and yes."

"My girlfriend Dru Ann will be thrilled. She says we spend too many evenings in."

Giulia blew out a breath. "On your heads be it."

Three

Owen and Blossom signed both copies of DI's standard client agreement with unconcealed satisfaction.

"If you'll write a check for our retainer as indicated in paragraph 'e' on page two," Giulia said, "we can conclude business for today."

Owen laid the stack of twenties on DI's copy of the agreement. "Nope. Blossom and I discussed the money beforehand. This is your retainer. You have to spend money to make money."

"Don't forget inheriting money counts too," Blossom said.

Owen chuckled.

When the clients left, Giulia balanced the banded twenties in her hand in the middle of the main office. She was rewarded with a jaw drop and a gasp.

"Do I dare ask how much?" Sidney said.

"The violet strap means I'm holding two thousand dollars."

Zane whistled. "Lunch on the new clients?"

"Really good lunch on the new clients?" Sidney waved the folder of menus she kept at her desk.

"As tempting as lunch sounds, we will be upping our game to account for every penny of this retainer." She set the cash on Zane's desk. "I don't trust these clients not to turn on us. They're angry, greedy, and were backstabbing each other in my office."

"Maybe it's time for another ghost." Zane winked at Giulia.

Sidney glared.

Giulia bit her lips. Even after several months and a handful of unequivocal ghostly cases, Sidney was not quite reconciled to DI's new venture. At least the ghosts handled all the advertising for the supernatural arm of the business. From what Giulia understood, the dead communicated through a superpowered version of The Twilight Bark.

Since Sidney was a huge Disney fan, Giulia didn't mention the ghostly comparison to the dog messaging scene in *101 Dalmatians*.

Zane reached for his coat. "I'll deposit this. Should I make a side trip for coffee?"

"Always," Giulia ran into her office and returned with three dollars. "Any syrup."

"Chamomile smoothie, please." Sidney added her offering.

"It's a good thing the baristas downstairs know us."

The phone rang. Zane picked it up with the hand not tangled in his peacoat. "Driscoll Investigations. How may I direct your call?...One moment, please." He hit the hold button and took a second to compose himself. "It's *The Scoop*. They want to make an appointment."

"Maybe a new ghost would be better," Sidney said. "No, I don't really mean it. Ken Kanning is predictable. I wouldn't mind a little predictability in my workday."

Zane kept his inquiring gaze on Giulia. The seconds lengthened.

She made a gesture of acquiescence. "Give them an appointment."

Seven Days to Mardi Gras

"Welcome to Part One of *The Scoop*'s in-depth report on the life of Cottonwood, Pennsylvania's favorite eccentric philanthropist: Vernon Jevens."

Ken Kanning flashed his gleaming smile at the camera. The thin February sun struck highlights from his rich brown hair and emphasized the cold, red tip of his nose. His bronze blazer contrasted with the withered post-winter grass. The ruddy stone wall behind him offset his burnished skin. His cameraman, Pit Bull, approved of the effect. More so because he'd set up this shot on purpose to minimize his editing time.

The face of Cottonwood's most popular—or most controversial, depending on whether its host had ever launched himself and his camera at them for a story—local TV show gestured to the niches in the stone wall.

"For any Scoopers who haven't been to the First Church of Cottonwood's cemetery in a while, this is an urn garden. No more taping flowers to a mausoleum wall where they wither in a couple of days. Out in the sunshine you can plant actual flowers around your loved one's final resting place."

The camera zoomed in on a cookie jar-shaped urn decorated with multicolored swirls like a psychedelic Easter egg. The more sedate urns on either side were plain chrome and wood. The camouflage urn beneath it looked drab by comparison.

"Vernon Jevens loved art and he loved to shock people. Only he would commission an urn decorated by a hippie on acid." He paused. "That'll never fly. Bull, you'll have to cut the last sentences. I'll start again." A pause. "Three. Two. One. Vernon Jevens loved art. He commissioned this unique urn to put a smile on the faces of people coming here to remember him." Another pause. "Crap. Woman and two kids headed this way. Let's shoot an intro over by the garden sign."

Four

Ken Kanning arrived at nine o'clock on the dot Tuesday morning, without Pit Bull in tow. As soon as Giulia heard his ultra-smooth voice in the outer office, she knew she still hadn't hit on an effective prep method for withstanding lengthy Kanning time. She slugged more French roast with crème brulée syrup and opened her door.

"Good morning, Mr. Kanning. Please come in."

Zane kept a poker face but Sidney ducked behind her monitor. Giulia knew her own professional mask was the cause. It was the opposite of her attitude toward *The Scoop* every other day, but this was business. She closed herself in with Kanning.

"Giulia, you're looking terrific." Kanning leaned back in the client chair. "My ex didn't bother to get back her figure until Kord was three. He's my youngest."

It would be a waste of excellent coffee to "accidentally" tip her cup into his lap. She repeated this to herself twice as she took out a legal pad and sat with the desk as a buffer between them.

"Mr. Kanning, how can DI help you?"

He sat up in the chair. "You're right. Family stories are for beers during Happy Hour. I want to talk to you about Kord." He poked his phone and turned the screen toward her. "Spitting image of me, isn't he? My ex is good-looking, but both the kids inherited the never-fail Kanning charm. Kord will make it big one day."

Giulia waited with her pen still capped.

"Pull up YouTube and type in 'Kord's Kernels' with two *K*s."

She recited *a haon...a dó...a trí...a ceathair...*to herself as she typed. Counting to ten in Irish came as easily as Latin to her after two years of marriage, and it was just as effective a way to keep her temper. She didn't tell Kanning she'd already been exposed to one of his son's videos.

"What is it you'd like me to see?"

Kanning jumped around the desk and breathed down her neck. "This is my son's channel. Look at the kid. He's going to revolutionize the way the world sees news." He took the mouse and scrolled down the list of videos. Giulia had to count all the way to *a deich* before she allowed her hand to unclench.

"Here's his series on bullying. These are a two-parter on school lunch nutrition. These four are movie reviews. See the football fields? He's a sideline reporter for his brother's JV games." The pride in Kanning's voice sounded different from his usual innate egotism. Giulia was almost prepared to believe something was more important to him than *The Scoop*.

"This is the series I need you to see." He scrolled back to the top of the list and clicked on a video series titled "The Epic Science Fair Project."

Excitement and geekiness radiated from the scrawny middle schooler on the screen. Listening to his high, boyish voice right after his father's deeper one emphasized the similarity of inflection, sensationalism, and reporting styles.

"He's modeled himself after you."

Kanning's grin threatened to split his face in half. "Isn't he something? Here, let me get to the important part." He paused the playback, clicked on the third video in the series, and hit "play" again.

"We got the supplies in yesterday and we're ready to start making Kord's Whiteboard." Mini-Kanning winked at the camera. "The other name for this red plotting toy with the big white knobs is copyrighted, so this project will be 100 percent my very own, right down to the name."

Giulia retrieved her mouse and paused the playback. "Mr. Kanning, a summary would be appreciated."

Kanning *humphed*. "Bull said motherhood would mellow you. He owes me five bucks." He backed off but stayed on Giulia's side of the desk. "Kord's mother cleaned out the attic and tossed a pile of old, broken toys. He got the idea to recreate that particular toy for his science fair project. Can you draw anything with it? I can't even make a straight line on one. Kord loves to take things apart and see how they work. For this project he corralled his sitter into helping him. He's got a crush on her so bad he might as well tattoo her face over his heart."

Giulia started writing. "He looks too old for a sitter."

"My ex works at one of the big hotel chains. They all have to take turns working the lousy shifts and she doesn't want Kord and his brother alone late at night. Before you ask, the divorce was as friendly as possible. We put the kids first. This girl's been his sitter since Kord was eight." He poked the legal pad. "Keep writing. I'm on point. Kord did the lion's share of the work because it was his science fair project. He won, of course. Offered his sitter half the prize money, but she wanted the toy instead. He figured he could always make another, so he gave it to her."

Giulia stopped writing. "Mr. Kanning."

"Have faith. Hah. See what I did there? Here's the payoff. The sitter was a real daddy's girl, but her dad kicked off last summer. She's been moping ever since. A week after the science fair, she came over and babbled that she talked to her daddy. Kord swears sparks were shooting off her."

Giulia wondered what recent sin she'd committed to bring Ken Kanning plus a potential ghost into her life.

"Kord was all over it like a rash. My ex, not so much. She was born with a pole up her butt. Says I only married her because her name begins with a 'K.' With that attitude, you're probably wondering how we lasted long enough to make two kids."

"I am not."

Another annoyed noise. "Fine. So the love of Kord's adolescence claimed she got a message from her dead father on the drawing toy. Here's the twist: She couldn't get it to work when I was there, but two days later, Kord called me. He couldn't stop squeaking, poor kid. He's dying for his voice to change. He said his sitter got another message on the science project and he filmed the whole thing."

Five

Playing Devil's Advocate against *The Scoop* came as easily to Giulia as drinking French roast coffee. "Mr. Kanning, I could give you four ways such a message could be a hoax without batting an eye."

"Bingo." Kanning grabbed her left hand and shook it. "You grate on me like a piece of sandpaper sometimes, but I knew you were the only person for this job. Go to the video with the clickbait title."

Giulia scrolled. "The one titled 'You Have to Watch This?'"

"Yeah. Kord's smart, but he's not Internet-savvy yet. It's okay to click. I've checked everything. He's virus-free."

Anything to get Kanning out of her office. She clicked.

"Guys, guys, guys, you are not going to believe this!" Kanning had been right. His son was squeaking. "This is Kord Kanning with today's installment of Kord's Kernels. Sit down, guys. I mean it. Remember my first-place science project? The Whiteboard?" He pointed to his left. "Scroll through my video thumbnails on your right and you'll see the series. Do that later, okay? Listen to me now." He bounced in his office-style chair but when the picture jiggled, he settled down. "Sorry about that. My camera has a warning light when it isn't stable. My dad, Ken Kanning of *The Scoop*, installed it for me." His skinny hand reached for something off screen. "Come on, Shiloh." Another voice whispered off screen. "Come on. This could be your big break." The whispering got more intense and Kord released what he'd been tugging. "Okay. Cool. I got it. My friend Shiloh says she wants me to keep the spotlight." He held up a white plastic square with a clear glass or plastic center inset and two white knobs in the bottom corners. "Here's Kord's Whiteboard. It's a cool project, yeah, but there is so much more to it now!"

Against her will, Giulia found herself liking this miniature Ken Kanning. His sincere enthusiasm was a welcome change from his father's manufactured excitement pasted on for Pit Bull's camera.

The middle-schooler demonstrated how his project worked, then leapt into his news. "Shiloh's dad died last July and she misses him a lot. She's really into those ghost hunting TV shows, too. So when I gave her my Whiteboard, she tried to talk to her dad's ghost." He looked to his right again. "Please?" More whispering followed by a pout. The pout changed to an "on camera" face a moment later. "Shiloh says she's not into cameras but she'll work the knobs for me. Okay, here we go."

He set the toy on a work table. The video's perspective swooped up until the viewer was looking down at the table.

Kord's voice continued: "I'm going to ask a question and Shiloh will write it out for me and then you'll see something amazing. My question is: Where are my lucky socks?"

Thin fingers with chipped black nail polish reached into the picture and manipulated the round white knobs. They twisted and turned, writing out Kord's question in a long, connected string of letters in the top half of the screen.

Kord's voice again: "Now we have to wait. I hope it won't take too long, because I can't stop recording and start again. If I do, I'll get a hundred comments calling it 'fake.'"

A shaking finger pointed to the screen.

Kord's voice jumped an octave and a half. "Look! Look! We're getting an answer!"

The knobs turned on their own, drawing a shorter string of connected letters: *Basketball bag.*

Giulia reached for the mouse, but Kanning said, "Wait."

The video careened down as though it was riding the Cyclone on Coney Island. "Shiloh, record me." The video swung to the left. Kord was rummaging in a closet. A generous person would call the space "chaotic."

"I looked through my bag on Saturday." He dug through the shambles and pulled out a large green gym bag. "They're not in here." He dumped the contents of the bag on the floor. "See? No lucky socks. I even checked the zipper pockets." He turned the outer ones inside out and punched his hand into the empty bag. "The one inside here for shoes is always empty—wait a sec." His eyes widened. "Bring the camera closer. Not too close. Keep the bag in the shot."

The camera stopped moving. Kord yanked the entire bag inside out. A third zipper pocket at the short end of the bag appeared to have a slight bulge. "I checked everywhere, I swear." He pulled the zipper around the end and a pair of bright blue socks with an allover pattern of basketballs fell to the floor.

Kord stared at them open-mouthed.

Six

Ken Kanning took over the mouse again and paused the video.

Giulia clipped every word of her next sentence: "Mr. Kanning, keep your hands to yourself."

He laughed. "That could be interpreted the wrong way."

She looked him in the eyes. "My statement was perfectly clear."

"Yeah, in context."

"Mr. Kanning, in one sentence, what is your request?"

Her aura, if such things existed, must have reacted against his the way similar poles of magnets repel each other. He retreated to the opposite side of the desk. "Kord set up a live test of his science project. I want you there as the control group."

She pretended to misinterpret. "Crowd control is a job for a security company."

"No, no, no. Come on, you know about scientific experiments. Kord needs a reputable and impartial observer to prove he's not rigging his gizmo."

Giulia's common sense held a megaphone to her ear and yelled "Say no."

She said to Kanning, "Will *The Scoop* be there?"

"Do you have to ask?" I'm compiling an episode about ground-breaking local students. It wouldn't look right for me to give Kord an episode all to himself." The Smile appeared. "If my son really trapped a fortune-telling ghost, you're the perfect inquisitor for his challenge."

Giulia tried again. "There are several other detective agencies in the greater Pittsburgh area."

The Smile gleamed. "None of those other detectives dislike me enough to be completely impartial."

Giulia didn't even blush. By that logic, he had a point.

"Point to me," he said as she thought it. "If it turns out Kord did something stupid to entertain his subscribers, one of my fans might be tempted to spin the story to kiss my butt."

"You do have enthusiastic fans."

He leaned across the desk. "This is my son we're talking about. He thinks he's got a pet ghost and you're the ghost detective. We both know not all ghosts can be trusted. I want you to protect my son."

If Giulia ever cursed, she'd be heaping profanity on herself right now. She opened her mouth and said, "What day and time is this live challenge?"

Kanning pumped his fist in triumph. "I knew I could reach you. It's tomorrow at four o'clock after school. His mother would have a cow if I pulled him out of classes again."

Giulia opened the master calendar on her computer. "A little more notice would have been preferable."

"You can handle it. Besides, Kord only issued the invitation the day before yesterday. He told me about it when he asked us to film it." Kanning shook his head with an indulgent expression. "The kid is constitutionally incapable of planning ahead."

"Four o'clock tomorrow. Location?"

"The town soccer complex, field A. Wear boots. Sunday's thaw turned the turf into a mud pit."

Giulia pressed the intercom button. "Zane, please print out our client agreement for Mr. Kanning."

Zane brought it in with the straightest face she'd seen on him since his initial interview.

Kanning skimmed it. "You should charge more. People will think you're second class."

Giulia said, "Please sign on page two. How will you be paying our retainer?"

He handed her a Mastercard with a grimace. "If my self-esteem relied on how others perceive me, your attitude would drive me to drink."

Giulia took out her phone and attached the card reader to it. A minute later she emailed Kanning a copy of his receipt. "It's always good to be comfortable in your own skin." She said the cliché without gagging.

Her new client indulged in a gagging noise as loud as a belch. "I can't stand greeting card sentiments." His phone chimed. "Got the receipt."

Giulia stood. "We'll meet you at the soccer field before four tomorrow."

She walked him to the door more to make sure he left than out of politeness. As soon as the downstairs door screeched shut, a series of beeps came from Sidney's phone.

"911? Our boss just took on *The Scoop* as a client. She's obviously hallucinating. Send help quick."

Seven

Giulia described the project after they all stopped laughing. "Zane, I'd like you with me on this."

"You got it, Ms. D. Expecting trouble?"

"From our client if his son turns out to have faked the ghost messages." She held up a hand. "I'm not saying this simply because he's a Kanning. He might have fallen under the compulsion to amass more and more YouTube followers."

Kord Kanning's voice came from Sidney's speakers. She frowned at the screen. "Could be magnets from this angle."

The high voice overlapped as Zane's speakers started. Zane's frown mirrored Sidney's. "I can't see a fishing line in real time, but if I download the video and slow the playback I might."

"Add to those the obvious possibility of a Kanning indulging in a spot of video manipulation." Giulia ticked off the theories on her fingers. "What if he planted the socks in his gym bag ahead of time? He could be a great actor."

"You sound like the masked magician who reveals all the magic trick secrets." Sidney made a face. "When you know how the trick is done, all the fun goes out of it. I mean, I know the magician planted a sugar packet in the middle of the lemon before he started, but it's so cool to watch him pretend to cut it open and see the look on everyone's face."

Zane stared at her with one eyebrow raised. "What are you talking about?"

"Table magic. It's the perfect choice for a date night. Giulia, do you really think the little Kanning would be unethical just to get more followers?"

Giulia came around to Sidney's monitor. "Can I drive?" She froze the video on the feminine hand with chipped nail polish. "If not for views, he might exaggerate to impress the owner of these fingernails."

Zane got a faraway look. "When my parents divorced, I went to live with my dad. I was ten and he spent every weekend with one of his girlfriends. He hired our next-door-neighbor's daughter to stay with me every Saturday morning through Sunday afternoon."

"Did she break your pre-pubescent heart?" Sidney said.

"Not on purpose. Her family moved to California when I was twelve and a half and she was sixteen." The reminiscent expression lingered. "She was tall and her skin was the color of chestnuts fresh out of their green prickly shells. I stayed awake coming up with ways to touch the smooth, soft skin on her hand. She liked to dye her hair in layers of color, usually red, blonde, and black. We played *Final Fantasy* and *Zelda* for hours. It took me four months to finally beat her in a game."

Giulia and Sidney stared at him, mouths open. His colorless face had a pale red tinge. A minute later he shook himself and the tinge receded.

"So, yes, it's possible Kanning's kid may have falsified data to impress the girl."

Eight

Giulia beckoned everyone into her office. "Since I plan to jettison *The Scoop* after tomorrow's event, on to our real client." She slid the photos toward them. "This is the Mardi Gras house."

"You're kidding," Sidney said.

"Someone lived in this artist's nightmare?" Zane studied one of the photos. "The stuffed doll riding the tricycle nailed to the ceiling looks like my cousin on a bender."

"Is the whole house like this?" Sidney leaned over Zane's arm to see the other picture.

"As far as I know the place is a hoarder's nightmare. I've asked the clients for the blueprints so we can strategize without distractions. They're having them couriered over."

Zane radiated innocence. "If the house is haunted, you could get the resident ghost to give us a hand."

Giulia's radiation matched his. "If the house is haunted, I could ask the resident ghost if there are any hidden valuables and this will be the easiest two thousand we've ever earned." She thought a moment. "The family says they're suspected of having caused Jevens' death. The ghost could help us with that, too. Or I could call my personal police detective. She dialed. "Frank? Can you tell me if Vernon Jevens' family are still suspects in his death?...Thanks." She put down the phone. "We'll have the answer by tomorrow."

A knock at the outer door. "Faster Than Light Delivery."

Sidney opened it. "At least they're quick." She signed for the package. "Stop laughing. I didn't mean to make a joke."

They spread the blueprints out on the table beneath the window.

"On paper it looks like a normal house," Sidney said.

"A normal house with four bedrooms, two bathrooms, an outdoor kitchen, and a separate apartment in the basement." Giulia calculated the mortgage payment and utility bills and shuddered.

Zane jabbed a finger on the backyard layout. "Look at the pool they planned."

Sidney bent over it. "Somebody give me a napkin so I don't drool on the blueprints."

Giulia brought a pen and legal pad from her office. "Four bedrooms, two bathrooms, family room, dining room, game room, library, kitchen..." She stopped writing and dialed the client. "Mr. Jevens? Giulia Driscoll. Thank you for the blueprints. Will all rooms in the house be open for the event?...I see. Thank you." She pocketed her phone and picked up the pen again. "The good news is all entrances to the downstairs apartment will be locked for the party. The bad news is we still have to cover nine...eleven...twelve rooms, plus bathrooms." She picked up the top page and compared the two floors again. "Zane, how's your progress on cloning and teleportation?"

"Behind schedule, I'm afraid. The permits are all tangled up in red tape."

"We'll have to handle this the old-fashioned way, then."

"Wait." Sidney held her hand between them like a crossing guard. "What are you talking about?"

Giulia's smile was rueful. "We're fantasizing about science fiction methods of being everywhere at once for the party."

Sidney returned the smile. "After all this time with Zane, I should've known. Pretend I didn't say anything."

Giulia began again. "First, schedules. My in-laws will watch Finn overnight. Sidney, what about Jessamine?"

"Olivier's mom and dad have volunteered to spoil her rotten. This will be our first night out in two and a half months, woohoo!"

"But it's a working night out."

"Out is out. You'll understand soon enough. I'm sure we'll have time for one dance. We haven't danced since I got so pregnant my arms couldn't reach his shoulders."

"Frank said the same thing, especially about Finn interfering with our nights out. Zane, is Dru Ann okay with the plan?"

"Yes, if we get to dance." He made a helpless gesture. "Are all women hard-wired to dance at parties or it doesn't count as a real party?"

Giulia and Sidney laughed. "Maybe," Giulia said. "Now for costumes. We have to be able to move about freely, so no Bronies."

Sidney stamped her feet in laughter.

Zane said with obvious restraint, "Ms. D., if I didn't value my job, I'd reply. As it is, I didn't hear the 'b' word."

Giulia fist bumped him. "There's hope for you yet."

Sidney pouted. "I guess I can't indulge my Disney fantasies and go as Belle."

"Why not?"

"Hoop skirt. I want to do it right or not at all."

"My secret wish to create an authentic Godzilla costume must also remain unfulfilled."

"You could've saved yourself a lot of money in padding if you'd dressed as the big lizard last Halloween when you were pregnant." Sidney made a picture frame with her thumbs and index fingers and scrutinized Giulia through it. "Now you'll need two king-sized pillows, at least."

"I'll keep it in mind for the next pregnancy. The real trouble is we have less than a week to come up with costumes. The rest of Cottonwood has most likely left nothing on local shelves we can use."

Zane returned to his desk. "Amazon to the rescue."

"Good idea, but not right now," Giulia said. "Otherwise we'll spend all afternoon down the online rabbit hole. Today's task is our preliminary strategy for next Tuesday."

"I've got it," Sidney said. "We'll all go as Power Rangers. I call pink."

"Stop," Zane said. His fingers flew over the board. "I remembered something important."

They waited.

"Here it is. Our dysfunctional clients weren't exactly honest with you, Ms. D. Vernon Jevens didn't stop at collecting kitsch and amateur art. He was also a patron of haunted objects."

"They mentioned it."

"Only a mention? I went down a rabbit hole while I was

researching the family. One of the paranormal organizations he willed money to gave an interview to their local paper about how they helped him acquire a possessed doll they'd investigated." He looked across the room. "Sidney, I won't show you the video clips."

"You're on my friend list again."

Zane continued. "Another reporter got him to show off his collection. No pictures of the house as it is now, but we have glamour shots of two dolls, one dollhouse, a mirror, a wedding dress, and a rotting Bible."

"He was taken for a ride," Giulia said. "I guarantee half of those are exactly what they appear to be and nothing else. No. Three-quarters."

Zane said, "What about the other quarter?"

Giulia headed for her computer. "I'm going to find out."

Nine

Giulia was crying on the couch with Finn in her lap when Frank came home at six p.m.

"*Muírnin?* What's wrong?" He dropped his car keys on the foyer floor and ran into the family room.

"He *booped* my nose," she blubbered. "Gabrielle said he did it to her today and she said not to worry, that I didn't miss the only time he'd do it and she was right." A huge sniff. "He's so adorable."

Detective Frank Driscoll looked like he needed to make an emergency phone call to Dear Abby. "I'll get you a tissue."

When he returned from upstairs Giulia was finishing Finn's supper. She took the tissue in her free hand and blew into it. "Thanks. Sorry I freaked you out. I think my hormones aren't quite re-regulated yet." She stroked the baby's cheek. "He was starving tonight."

"So am I." Frank pulled a pitiful face.

"Chicken and rice casserole in the oven. Should be ready in fifteen minutes."

He kissed her forehead. "You're the perfect wife." He kissed his first-born's forehead. "Wait 'til you taste your mom's cooking."

Giulia flung a cloth over her shoulder and hoisted Finn up to it. Frank snatched up his phone and hit the record button as Giulia patted the baby's back. An epic belch issued from the tiny mouth. Frank high fived the small hand.

"Dear, please don't post that online."

"No worries. I'm only sending it to my brothers."

She rearranged her clothes. "Will your brother the priest appreciate it?"

"He'll thank me for reminding him why he's not married." When the picture had been sent, he said, "Vernon Jevens. Coroner said death was caused by heart failure, probably after a lamp he touched shorted out. Guy was almost one hundred years old. That being said, his loving family were waiting with bated breath for him to kick off, and any one of the three could've messed with the lamp."

"Is the case still open?"

"Technically, but the homicide guys said it's more likely the house poltergeist killed him, because the family's too shrewd to risk losing their share of the estate."

"The house poltergeist?"

"So the rumor says."

"Wonderful."

Six Days to Mardi Gras

The last cleaning shift finished before sunset. The cheerful paralegal paid the head of the crew and locked up the house.

Two minivans and one compact drove down the long, curving driveway. The paralegal pulled to the side and locked the entrance gates after the procession.

At dusk, a family of deer wandered into the landscaping and dined on the arbor vitae. When night fell, groundhogs moved in to nose through the dead winter grass.

Hours after the animals returned to the woods, a light appeared in one of the second-floor windows. It glowed like a candle yet moved from window to window without flickering. If the house had been built near a swamp, observers would have called it a will-o'-the-wisp.

Ten

Late February weather pulled its third about-face of the week. This morning it produced forty-mile-per-hour winds, which threatened to turn the Nunmobile into Dorothy's house from *The Wizard of Oz.* The single bag of cheap cat litter in the trunk needed a companion. The thought of trading in the Nunmobile for something with more bulk was blasphemy, plain and simple.

The Cottonwood Herald had survived downsizing, a takeover by the Pittsburgh *Post-Gazette,* and wrenching itself into the digital age. *The Cottonwood Post-Herald* occupied an office building half its former size with room for a single small web press in its basement.

Giulia waited for the receptionist to remove the jam from her desktop printer. "Good morning. I have a nine o'clock appointment with Opal Watson."

A perfunctory smile. "One moment, please." She stabbed the phone buttons with a tiger-striped fingernail. "Opal? You have an appointment not in the system?...Could you please remember to add all appoints to the calendar? Thanks." The tiger nail pointed to Giulia's left. "She's through there, down the central cubicle aisle. Fifth one on the right."

"Thank you." Giulia guessed a fight with the significant other, the printer on its last gasp, or a recent lecture from the boss. Perhaps she should print up business cards with her Polite Smile list and slip them surreptitiously where they'd be most useful.

She pushed open the door and entered a full-color version of *His Girl Friday*, with cubicles. Multiple keyboards clacked as loud as old-school typewriters. She picked out at least five different phone conversations. Snippets became clear as she walked the aisle.

"Can I quote you?"

"What were the words on your garage painted with?"

"Do you have her voicemails?

"The giraffe is in labor? Be right there."

"Western omelet and home fries, please. My card's on file."

Giulia stopped at the lunch order cubicle. A skeletal woman held together by skin tanned to bronze leather hung up a standard black office phone.

"Ms. Watson?" She pitched her voice to cut through the surrounding noise.

"Yeah? Oh, you're the detective." She kicked a narrow chair toward Giulia. "Come into my soundproof booth."

Giulia sat. The reporter completed a paragraph, saved, and closed the document. "Call me Opal." She opened a packet of nicotine gum and chomped down on a piece.

"Giulia."

"Like Julia Child? Can you cook?"

"It's spelled the Italian way, and yes."

"Good. I'm so tired of young women who think five-minute microwave recipes will get them through life." She moved the gum to her cheek. "If only these things worked or we returned to the halcyon days when they allowed smoking in here." The gum traveled to her other cheek. "What did you want to talk to me about?"

"The haunted items collected by Vernon Jevens. You wrote a feature article about them in conjunction with the Pittsburgh Ghost Tracking Society."

A deep chuckle. "I remember them now. A bunch of teenagers at heart, hoping to see a real, live ghost. You know what I mean." She opened an archive link and typed in its search window. "Here you go. See her? She's the one at magic shows who's positive the magician didn't palm an adult rabbit into the hat. Penn and Teller could explain the trick in detail and she'd insist the explanation was all part of the act."

"She doesn't appear gullible." Giulia liked the look of the smiling young woman in the photograph.

"She combines a hard-headed business model with Twilight

Sparkle. I like her." Opal glanced at Giulia. "You familiar with *My Little Pony*?"

"I am." Giulia wished she knew Zane's girlfriend well enough to dress him as one for Mardi Gras. As long as he could move in it, the effect would be epic.

"You get the reference then. My granddaughters live, sleep, and breathe the critters." She clicked on the photograph, which brought up a dozen more. "I liked her. She'll get over this trend and run her own business in ten years. Here're the supposedly haunted artifacts." She scrolled through pictures. "Look at this wedding dress. Back in the Dark Ages when I married my first husband, I wore something like it. I say they should hold it in front of the supposedly haunted mirror and see who appears. You skeeve old china dolls?"

"Not particularly."

Two separate one-sided arguments started in the cubes on either side.

"Shut your traps, you hacks! I got a detective here. She'll subpoena your records if you tick her off." Opal winked.

Friendly vulgarities floated over the cubicle walls. The conversation volume dropped by half.

"They listen to the old broad. I bake cookies." When she smiled, it was apparent her whitening toothpaste was still waging war with her smoking habit. "The kook—that'd be Jevens the patriarch—brought all these to Pittsburgh to have them examined. Our gullible friend and her cronies vetted 'em all and called in *The Scoop*. Heard of them?"

Giulia closed her eyes for an instant. Opal guffawed. "Hey, gang, the detective wants to hear all your stories about *The Scoop*."

"No, really, I don't—"

Three women and two men crowded the cubicle opening.

"They ruined one of my best stories—"

"They showed up at my kid's school during a lockdown—"

"They—" "They—" "They—"

"Stop." Giulia held up both hands. "You're preaching to the choir, but I can't fit all your stories into my schedule."

The voices staggered to a halt.

A bald man with a pencil-thin mustache said, "Opal, you're a wicked temptress."

Opal said in a low voice, "I'll make snickerdoodles tonight. They'll be fine." She beckoned Giulia. "Scoot your chair over here. Those are the dolls."

The dolls resembled each other only in their porcelain heads, stuffed bodies, and disturbingly realistic hair. The first smiled and winked, which gave it a drunken air. The second might have been a newborn from its frown and lifeless eyes. Giulia wondered if the second was a Victorian mourning doll, which would make the head wax, not porcelain.

Giulia put more space between herself and the images. "I wouldn't be surprised if they really were haunted."

"Me neither. There's one other object. Oh, yeah. A Bible. Takes a pretty ballsy ghost to haunt a Bible, don't you think?" She snapped her fingers. "We got distracted. The ghost people called in *The Scoop*, but their hope for local fame was trumped by some Doomsday Prepper group getting raided by the cops and Mr. Scoop himself getting winged by a stray bullet..."

The reporter brought her face closer to Giulia's. Closer still.

Giulia waited, resigned.

"Well, shut my mouth." Opal climbed onto her desk and announced, "Get off your flabby butts, you hacks, and meet the detective who starred in the only satisfying Ken Kanning show ever recorded."

Eleven

Not wanting to alienate potential sources of information, Giulia told the story of last summer's undercover Doomsday Prepper cult case. She used no client names and skimmed over personal details, but the reporters were still the best audience she'd ever had. Even her two most grateful haunted families didn't come close. Although the families had paid for her services, which evened things out.

Opal shooed them all away after a long twenty minutes. "We both get paid by the hour and I've taken up too much of your time. What's your email?"

Giulia spelled her work address.

Opal typed. "I'm sending you a link to my story. Added to it," she opened another window and copied part of an address file, "is the contact information for the head of Kooks Are Us."

Giulia smiled. "The paranormal society?"

"Yeah. You'll like her, but she might try to hard sell you. I think they want those pieces for their collection."

"I can handle it. If they're serious, I can put them in contact with the current owners."

Opal hit Enter. "Sent." She pointed to herself. "I looked you up when you made the appointment. Reporters. It's ingrained. You're on the opposite side of the haunting business. Keep up the good work. People who con the gullible deserve a special place in Hell."

From the newspaper, Giulia stopped for more cat litter before making an appointment with the Pittsburgh Ghost Tracking Society. The wind gusts were getting stronger and her car was light.

The additional forty-pound bag in the trunk seemed to keep the Nunmobile in closer contact with the highway. Giulia drove along an overpass the height of Godzilla and tried not to picture blowing off it, car and all. The resulting *splat* would trigger a large life insurance payment to Frank and Finn, but her preference would be to postpone her moment of Divine Judgement for a few decades.

She reached solid ground in one piece. "Thank you, Dollar Store cat litter."

Siri answered from her phone in the center console, "Routing to the Dollar Store. In half a mile—"

"No! Cancel." She laughed too hard to be understood and had to repeat "Cancel."

"Ending route," her phone agreed.

The rest of the drive was without incident or disembodied voices, robotic or otherwise. Silence meant her ghost rules were more or less inviolate. No surprise visits during the following: driving, during husband and wife time, or while carrying the baby. Male ghosts always sniggered at the middle rule. Word of mouth among ghosts was powerful, from what they'd deigned to tell her. But the dead, like the living, had its share of personalities who thought the rules didn't apply to them. Once she accepted the existence of ghosts as fact, she instituted the rules, but also drove with extreme caution. No insurance company would believe an accident was caused by "driver startled by ghost."

An attitude-laden ghost once told her the reason most of the dead respected her boundaries was because she respected the dead. Giulia'd kept to herself her amused comment about teenage attitude being stronger than death. Teenage talkativeness was an unexpected benefit to the ghost taming part of DI, though. Word of mouth brought in more living and dead clients.

The Society possessed a three-story brick house with a wraparound porch, a bay window on the first floor, a second-floor balcony, and a stained-glass window beneath the front peak. The Society's name in understated copper letters on a black sign hung next to the doorbell. A beautiful house which didn't tempt her. Beautiful old houses almost always needed tens of thousands in repairs and were woefully under-insulated. The heating bills alone negated any temptation to relocate her family from their snug little Cape Cod.

The ultimate goth answered the door. Black shirt, jeans, sneakers, hair, eyeliner. He reminded Giulia of one of the contestants on *American Idol*. She wasn't sure which season.

"Hi. Welcome to the Ghost Tracking Society. Enter and be enlightened."

When he didn't sing the welcome in a throbbing tenor, the comparison fell apart.

"Hello. I have an appointment with Ms. Comette."

"Sure. I'll be right back."

This might have been his first day. He left Giulia in the foyer without offering her one of the four wing chairs upholstered in different floral patterns. He even forgot to steer her to the brochures or the scrapbook of articles on the curly walnut coffee table. Since diffidence was not part of a good detective's repertoire, Giulia stashed a brochure in her messenger bag and opened the scrapbook.

Shiloh's soulmate returned with his older sister. Had to be. Black shirt with lace collar and cuffs, black pants, flats, hair, eyeliner, mascara. Both had the same deep blue eyes and natural pout. She wondered if they secretly hated those two blots of color in their ensembles and were saving up to buy the darkest colored contact lenses available.

"Ms. Driscoll? I'm Haley Comette. Welcome to the Society."

Giulia shook hands with a straight face.

"You're dying to know." The Society's Director sighed. "I'll explain on the way to my office. I was born the day Halley's Comet appeared in 1986. My dad, the lover of puns, insisted I have the most memorable name possible." She gestured Giulia to a wing chair in yet another floral pattern. "Thanks, Dad."

"Would you feel better if I mentioned my great-great aunt who named all her children after the Mysteries of the Rosary?"

Haley sat in her own wing chair behind a lovingly restored walnut desk. "You mean like, wait, my Mom tried to raise us Catholic...You mean like Scourging and Crucifixion?" Horror filled her face.

"Not Scourging, but I had Great Aunts Crossifisa and Annunciata and Great Uncles Risurrezione, Ascensione, and Assunzione."

"Christ on a bike." Embarrassment supplanted the horror. "I beg your pardon."

Giulia grinned. "Exactly how they used to express it in front of us kids when our parents weren't around. Some parents ought to be slapped."

"I volunteer mine as tribute." She clasped her hands on the desk. "What did you want to see me about?"

"Vernon Jevens and his haunted object collection."

A quick shudder of revulsion. "We couldn't get him out of here fast enough to suit me." Another look of horror. "You're not a relation, are you?"

Giulia projected a bubble of calm. "No. We're working for the family during the charity Mardi Gras party at the Jevens house. I never met Vernon."

"Be grateful. He was an evil, creepy little man. Not in stature, because even in his eighties he was probably six foot two. I kept a piece of furniture or one of our male Society members between us at all times."

They shared an "eww" look.

"Evil in what way?" Giulia said.

"You know he brought us several items he'd collected to confirm the sellers' claims the items were haunted?"

"Yes." Giulia didn't want to lead her on or express skepticism.

A beat, as though Haley had picked up on Giulia's reticence. "I have the pictures we shared with *The Cottonwood Post-Herald*." She typed for a few seconds and turned her monitor so they both could see it. The dolls came up first, one after the other. "Haunted and possessed dolls are the biggest cliché. One of the reasons I'm head of the Society is I'm an antiques expert. My family's been in the business for generations. People contact us about dolls seven or eight times a year."

Giulia fed her the straight line. "And your conclusion?"

Haley tilted her head as though trying to read into Giulia's response again. "Are you a skeptic?"

"I keep an open mind." This appointment wasn't about Giulia's ghost skills.

Haley straightened her head. Faint trails of sunny yellow overlaid her blue-black hair. Giulia closed her eyes, exhaled, and opened them.

No yellow. She was going to have to have a serious talk with Rowan, the proprietor of the Tarot Shoppe across the street from Driscoll Investigations, and Giulia's mentor in all things supernatural. This whole "seeing auras" thing was getting out of hand.

"The smiling doll wouldn't bring much at an auction. It's from the early era of mass-produced toys and hasn't been treated well. The other doll, though, is a real treasure. It's an authentic wax mourning doll. Its owner made a porcelain mask to protect the wax, but everything else is original. The dress alone—" She cut herself off with a self-conscious laugh. "Don't let me get started or we'll be here until closing time." She clicked on a picture of a three-foot tall mirror. "Look at the carvings. See the cherubs at the corners? Raphael's cherubs are my weakness. They always look like they'd rather be watching rugby or reading a detective story. Anything except play in the cherub orchestra or stand in for Cupid. This piece commanded serious money at the auction where Jevens picked it up."

Giulia took out her iPad and began making notes. "I guess we shouldn't say 'Bloody Mary' into it three times at Mardi Gras."

Haley's eyes turned into chibi manga eyes. "Oh, no! Never do that!"

"Don't worry. We're counting on most of the partygoers being too drunk to do anything dangerous." A new note: paranormal enthusiasts and humor don't mix.

A picture of a yellowed wedding gown with a partially rotted lace bodice replaced the mirror. "Doesn't this scream 'Miss Havisham' to you? It reeked of mothballs when he brought it in. My younger brother—he's our part-time receptionist—had to leave the room to throw up. He's sensitive to chemicals, although if I combined the words 'him' and 'sensitive' in his presence his masculinity would take extreme umbrage." She winked at Giulia. "Here's the Bible Jevens bought. The mildewed pages stunk as bad as the mothballs. Bookworms had been using it as their lunch buffet for quite a while as well. Now—" another click "—here's the showpiece of his collection."

The dollhouse was a work of art, if by 'art' the designer meant 'Halloween should be celebrated all year long because nightmares are good.'

Three stories tall with a peaked roof and two chimneys, missing several gray shingles and with the front door hanging askew, the dollhouse needed only an imaginative observer to inspire shrieking night terrors. The next pictures showed room details: broken furniture, peeling wallpaper, miniature dolls, tables set for dinner. Dishes and food were covered with cobwebs. Intricately detailed spiders, bats, and rats had been poised at strategic spots. Nothing so obvious as a ghost-shaped sheet hung in any room, including the attic. Rather, the overall effect was "Don't look behind you—run, run now!"

Giulia wanted to own it.

"We hated it," Haley said. "Our photographer kept thinking she saw something move every time she took a picture. We even took a video, but nothing appeared. Not that that means anything."

"I wish I could afford it." Giulia sighed with regret.

Haley's eyebrows performed gymnastics. "You like the dollhouse?"

"I enjoy horror movies."

"Wow, you don't look it."

Giulia refrained from the obvious reply: if I had a dollar for every time someone said that to me...

"To each their own, I guess." Haley clicked once more and returned to her desktop wallpaper. "Right when we were trying not to freak out over the dollhouse, *The Scoop* arrived. You know them? The local version of *TMZ*?"

"Better than I'd like to."

Mentioning *The Scoop* always caused one of two reactions: a snort of derision or a star-struck exclamation. Until now. Gloom descended on Haley, the gloom of loss and disappointment.

"Vernon Jevens was a big fan. We didn't really want them here, but all four of us realized the opportunity. If the show featured our Society, it would be the biggest membership boost we'd ever have." A wry smile. "And thus we sold out."

Giulia shook her head. "No. And thus you took advantage of a business opportunity."

The wryness deepened. "It would have if a bigger story hadn't dropped in their laps the same week. We would've been part of a show on multiple local interest groups. I don't know what happened to the footage they shot of us, but the promised show never appeared."

Giulia leaned forward. "Are you attending the Mardi Gras party?"

"I thought about it, but I'm not a crowd person. Besides, *The Scoop* is the party's official videographer. It'll be like having to watch the game winner get interviewed while you stand on the sidelines in second place." Haley had the indefinable look of someone who needed a stiff drink.

"Think of it this way." Giulia, not a sales person, tried to sell her idea. "*The Scoop* will be everywhere in the house, filming everyone. If you come dressed as the head of the Pittsburgh Ghost Tracking Society and tell the story of the haunted objects to as many people as will listen, *The Scoop* will take notice. They're drawn to crowds the way I'm drawn to coffee."

Haley gloomed. "It's probably not going to happen. I'll end up contacting the family after the party and trying to charm them one on one."

Giulia finished typing. "One last question: Did you determine whether any of the objects were haunted?"

"Perhaps." She opened another folder and clicked on a video. "My co-founder and I attuned ourselves to the vibrations of each item."

The video began with Ken Kanning introducing Vernon Jevens and the Society personnel. Then Haley and an older, bald man held their hands over the mourning doll. Haley described the atmosphere she felt around the doll. The man shuddered and pulled both their hands away.

"There is great anger in this object." His Bronx accent came through in "anguh" instead of "anger."

Haley re-centered herself before the doll and closed her eyes. "Yes...yes, I'm sensing it now."

Giulia was a nice enough person not to ask Haley if she was especially susceptible to strong personalities.

The video continued with the pair performing the same actions for the other objects. Vernon Jevens poked his face into the shot when Haley moved onto the next object, describing how he acquired it. Every so often Ken Kanning's voice added some excitement to the show. At the end of the performance, Haley faced the camera alone.

"Based on our combined years of experience, we've concluded that the spirits in the antique mourning doll and the wedding dress are strong enough to make themselves felt. The spirits in the other objects, if any inhabit them, are either too weak or too uninterested at the moment to reach us. We recommend extreme caution be taken with the first two objects we mentioned."

Haley closed the video. "Jevens and his...nephew, I think, packed up all his treasures as though we were going to steal something. My brother offered to help but if looks could kill, he'd have been our family's first ghost, for real." She tapped her fingers on her desk with a thoughtful air. "I wonder if we can afford to buy these from the family?"

Giulia put away her phone. "The family will be hosting the party. To indulge in a generalization, two of the remaining three are up there in age. They also don't appear to want to live in the house." Understatements were becoming a new specialty of hers. "You might want to capitalize on the hours of noise and music and chaos toward the end of the party and make your proposal then."

Crafty delight filled the Society Director's face.

Twelve

Giulia's phone rang while she was on the Turnpike. Her long-held refusal to install a hands-free device in the Nunmobile had been jettisoned when Finn was born. What if something happened to him while Sidney's mom was watching him? If she needed to drop everything and race him to (God forbid) the ER? Her old method of waiting until she reached her destination before checking messages became irresponsible the moment she returned to work.

Sure, most of the time the callers were spam disguised as local numbers, but in the car at least she was willing to answer instead of ignoring them. She glanced at the screen.

Sidney's mom.

She cracked her fingernail stabbing the green icon. "Gabrielle? What's wrong?"

"Nothing. Don't drive off the road. I know you're in your car because I can tell you're on speaker. I'm calling to tell you Jessamine has decided Finn belongs to her and she's never letting him go."

Giulia laughed with relief. "Can you let her know he won't be sleeping over for about twenty years, until they're married?"

"I'll try to convey such a large amount of time to her. So far anything longer than three minutes equals forever. I'll see you in a few hours."

"You're the best."

After this, the drive to the courthouse was a breeze. The court clerk kept one eye on the clock as it ticked to noon and exchanged a copy of Vernon Jevens's will for cash in less than fifteen minutes. She walked in Giulia's shadow all the way to the parking lot and zoomed into the street before Giulia's seat belt was buckled.

She opened her own office door at 1:20. Sidney and Zane were studying the Spirit Halloween website on Zane's computer.

"Ms. D., what if we all went to the party as Agatha Christie characters? I could be Hercule Poirot."

"I could be the kooky writer lady, Ariadne Oliver," Sidney said. "I like her. She eats apples all the time. You could be Miss Marple."

"Frank could be Captain Hastings." Giulia contemplated the idea and discarded it with regret. "Too obvious. Detectives dressing up as detectives to detect." She hung up her coat. "Maybe for Halloween. It'd be a good joke on anyone coming into the office."

Sidney eyed her. "Something's up."

"I brought a little light reading." She held up the folded paper. "Vernon Jevens's will."

Zane closed all tabs. "Group reading at the window table?"

"Of course."

When Giulia spread the pages across the table, their heads moved in sync as they read like they were watching a tennis match.

"Holy gods," Zane said. "No wonder the family's screaming for more of his money. A twenty-thousand-dollar scholarship to a taxidermy school? Five thousand each to five different paranormal groups? Look at this: money and housing to fifteen atelier startups. The man loved his art."

"Only a thousand to each of our clients? What an insult," Sidney said. "Why give them anything if they all hated each other?"

"Because he's smart," Giulia said. "If he left them nothing, they could have argued the will was invalid because he ignored his only living relatives and left all his money to 'crackpot' organizations. The video I saw today at the Pittsburgh Ghost Trackers Society would make great ammunition. Jevens comes across as obsessed enough for the family to try and claim he was mentally unstable."

"Devious." Zane ran a finger along one of the bequests. "Devious runs in the family. Also sarcasm: the sum of one thousand dollars to my sister, Blossom Burd, whose love of the color gray made every day as bright as the summer sun."

Sidney snickered. "The sum of one thousand dollars to my only surviving son, Owen, secure in the knowledge that he won't waste one penny of it on frivolity."

"He seemed to hate one of them the least, "Giulia said. "The sum of one thousand dollars to my nephew Randy, known as RJ, who no doubt will spend it on frivolity. Were it possible, I would rise from my grave so he could continue to regale me with tales of his exploits.""

"He sounds as unpleasant as the two who came in here," Sidney said.

Giulia added in her head. "This isn't enough money. I only get ninety-two thousand dollars. Jevens was worth boatloads more."

"Only ninety-two thousand?" Sidney said. "I could pay off the balance of my student loan with a quarter of it."

"I shudder at the potential cost of college by the time Finn turns eighteen." Giulia ran into her office and returned with a file folder. "Vernon's pattern of withdrawals. They gave us a copy of the investment and bank statements."

Zane ran his finger down the list. "If we were in an episode of *CSI*, I'd say he was being blackmailed."

Giulia made notes on the investment statement. "Based on my meeting with the Director of the Pittsburgh Ghost Society, Vernon would more likely be the blackmailer." She listened to herself. "It's a good thing the dead can't be libeled."

"Have you discussed the idea with an actual ghost?" Zane seemed interested rather than trying to get a rise out of Sidney.

"Not yet, but since I'm not a lawyer I'll be able to dodge the issue."

Sidney shook an admonishing finger at her. "I remember when you wouldn't even have thought about libeling someone, let alone say it out loud."

Giulia batted innocent eyes at her. "Clinging to the past is counterproductive. On point, it appears our clients are more than vindictive. They might also be correct. Their patriarch appears to have been squirreling away money from them."

"A mistress?" Zane said.

Giulia opened her phone and dialed. "Mr. Jevens? Giulia Driscoll. Regarding the missing money: Did Vernon Jevens have a companion?"

The answering guffaw was so loud Giulia yanked the phone away from her ear.

"Wait'll I tell RJ this one. Forget it, Driscoll. My father hated everyone. Before you say it may have been an act, I put a detective on him last year when we thought he needed to be confined to a home."

"And the detective found?" If Giulia took away anything from her decade in the convent, it was the skill of the polite response when the other person deserved a blistering lecture.

"The only human interaction my father had was with antique dealers, phony psychics, and starving artists. Open his bank statement."

"I have it in front of me."

"We traced about a third of the money he withdrew. We expect you to find us the rest. Call me the next time you feel the need to make me laugh." The phone went dead.

Giulia glared at her screen. "Sir, you are of an age when etiquette was still taught in schools. A refresher would be to your benefit as a businessman."

"Once a schoolteacher," Sidney said, "always a schoolteacher."

"Finn will benefit from it," Zane said. "My parents left our education completely to the school. I got stuck with a geezer counting the days to retirement for fourth and fifth grade."

"So a dual major magna cum laude from MIT was revenge?" Sidney said.

"English was my worst subject, thanks to those two." He bowed to Giulia. "I worry all the time I'll mess something up."

"It's not worth the worry. I live to correct grammar." She set the list of stocks next to the other two documents. "I don't see any sell-offs."

Sidney paged through the Will. "Here it is. Stock in IBM, McDonald's, Proctor & Gamble, AT&T, and Disney, all go to the family business."

"Which would be Owen Jevens." Giulia looked around for a pen and paper to doodle on.

"Those are all blue chip," Zane said. "I guarantee Owen won't sell those. He must be after more liquid assets."

"As his aunt said, thus the continual business deals." Giulia let her eyes unfocus on the documents for a long minute. "They helpfully volunteered the information that the police suspected each of them to have killed Vernon, who died of a heart attack when a lamp shorted in his hand. From the little we know, Blossom would squirrel away money and Owen would use it to buy more businesses."

"I vote Owen," Sidney said.

"Same here," Zane said.

"I agree, but why?" Giulia said.

"Don't be offended," Zane said, "but women of her generation were expected to have babies and sew clothes, not run a business."

"Sidney?"

"I'd need to see more of her, but Zane's theory is a good start."

"All right. We need more on Owen. If I could trust Vernon Jevens' ghost, I'd almost consider trying to contact it, but it seems only a fool would've trusted him alive or dead."

No further reply. She turned around. Sidney was holding a hand-lettered table tent: Ghost Tamer At Work.

"I like it," Giulia said. "It'd look great on the door. Driscoll Investigations: Ghost Taming on Request. No Divorces. Deceased clients must have a living relative to ensure payment. No jump scares allowed."

Sidney stepped toward her. "You mean it?"

"I do not. We have a positive reputation as a legitimate detective agency. I could've sworn I told you both about the way ghosts have been advertising the ancillary part of the business through word of mouth."

Sidney turned the sign face down on the table. "More than I want to know."

Thirteen

"May I speak to Edward Nelson, please?"

Giulia held the phone to her ear with her shoulder while she made notes. An hour of digging, with the assistance of Zane's special talents, had unearthed Owen's most recent half-dozen business deals. The results confirmed her suspicion: Owen's ruthlessness had little in common with fair play.

The brief article buried in *The Cottonwood Post-Herald's* Sunday business section was little more than filler:

Jevens Holdings Ltd. Merges with Balalaika Inc.

Jevens Holdings Ltd., Cottonwood's low-profile business powerhouse, has completed a merger with Balalaika Inc., owned by opera singer turned entrepreneur Edward Nelson. This is the fourth merger in the past sixteen months for Jevens Holdings, which has retained its family name throughout. CEO Owen Jevens declined to give details regarding the two companies' plans to integrate. Nelson's spokesperson was not available for comment.

Everything the article didn't say could fill a Mack Truck. Angry people liked to talk. Giulia had learned this useful piece of wisdom from Amazon reviews.

"Nelson speaking."

"Mr. Nelson, I'm calling on behalf of Driscoll Investigations. We're looking into the background of Jevens Holdings. Would you have time for a brief meeting later today?"

Silence.

"Mr. Nelson?" Line one's button was still lit on her desk phone, so the call hadn't dropped.

"I'm here. Let me put you on hold." Waiting in the empty silence, Giulia pegged him as a chorus baritone: a voice good enough in a group but not powerful enough for a solo. Even his speaking voice lacked diaphragm support.

No click warned her of being taken off hold. "Who did you say you were?

"Giulia Driscoll with Driscoll Investigations."

"Thought I'd heard the name. Fine. When do you want to meet?"

She wanted to know the context of his recognition. Regular clients or ghostly ones? "Are you free after seven tonight?"

A tired laugh. "No problem. Where?"

"The Pine Duff Diner?"

"Sure. I know where it is. Eight okay?"

Fourteen

In the end, Giulia was glad to escape a day-long deluge of emails, billing, and fending off divorce cases. She hit the intercom.

"Zane, it's a good twenty minutes to the soccer complex. We should get there extra-early."

His Humphrey Bogart baritone reverberated through the speaker. "But not so early we get ambushed by *The Scoop*."

"I like the way you think."

Giulia drove the Nunmobile since they didn't need to hide their presence. The parking lot by Field A was two-thirds full at quarter to four.

"This does not bode well," Zane said.

"I suppose there's no chance schools are having early tryouts." Giulia parked next to *The Scoop*'s white van. "Kanning should put their logo on their vehicle."

"But the creeper van look is so classic."

She turned off the ignition. "Are you prepared to be our defensive line if the crowd is aggressive?"

He flexed.

"Here we go." She unbuckled her seat belt. "Our single moment working for *The Scoop*. May it be shorter than we hope."

They exited the car in sync. Giulia dropped the keys in her messenger bag. Now that she'd returned to her pre-pregnancy self, she was able to fit into her beloved violet wool coat again and move with ease. Zane's black peacoat offered similar freedom of movement.

They heard singing as they climbed the ridge surrounding the soccer fields. Shouts and chants disrupted the singing the higher they climbed. When they reached the top, they both stopped.

"It's like a casting call for a Monty Python movie," Giulia said, awe in her voice.

"Spam, Spam, Spam, Spam," Zane sang under his breath.

In the ten-yard circle in the center of the field stood Kord Kanning and a thin girl dressed all in black with dead-white makeup accented by deep purple eyeliner and lipstick. She looked familiar, but the cosplay festival crowded out the memory trying to surface. Giulia filed it for the next quiet moment. The crowd seemed to treat the circle as a barrier, because they swarmed around the rest of the field without crossing the faded white circle of paint.

Half a dozen young men wearing sweatshirts with large Greek letters stood at the farthest end from Giulia and Zane.

"What are they singing?" Giulia cocked her head. "It sounds like 'Red Red Wine.'"

"They are. I was in the same fraternity at MIT. It's our unofficial drinking song. If they have flasks in their pockets, wait until you hear the lyrics when everyone starts to slur."

"Joy. Drunks at this hour of the afternoon. I wonder if the Bible thumpers on the right will try to lecture them."

Zane followed her gaze. "How do you know they're Bible thumpers?"

"They're wearing the uniform."

A bearded man in brown pants, a white shirt, a bolo tie, and a dark blazer waved a black book toward Kord and his companion. His lips moved, but the singing drowned him out. On his left stood two women in prairie-style dresses. On his right, a girl and a younger boy, their clothes identical to the adults'. At intervals the leader's mouth closed and his acolytes said something in unison.

Giulia said, "I recognize their pattern. He's reciting a Psalm and they're coming in on the responses."

"Why aren't they wearing coats?" Zane shivered. "They're making me cold just looking at them."

"Don't get me started on extremist Christian sects. We'll be here until next week."

Zane jogged her elbow. "Other side of the field from the Bible group. Are they identical twins cosplaying *Call of Cthulhu*?"

Despair stabbed at Giulia as she read lips. "Nothing so simple. They're actual cultists."

"Ms. D., it's a game."

"It's also a religion. The few adherents I've encountered were harmless, but they're hard to shut up. I recognize the emblem on their shoulders." She indicated the small group near the fraternity with a nod. "Did you notice the Deadheads?"

"No, I was...holy gods, they are stoned out of their gourds." He lowered his voice. "I might try to score a joint off them when we're done."

"You did not say that and I did not officially hear it. Except for the 'when we're done' part."

Off to their left by the bleachers, Ken Kanning and Pit Bull narrated and filmed the swelling chaos. More cars pulled into the parking lot.

Giulia started down the ridge. "Let's get to our client before someone brings out a starter's pistol."

Fifteen

Giulia and Zane walked the field's perimeter to get to *The Scoop*. Kanning shut off his microphone as they approached.

"Giulia good to see you here early, but I knew you would be." He pointed with his microphone. "Twenty-three so far. Not a bad turnout. Bull can make it appear larger."

"Hi, Giulia. Hi, Zane." Pit Bull eased the camera off his shoulder. "What's your opinion of the kid's ghost?"

Tired new mom Giulia chose at last to give up the battle to keep *The Scoop* referring to her as "Ms. Driscoll." Frank was going to rag on her something wicked tonight when she told him.

"I'm reserving judgement until I see it myself," she said to Pit Bull.

The Smile split Kanning's face. "You're worth every penny."

"Incoming," Zane said.

A dozen students wearing different fraternity and sorority sweatshirts joined the original six. They appeared to be sober. Two of them carried backpacks.

Pit Bull said, "Four o'clock on the dot."

Ken Kanning smoothed his immaculate hair. His leather bomber jacket must have been warmer than it looked, because the tip of his nose showed only a hint of red. Giulia wondered if he'd found a new brand of pancake makeup. Kanning waved to his son, who gave him a thumbs-up. Kord bounced on the balls of his feet and talked incessantly to the girl beside him. Every so often the girl opened her mouth for the length of a monosyllable.

Kanning led them in procession through the crowd: himself,

Giulia, Zane, and Pit Bull in the rear filming it all.

The newcomers slipped off their backpacks. Giulia and Zane shared a look.

"I've got the kid," Giulia said. He was shorter and lighter if DI needed to swoop in for a rescue.

"I'll watch the girl," Zane said.

Giulia didn't regret leaving her Glock in the glove compartment. She was a good shot, but if the backpacks contained weapons, she'd be more use protecting the kids.

"Good afternoon, everyone!" Kanning's voice carried far enough to temporarily halt the Bible thumpers, the Cthulhu chanters, and even four of the six singing frat boys. "I'm Ken Kanning. Welcome to our challenge. Remember to smile, because you may be on the next episode of *The Scoop.*"

He handed the mic to his son. Kord squeaked once and shut his mouth. Kanning made a calming gesture and Kord took a deep breath. "Hi, everyone. Thanks for following my YouTube channel. This is Shiloh." He indicated the glum teenager with his other hand and accidentally smacked her arm. "Oops. Sorry. Okay, I know everyone's waiting to see my Whiteboard in person, so here it is!"

Kanning shook his head, The Smile rueful. Giulia was certain his son's next lesson would be how to work the crowd. She scanned said crowd. Several pairs of teenagers had arrived. The boys looked bored, the girls *tee-hee*'d. Behind them, three old women and a middle-aged man in a khaki raincoat.

The sorority sisters revealed the contents of their backpacks: several white sheets. Giulia nudged Zane and they both nodded with relief. The women draped the sheets over everyone wearing a Greek-lettered sweatshirt, drunk and sober. The student documenting everything on her phone stayed herself. When the eyeholes in the sheets were aligned, the group looked like a gaggle of Charlie Brown imitators in *It's the Great Pumpkin, Charlie Brown.*

Pit Bull said, "Ken," and motioned with his head.

Kanning glanced away from his son and back to the cameraman. He shook his head once.

Kord had overcome his stage fright and was telling the story of the first Whiteboard message. Giulia kept one eye on the swaying, signing ghost and the other on Kord and his friend. The uber-Christians and the Cthulhu cultists raised their voices as the majority of the audience moved to the perimeter of the ten-yard circle. Both groups were so intent on shouting everyone down they didn't appear to notice all the Charlie Brown ghosts.

Giulia moved through the packed crowd like she was the rudest player ever of "Go In and Out the Window." Zane shadowed her until they were positioned in a direct line with their chosen charges.

One of the ghosts tapped Kanning on the shoulder. "Boo!" Kanning's glare didn't stop its slurred serenade of the first chorus of "Red Red Wine" as it moved on.

Kord held up the Whiteboard and demonstrated how the knobs worked.

An old woman next to Giulia shouted, "Children should play with toys, not pervert them!"

Kord the neophyte engaged with the heckler. "Come on, lady, where would we be without Edison and Tesla?"

Kanning's irritated growl was loud enough to be picked up on Pit Bull's feed over the singing and chanting.

The glum teenager elbowed Kord. He caught the look on his father's face, stuttered, and fell silent.

"Ignore her," Kanning said. "Keep going with the demo and issue your challenge."

"Got it, Dad." Kord fumbled the microphone back into position and gave the camera a passable imitation of the Kanning Smile.

A taller ghost tapped the old woman on her shoulder. "Boo."

The heckler shrieked. The ghost and several people surrounding the old woman laughed. She aimed her purse at the ghost's head. It dodged, caught its heel on the sheet, and fell onto its back in the mud. A word Pit Bull would have to bleep for the final cut issued from the ghost. The unmistakable sounds of retching followed.

The old woman did an about-face and yanked up the sheet. "You are a stupid young man." She wiped his face with the hem of the now-muddy sheet and helped him sit up.

More ghosts gathered around calling for "Heather" to get this on film and asking the old woman if she'd come live with them and be their love.

Kord shouted "Hey!" so loud into the mic it gave a high-pitched feedback squeal. All other sounds ceased.

Kanning took back the mic. "Scoopers, I know you remember our exclusive footage of the convent poltergeist. It's archived on our website if you want to check it out again. So, are you ready for today's Big Reveal? If the stars align—"

The phrase triggered the Cthulhu cultists. They flanked Pit Bull and chanted into the camera. "The stars are right! Iä! Iä! Cthulhu fhtagn!"

The Christian extremists, not to be outdone, moved in for their share of the spotlight. Their leader began Psalm 119 and his family of followers came in at the proper cues. As the young boy recited, he adjusted his position to watch Kord with his peripheral vision. The teenage girl saw it and pinched him out of the patriarch's line of sight.

Kord took the mic. "Attention!"

No feedback this time. The shout caught the Cthulhu twins between "Iäs" and the Psalm-chanters at the end of a verse-response cycle.

Kord pressed his advantage. "Who came here to check out the ghost in my Whiteboard? Raise your hands."

A dozen arms shot up. Pit Bull sidestepped his new friends to get a clear panorama. A new ghost photobombed the shot. Pit Bull swiveled one eye toward the interloper. "Move." The ghost vanished as though it was an authentic visitor from the Other Side.

"Everybody who raised their hands, come closer." Kord made sweeping inclusive gestures with both arms.

All the ghosts pushed forward. Several dragged off their sheets and dropped them on the muddy grass. The evangelical boy twitched toward the circle. The older girl stepped on his foot. Two couples and the man in the raincoat joined the front row. Giulia frowned, distracted. He looked familiar.

"Get ready, you guys. We're going to ask the ghost a question. This'll prove I'm not using magnets or camera tricks on my videos. Who has the first question for the ghost?"

Five voices shouted at once.

"One at a time, guys." Kord pointed to a girl wearing a bright pink ski jacket. "You first, miss."

She giggled. "Will I get an A in Physics?"

The young man whose arm she clung to said, "Your physics rate an A with me, baby."

She aimed a fake punch at his chest. "Stop."

"Me next." A middle-aged woman in what looked like three layers of winter clothes stepped in front of the pink jacket. "Where did Mr. Fuzzybutt run off to?"

Laughter on all sides. Pit Bull zoomed in on the woman's round face.

"I don't care what you millennials think of me. I want Mr. Fuzzybutt back."

Kord made bizarre faces in an obvious attempt not to laugh.

The glum girl finally spoke. "The guy with red hair." Her soft voice hardly carried, even with the microphone.

"Me?" A former ghost pointed to his chest. "Okay. Is there booze in the afterlife?"

Another former ghost: "What about sex?"

A different old woman: "Are my tropical fish waiting for me in Heaven?"

An angry young man, not one of the students: "When will my parents die and leave me all their money?"

A high-pitched giggle cut through the barrage of questions. The owner of Mr. Fuzzybutt shot a dirty look in the giggle's direction.

Giulia looked behind her at the giggler and back at Kord. Recognition of the giggle had almost worked its way to the front of her brain.

"I'll see if this stupid toy is for real." One of the former ghosts stepped over the soccer circle. "Come on, gang. It's empirical research time." He snatched the Whiteboard from Kord's hands.

"Hey!" Kord and the girl grabbed at it, but the former ghost held it up out of their reach.

"How do you write with one of these things?" He twisted the knobs.

More ghosts and former ghosts broke the plane. Giulia elbowed a lunging Cthulhu twin in the ribs. Zane shoved two ghosts out of his way. Kord kicked the thief in the shin. The girl screamed, "Give it back! Give it back!"

The thief turned and ran. Kord and the girl chased him like a pair of Keystone Kops. The entire crowd surged after them. In the chaos, the preacher's young son shadowed the thief, talking a mile a minute. All the teenage couples joined the fraternity and sorority squad in a raucous reprise of "Red Red Wine." The backpacks opened again and yielded several wine bottles.

Zane and Giulia converged on the Whiteboard thief.

"Piss off," he shouted, still fumbling with the knobs.

Giulia punched him in his nascent beer gut. As the thief doubled over, Zane grabbed the Whiteboard and tossed it to Giulia. Mr. Fuzzybutt's owner reached out to shove Shiloh out of her way. Zane swept the girl up in a firefighter's hold.

She squawked and beat his back with her fists. "Let me go! Help!"

Zane said over his empty shoulder, "Shut up. I'm one of the good guys."

Giulia hooked her arm around Kord's ribcage. "Move." She hustled him over to the sideline bleachers where Kanning and Pit Bull were filming the melee.

Over the shouts and singing, Giulia heard a woman screeching. She couldn't understand a word, but every so often Ken Kanning winced.

The evangelical preacher poked a righteous finger at the Cthulhu twins. The finger dislodged her badge, which fell into the mud. The twins each made a fist and punched both sides of the preacher's face in unison. He fell backward like a tree: *thud-sklorp*. The women and the young boy with him attacked the twins. More screeching augmented the single voice Kanning didn't seem to want to hear.

The sorority girls made a circle around them. "Knock their teeth out! Pull out their hair! Go! Hit 'em harder! Go!"

A woman with a face like an open-mouthed Greek tragedy mask snatched at Kord. Giulia held onto him.

"Mom?" Kord said.

"Kord Christopher Kanning, what do you think you're doing? I know I shouldn't have let your father talk me into this nonsensical stunt." Her trendy platinum hair stuck out like it had been electrified. The red hive blotches on her cheeks and neck ruined her tasteful makeup.

Giulia released Kord and moved behind the bleachers to use her phone. Ninety seconds later she returned to Kanning and Pit Bull. "I called 911."

The main fight had spawned two other fights between various students and other paranormal enthusiasts. Within three minutes the first police car squealed into the parking lot, siren blaring. Everyone not fighting scattered, jostling Giulia, Zane, and all Kannings in their way.

"Run!"

"I've got weed in my car."

"Mom will kill me if I get arrested again."

"Who's not too drunk to drive?"

A falsetto giggle passed Giulia. The guy in the trench coat cut behind the bleachers and joined the panicked rush to the parking lot. She should know him and Shiloh. Something recent...

It started to thunder.

Sixteen

Kord's mother draped her winter coat over her son. "Mom, come on." He tried to wriggle out from under it. "Everything was going fine. The drunks would've tripped over their own feet in a minute."

Ken Kanning touched Giulia's shoulder. "Thanks."

Giulia pulled up her collar. "We'll add rescue services to the bill."

He laughed. "Ever think of coming on board *The Scoop*? You'd be great comic relief on our darker shows."

The atrocity of the suggestion rendered her speechless for a moment. She said through a dry mouth, "Thank you, no. By the way, DI is keeping the Whiteboard."

"What?" Kord made a final heave and escaped his mother's clutches. "It's mine. I created it. You can't have it."

Giulia turned him so he faced the soccer field. Three uniformed police were handcuffing the remaining frat boys. Two more slipped in the puddles of slush as they wrestled the Cthulhu twins into cuffs. One officer had a split lip and another's nose gushed blood. A sixth was calling in for backup with extra cuffs. Sleet pinged off his coat as he stood over the preacher and his clan. The clan sat in the muddy slush reciting Psalms. The women's dresses were torn and their tight, braided buns were tangled messes. Blood trickled down the older woman's forehead from a new bald spot on her scalp. The preacher was missing a front tooth and both his eyes were swelling up.

"You initiated this chaos," Giulia said to Kord. "If anyone else who saw your YouTube invitation comes after your Whiteboard, we're equipped to handle it."

"But it's mine." A whine crept into his voice.

His mother yanked him back by one arm. "I never want to see that thing again."

Ken Kanning bent his six-foot height down to his son's almost five. "Kord, listen. The cops are coming over to ask what happened. If Giulia sticks the Whiteboard into her bag there, we can tell them we gave it to Driscoll Investigations for safekeeping because we wanted to stop any more violence."

More thunder but no rain followed when backup arrived. The preacher and his clan had been cuffed and were being escorted to the cars. One of the officers approached the bleachers. "Did one of you call this in?"

Giulia stepped forward. "I did."

The officer's forehead wrinkled. "Have we met?"

She smiled. "Christmas Potluck."

"Cannoli. Now I remember. Giulia Driscoll." He put his back to the sleet and took out a pen and a small notebook. "What started this donnybrook?"

She ignored Kanning's signals and put a hand on Kord's shoulder. "This young man unwisely issued a challenge to his YouTube followers."

The officer glared at Kord.

Giulia continued. "To no one's surprise, extremists of every stripe crawled out of the woodwork."

He maintained his stern gaze. "Didn't your parents warn you about the Internet?" He turned to Giulia. "What got this bowl of mixed nuts out here in this weather?"

"The young man invented a new type of ghost box."

He stopped writing. "A what?" Light dawned. "You mean like something they use on those ghost hunting TV shows? No wonder." He wrote several notes. "Do we have a problem?"

Giulia patted her messenger bag. "I'm glad you remember my cannolis, but did you also remember I'm a private investigator? This young man and his father are my clients."

His glance at Kanning and Pit Bull was not that of a fan. *The Scoop.* I thought I recognized you."

Giulia immediately liked this officer. "Since my client's son acted in ignorance?" She let the question hang.

"Yeah, I'm not about to issue a citation for disturbing the peace to a ten-year-old."

"Eleven and a half," Kord said. His father stepped on his foot.

The officer continued without a hitch. "To an eleven-year-old, when the real troublemakers are leaving dirty wet splotches in all our cars." To Kanning: "I'll give you the benefit of the doubt."

Kanning exuded innocence. "I don't know what you're talking about, officer."

"As in, I hope you didn't stage this circus for an episode of your show."

Kord made himself into a skinny shield in front of his father. "Officer, I went live on YouTube and challenged anybody to come here and prove my Whiteboard is a fake. I didn't think all those morons would crash it."

Despite the wind and impending rain, the atmosphere within the group warmed.

"Check with your parents before you wave a red flag at the Internet next time." The officer put away the notebook and said in a chillier voice, "Mr. Kanning, please be available with your son in the next few days to make a statement."

"*The Scoop* is always ready to cooperate with law enforcement."

Giulia and Zane found reasons to look at the state of their coat fastenings.

The officer was halfway back to the parking lot when Kord's high voice began, "Dad, what about—" and stopped when Kanning stepped on his other foot.

No one spoke until only the DI and *The Scoop* contingents remained.

"Kord," Kanning said, "never offer the cops more than you have to."

"But Dad, you said you wanted to help the police."

Giulia needed to get far away from Ken Kanning's idea of parenting advice. "We'll contact you tomorrow."

The goth girl followed Kord and his mother to a beige minivan. Kord was already talking about his next YouTube episode. If the girl replied, her voice didn't carry as well as his.

Seventeen

Giulia and Frank reached home simultaneously. Frank opened his door and the wails of a starving wolf cub filled the garage.

"Thank God. His diaper's clean, and I don't possess the necessary equipment. Finn, the waitress is here with your supper."

Giulia unbuckled the baby from his car seat. "You'll be giving him incorrect ideas. I am so much more than a milk jug." Finn's wails subsided to whimpers the moment he nestled against Giulia's shoulder. "Did I make a tasteless joke?"

Laughing, Frank kissed her. "You did, and it was probably the mildest one I've ever heard."

Giulia murmured nonsense to Finn, whose voice had revved up again. "I have to get inside, little one."

Finn was having none of it. Giulia dropped her wet coat and messenger bag on the rug and took a clean dishtowel from the kitchen on her way to the couch. Frank closed the door to the garage and cupped a hand behind one ear.

"What's this I hear? I believe it's silence."

"Men. Constantly hungry, no stamina, and zero patience." Giulia brushed Finn's cheek with one finger.

"Is this where you remind me I missed fifteen of your seventeen hours of labor because I was bringing in the Parking Lot Slasher, thereby giving untold numbers of citizens their first decent night's sleep in weeks?"

Giulia switched Finn to the other side. "You realize you will be reminded of those fifteen hours for the rest of your life."

"Now you know why men invented beer."

"I would be extremely happy to learn that the first ancient Sumerian to invent beer was an overworked woman who had in fact been trying to craft a recipe for better bread yeast." She smiled up at her husband. "He's a little vacuum cleaner tonight. I have a fast dinner planned, so please don't eye Scarlett and the grill."

Frank walked over to the three-foot square cage by the front door. "Your chameleon needs water. A need I can and will take care of."

"'Nurturer' is your middle name." She burped the baby and arranged him in the portable newborn lounger she carted around the house with her. "Frank, this contraption is the most amazing accessory ever."

He came into the room to tickle the baby's feet. "I dare you to call your old Mother Superior and tell her all about the wonders of modern baby conveniences."

She held out her phone to him. "Only if you call Captain Jimmy on speaker so he can hear you sing *The Addams Family* theme while you make Finn laugh."

He didn't answer right away because he was performing that exact ritual. "Touché. Instead, tell me all about your guest-starring role on today's episode of *Keeping up with the Kannings*."

Eighteen

At ten to eight Giulia entered the Pine Duff Diner and slid into the booth closest to the Pine Avenue door. This booth was also the farthest from the two families with boisterous children. She resented losing family time, even though Finn was sacked out before she left the house and Frank was letting her nephews beat him in *Halo* online.

The diner was three-quarters full and everyone was eating breakfast, the diner's specialty. The greatest hits of the 1970s pulsed through the sounds of clinking silverware and multiple conversations.

"Evening, and welcome to the Pine Duff." The server, a middle-aged woman with limp braids and pain lines at the corners of her mouth, set a paper coaster and glass of water in front of her.

Giulia experienced instant sympathy. "Have you tried Skechers?"

The server brightened. "New pair on order. I'm wearing my old, collapsed ones and they're killing me. How'd you know?"

"Recent pregnancy ankles."

"Kids. The gift that keeps on giving." She handed her a menu.

"Two, please. I'm expecting someone."

At that moment, Archie Andrews—the one from the comics, not the one from the new show—opened the far door. Giulia chalked up the ability to make the comparison to streaming old TV shows during late-night Finn feedings. She half-stood and waved.

"Giulia Driscoll?"

"Good evening. Please have a seat."

The server returned with a second water glass and perked up even more. "We're known for our home fries."

"Breakfast at this hour?" He glanced at the menu. "Why not? Let's see...The number three special with decaf, please."

Giulia said, "Hash browns and one egg over easy with coffee, please."

"Coming right up." A bigger smile for Archie Andrews come to life.

"Okay, Ms. Driscoll, before I forget to ask, do you own the business?"

"I do."

"I was hoping you'd say that." Archie—that is, Edward Nelson—cast an irritated glance at the ceiling speakers. "I am probably alone in my opinion, but 'The Piña Colada Song' is not on the same level as anything by Rodgers and Hammerstein."

Since Giulia enjoyed kitschy pop and 80s glam rock, she sipped water.

"Anyway," returning his gaze to her, "I started the chamber of Commerce's Small Business Initiative Committee. Been President Emeritus for a bunch of years, but always happy to see one more entrepreneur keep some money out of the coffers of the conglomerates."

Their server returned with food.

"Awful fast," Nelson said.

The server looked sideways at him. "Hon, is this your first time? The Pine Duff serves up the fastest and best breakfast in town." She set out their plates and mugs and stood with her arms crossed. "Take a bite."

Nelson speared a forkful of home fries and chewed. "I apologize, my taste buds apologize, and my stomach apologizes."

"Accepted." The smile returned. "Enjoy your food."

"Seriously, this is great food." Nelson sliced a fluffy pancake. "I'm going to make this a regular stop." The bite of pancake disappeared. "So what's up with He Who Must Not Be Trusted?"

He said it with a touch of the sardonic. Disappointment flashed through Giulia. She revised her plan, since he wasn't an angry contact.

"We've been hired by the Jevens family—"

He coughed into his coffee mug. "Get half up front."

Giulia stirred a teaspoon of blueberry syrup into her coffee. "Our policy includes an initial retainer."

He stared at her doctoring the coffee. "Good...uh...idea." More pancakes stopped further comment.

She began again. "We've been hired by the Jevenses to look into the possibility of assets not mentioned in Vernon Jevens' will."

Nelson regained his stride. "Are you a professional dancer? You sure pirouetted around your meaning." He tried to soften it with a grin. "Apologies for being a smartass, but I see where you're headed. Owen the Shark thinks his dear departed daddy hid some cold hard cash. Owen never met a dollar he didn't like."

"The same can be said for most of us." Giulia sipped her coffee. Not bad, but the syrup was a little too thick.

"Touché." He added ketchup to his sausages. "I'm directing opera now. I could use a cash injection to repaint some set pieces. You'd be surprised how much a decent artist charges."

The Bee Gees sang "Stayin' Alive" over their heads. The family in the next booth sang along. Nelson glared at the ceiling. "I may only come here when the playlist begins after 1990."

Giulia replied to his earlier comment, "I've worked in the orchestra pit for the Cottonwood Community Theater for several years."

"Then you know how it is. Consider the griping said." He chewed and swallowed an entire sausage link. "Let me give you the gory details of my company's 'merger' with Jevens Holdings." The quotes around "merger" hung in the air.

Giulia nibbled her fast-cooling home fries.

"I started Balalaika as a source for actors and musicians to rent specialty costumes, instruments, and set pieces at reasonable prices. You know how fast those expenses contribute to high school drama departments and local theater companies going belly up." He signaled for more coffee.

Their server refilled both cups. "Everything taste okay?"

"Better than okay. I'll be back." Nelson's Schwarzenegger impression was bad enough to be funny.

"After a rough beginning," Nelson continued, "the business started to take off." His eyes avoided Giulia's second fusion of syrup and coffee. "I gained repeat customers from around the country. I even turned a small profit eleven months running. American Theater dot com did a feature article on me." He stirred milk into his coffee. "Thus bringing me to the attention of Jevens. Ever read *Les Misérables*? One character scavenges valuables off dead bodies and gets rich enough to buy into the aristocracy." A thoughtful expression gave his freckles the aspect of huddling to discuss the play on fourth and one. "I'm talking about the stage musical. I've seen it a dozen times, but I don't know if the characters are the same in the book. What I mean is, Owen's business model mirrors that character arc." With an ostentatious gesture, he took his pulse. "I didn't think I was dead when his lawyer first contacted me, but we all make mistakes."

Giulia obliged with a chuckle.

"The lawyer floated the idea of a buyout. I wasn't interested. You'd think that'd end the discussion, but you'd be wrong. Owen's lawyer pursued Balalaika like a starving man goes after a steak dinner. He left messages, he sent emails, he called to make appointments, which I refused to grant, he even contacted my ex-wife."

"Added together those actions might be considered harassment."

"Not according to my lawyer and trust me, I nagged him even at his bargain price of seventy-five dollars per hour. Jevens' lawyer spaced his love notes far enough apart to skirt the rules."

Giulia reached the end of her coffee. "How long did this go on?"

"About six months. I reached a point where I started to consider the offer to get some peace. Especially from the ex-wife. Her angle was how much better off she'd be with the extra alimony and for the sake of the years we shared, didn't I want to do this one little thing for her?" His glare into his coffee mug could well have soured the milk. "By the fifth month, she was giving me delicate hints about involving her lawyer." He drank from the mug without spitting out curdled milk, proof his glare lacked power.

"What changed your mind?" Giulia knew several lawyers, and the aggressive ones weren't solely limited to Owen Jevens' arsenal.

"No offense to you, because I know there are detectives and detectives, but he hired one of you to dig into my past."

She said in a light voice, "Too many unpaid parking tickets?"

"One restraining order."

The Partridge Family from the sound system and the family in the next booth belted out "I Think I Love You."

Nelson cracked his knuckles one at a time starting with his left thumb. "You'll find this out if you want, so I'll save you the trouble. Back in college I was into experimentation. The younger brother of a friend of mine wanted to check out the music department, so I volunteered to give him the tour." He glanced at the singers and lowered his voice. "It turned out we were both into experimentation. I learned how to pick locks when I left my trombone in the practice room one Friday and needed it for a weekend gig. So I got us in there after midnight and we, uh, got a little too loud. The security guard heard us and opened the door. He—my friend's brother—got scared and jumped out the second-floor window into the bushes. He'd left his clothes behind and ran across the quad with everything flapping in the glow from the all the security lights." He switched to the as yet uncracked knuckles on his other hand. "I would've followed, but I tripped over a hi-hat and it came crashing down on top of me. I sprained my ankle and a cymbal fell on my dignity."

He tried to freeze Giulia with another glare. "I know what you're thinking, and you're wrong. The age of consent in that particular state is fifteen and he was seventeen. I was nineteen. The college suspended me for five days and the kid's parents took it to a judge who made me get tested for every disease known to medical science. Then they slapped a restraining order on me."

"I see."

The glare deepened. "Thanks for judging me. Look, I'm forty-two. We're talking about something that was dealt with twenty-three years ago. Jevens' legal fiend sent me a registered letter with copies of all the documents. He didn't waste time playing coy. If I agreed to the buyout, all would be forgotten. If I didn't, another set of copies would be sent to the local network affiliates, the bank holding my business loans, and American Theater dot com." *Crack. Crack.* "You see the trap? In this day and age any kind of sexual scandal is death to a business involving minors. It wouldn't matter that Balalaika's transactions only involved adults with credit cards."

All knuckles having been cracked, he reached for his water, drank its remains in a gulp, and slammed the empty glass on the table. The sound went unnoticed as the singing family was packing up and the booth on the other side was empty.

Giulia said only, "So you agreed to the buyout."

"They had me by the short—sorry. They had me where they wanted me. I took the money and informed my ex that as I was now unemployed with an outstanding business loan, she would owe me alimony if we went back to court." The sardonic smile returned. "That was a good meeting." He tossed his napkin into the congealed syrup and sausage grease. "Did I give you what you needed?"

She signaled for the check. "You did."

"Does this have anything to do with the big Mardi Gras thing I've been hearing about?" He reached for the check, but Giulia snapped it up. "Thanks."

"I'm the one who requested this meeting." While the server ran the DI credit card, Giulia folded her napkin and set it next to her plate. Years of waiting tables and washing dishes had conditioned her never to place paper into syrup of any kind. "Thank you for your help."

A shrug. His anger had abated. "I'm directing opera again. Weeks of frustration and diva-wrangling, but I'd forgotten how much I'd missed it. Nothing beats applause."

Giulia pocketed the receipt and her card, left the tip, and stood. "I wish you success."

"I'm directing Donizetti's *L'Elisir d'Amore* at Carnegie Mellon the first two weekends in April. Call me and I'll comp you tickets."

Nineteen

Giulia opened the Nunmobile's driver side door. Nine o'clock. Finn would be awake and hungry by the time she got home. It was nice of Nelson to offer her tickets, but she wasn't an opera fan. It'd take more than the prospect of free entertainment to lure her away from Finn and Frank for a night. It was bad enough she was losing next Tuesday night with Finn because of work.

The little car's interior was at least twenty degrees colder than the outside temperature. She inhaled slowly, containing her temper.

"I was told word had gone out about no surprises in the car."

A male ghost in a torn and bloody business suit materialized in the passenger seat. "You're not driving."

He wasn't as solid-appearing as Florence the Gibson Girl could become. She could see the seat details through his striped suit and gray skin.

"You were lurking."

"Only for a few minutes. It's hard to remember how time works for the living."

He had a point. The business suit was several decades out of date, as was his hairstyle. She started the car.

"You have until I open my garage door. This is way past working hours."

"I know. We all know your rules about family. Don't put the car in gear yet." He peeled away the suit and several layers of skin beneath it, revealing bubbled bones.

Giulia blinked. Few sights startled her anymore, but she still needed a moment to get used to certain methods of death.

"What are your answers to my three questions?" She drove into traffic partly to get home and partly to forestall any more horror movie special effect sights.

"Yes, I was murdered. No, I don't know by whom. Yes, I can direct you to a legal source of payment." He resettled himself in the bucket seat. "You remind me of my mother. Family always came first with her."

"Thank you, I think." She drove through a yellow light.

"You've probably heard this, but it's a relief to talk to someone who can see us and doesn't run away shrieking in terror."

"I grew up watching horror movies. They laid a foundation." The next light turned red while she was half a block away. "You have seventeen minutes, depending on how many green lights we catch."

"Time is a constraint on the living. I'll do my best. What do you know about lye?"

"I've made homemade soap with it."

"It has other uses, especially when my wife and my business partner decided I was in the way."

The light changed. Giulia didn't waste time offering sympathy. "Keep talking."

NBA basketball on the TV was the only sound in the house when Giulia opened the door.

"I'm home. Is it near the end of a quarter?"

"Four seconds," Frank said from the couch. "Three. Two. He goes for three...and misses." The buzzer sounded and the TV switched off. "Lakers win, no surprise to anyone. How'd it go?"

"The former owner of Balalaika hates 1970s music, loves opera, and provided useful information. The evening appointment ended with a new ghost appearing in the car."

Frank pulled her next to him on the couch. "A moaner, a curmudgeon, or a gory death seeking justice?"

"The latter. He remembered to appear before I merged into traffic. At least they listen." She snuggled closer. "I need to expand the ghost rules. If this keeps up, they'll crowd out my regular business."

"Eleven to eleven thirty a.m. on alternate Thursdays?" He kissed the top of her head.

"If only. I'm thinking three to five p.m. on weekdays and ten to noon on Saturdays during housecleaning time. They'll give me something to listen to while mopping the floors."

"Nineteen-eighties Saturday mornings on the radio isn't cutting it anymore?"

"Their playlist has become limited to 1983. A good year, but Prince, The Eurythmics, Madonna, and Springsteen had careers beyond a single calendar year."

Finn's FEED ME cry sailed down the stairs.

"I am summoned."

Husband and wife untangled themselves.

"Remember when you were only debunking phony hauntings?" Frank said. "I miss those days."

"At least I came back from maternity leave with a bang."

Twenty

Frank muted the eleven-p.m. edition of *SportsCenter*. "What are those crazy Jack Russells barking about at this hour?"

"I may be paranoid," Giulia said from her side of the bed, "but would you check? I'm tied up here."

Frank kissed the top of his son's head. "Never let it be said I deprived my son of his proper nourishment."

He left the bedroom door open. Giulia could hear the chameleon hissing like an angry steam pipe all the way upstairs. She held the baby tighter but didn't call downstairs in case Frank was stalking a housebreaker.

Silent commercials for ambulance-chasing lawyers and the latest copper cooking tool had never made Giulia want so much to heave a rock through the screen. Frank returned before she acted on the urge and wrecked the TV.

"I hereby resolve to acquire greater respect for your paranoia."

"Someone was trying to break in?"

"Correct. Either the loudmouth dogs or the giant lizard or both scared them away. Remind me to buy Snausages for the dogs and fancy mealworms for the lizard to reward them." He climbed into bed and pulled the covers up to his neck. "My feet are blocks of ice. By the way, our thief might have been either a him or a her. I only caught a glimpse of a skinny back as they ran under a streetlight."

Giulia cuddled Finn, who made an annoyed noise. "Someone doesn't appreciate having his midnight snack interrupted."

Frank turned off the TV. "This is bad. The neighborhood's been mostly crime-free up to now."

"I have a strong desire to buy a sign I saw on Etsy: If you wake my sleeping baby, I will cut you."

"I'll make a note for your birthday."

"Seriously, we should talk about a home security system."

Finn had fallen asleep. Giulia put him against her shoulder and patted his back. "Burp, young man. You're not waking me up at two a.m. from gas pain again."

Frank took a turn with the patting. "Setting aside the expense, home security—"

Finn let loose an epic belch. Frank raised his arms in victory. "I have the touch."

"Yes, dear." Giulia set the baby in the bedside bassinet. "You were about to say a security system is useful for the office but will make us feel like prisoners in our own home. Now if we could get a zoning exception to dig a moat...Wait a second." She picked up her phone and opened the app linked to the office security system. "Look what we have here."

At 10:04:45 the motion-sensing camera caught a dark, thin figure crouching at DI's door. At 10:04:55, the figure took a metal nail file from its pocket. From 10:05:11 through 10:16:19 the camera recorded a good dozen attempts to jimmy the lock. At 10:16:41 the figure stood and the camera stopped after capturing a clear image of its black-clad legs as it ran downstairs.

Giulia paused the playback. "The phone screen is too small for me to see details."

"Did a rich client give you a three-carat engagement ring to guard or something?"

"Heaven forbid. We don't want that kind of responsibility." She frowned at her screen. "In case you were wondering, looking for details in a video taken at night in a dark hall of a person dressed all in black is the security camera version of Schrödinger's Cat." She held out the phone to him. "Does this back look familiar?"

He studied it. "Maybe. Send me a still tomorrow morning before I get distracted."

She replaced the phone on the nightstand. "Since our wannabe thief or thieves failed to breach either door, I'm going to sleep. Zlatan is scheduled to wake me at five."

Frank pulled her against him. "You know because we used his soccer star nickname for your entire pregnancy we're going to slip and call him that when he brings home his first girlfriend. It's inevitable."

"Shh. You'll give him nightmares."

Five Days to Mardi Gras

Cottonwood's only costume shop posted its biggest sales month in its history. It surpassed even October 1977, the Halloween after the first *Star Wars* movie was released.

Twenty-one

Giulia, Sidney, and Zane pushed three chairs together and watched the security video.

"Stop," Zane said. "I think I see a profile."

Giulia enlarged the frame. "If only the tip of a nose and one cheekbone were enough. I sent several frames to Frank to see if any jogged his memory."

A knock on the outer doorframe. "Police."

Giulia opened it. "Good morning. Oh, hi, Sasha. Are you on solo duty?"

"Hey, Giulia. Rob is downstairs interviewing the coffee shop people."

Giulia indicated the door. "The thief wore gloves but we didn't touch anything, just in case."

"I knew you wouldn't. Have to go through all the steps anyway. You have security cam footage for me?" Sasha knelt and opened a fingerprint case.

"Second thing I did this morning." She handed the officer a thumb drive.

Sasha pocketed it. "You're a model citizen. Go on back to work while I take care of this."

"You got an email," Sidney said.

Giulia made a face. "Frank says the back looks the same but he can't swear to it."

Sasha said from the outer door, "You're not going to be happy."

All of DI came to the outer office.

"No fingerprints, right?" Sidney said.

"Not one. Your visitor didn't know how to pick a lock, but they knew enough to wear gloves."

"I blame TV," Zane said.

"Says the video game addict," Sidney said. "Giulia, any prints at your house?"'

"No. We thought it was because the dogs and the chameleon scared him away, but now that we know he wore gloves..." Giulia frowned. "We might need a system for the house."

"Ugh," Sasha said. "Way to be a prisoner in your own home."

"Great minds think alike."

Sasha packed up. "My instincts tell me the only prints I lifted belong to you three."

"Thanks anyway. Neat job. Frank leaves twice the residue when he takes prints."

Sidney brought paper towels and environmentally friendly spray cleaner from the bathroom. "I'm not getting dark powder all over my coat."

Sasha held out a hand for a towel and wiped her fingers. "For two years I've been telling Captain Reilly he should have me retrain the entire precinct in the proper way to dust for prints."

The downstairs door *skreeked*. "Sasha, you finished? We've got a call."

"All set. See you later Giulia. I'll let you know if anything comes of the video."

Giulia trudged back to her desk. "So much for any hope of identifying our useless thief."

"Assuming the same guy failed here and at your house," Zane said, "what was he looking for?"

Giulia tapped a pencil on the nearest legal pad. "What's your current caseload, you two?"

Sidney spoke first. "The VanAuken and Turner prenup searches."

Zane followed. "Serving subpoenas to three deadbeat dads and two parole violators."

Giulia finished. "Plus three background checks and two searches for pedophile priests for the Diocese of Pittsburgh, and one ancestor hunt for the Bishop."

"Don't forget the ghosts," Zane said.

Sidney stiffened. "Do you have to be so casual about them?"

"It's been five months since our first ghost," Zane said. "We've had more than enough time to adjust our paradigms."

Giulia smiled at Sidney. "There's no time limit on getting used to the supernatural. Remember, I put on a professional face, but you should see me over at Rowan and Jasper's."

Sidney's spine relaxed. "It's a good thing Rowan's everybody's perfect squooshy aunt. If she wasn't, I'd lock myself in the bathroom when she brings her Tarot readings and ghost stories over here."

Zane's Apple watch *binged.* "*The Scoop* has a new teaser."

Twenty-two

Sidney groaned. "You follow *The Scoop*?"

Zane shrugged. "Everyone has a vice. Want to bet this is about yesterday?"

Giulia facepalmed. "I'll bring it up on my screen." She chose *The Scoop* from her bookmarks.

This time Sidney gasped. "You bookmarked them?"

"Know your enemies." Giulia clicked.

Ken Kanning's mellifluous voice came through a black screen. "Have you ever seen a ghost?"

A moaning white shape floated across the screen.

"Have you ever contacted the dead?"

A black and white photo of a Victorian séance faded in and faded away.

"Have you ever wanted proof of life after death? Coming soon: Part One of *The Scoop* and the Ghosts of Cottonwood."

Giulia closed the tab.

Sidney said, "That was...restrained."

"Maybe they're trying for the PBS audience," Zane said.

Giulia snorted. "The day *The Scoop* woos away the PBS faithful is the day I give up coffee."

Zane's watch *binged* again. "Another one. They do this a lot."

Giulia pressed Play.

"The dead walk among us!" Ken Kanning's voice boomed through the speakers. Stock images of zombies and demons flashed on and off the screen in rapid succession. "How would YOU answer a message from the Other Side?"

A close-up of the Whiteboard and a quick cut to a different black and white illustration of a Victorian séance. In this one, the medium spewed ectoplasm.

"What if ghosts watch *The Scoop* from the afterlife? What if they contact us on live TV? Tune in and find out—soon!" Vincent Price's iconic laugh from the end of the "Thriller" video closed the teaser.

"I hope he got permission to use the laugh," Zane said.

"Should we call in an anonymous tip to ASCAP?" Sidney said.

Giulia said, "Sidney, are you practicing your disingenuous expression in the mirror every morning?"

Sidney put her hand over her heart. "It's a natural outcome of keeping my body and mind free of artificial ingredients of any kind."

"You can have my cherries jubilee coffee syrup when you pry it from my cold, dead, caffeinated hand." Giulia closed *The Scoop*'s window. "For the moment, since we can't recognize the intruder or confirm whether the same person tried both break-ins—" Her email roared. "Godzilla wants my attention." She enlarged the mail window. "Why is *The Scoop* emailing me? Which reminds me: Zane, please work up their invoice."

"What about the Whiteboard?"

"I'll hand it to Ken Kanning along with our bill." She clicked the email and read aloud, "Dear Giulia, here's the raw footage from yesterday. You kicked butt."

"Play it, play it," Sidney said. "You and Zane haven't told me anything about yesterday."

Giulia obeyed. Raw footage indeed, as Kanning's uncensored comments kept interrupting his usual *The Scoop* narration: "What dipshit cult do those twins belong to? Oh, wait, more idiot frat boys. They'll make for good footage."

Mini-Kanning took the mic and attempted to herd the cats.

"Kanning's son is going to be a star," Sidney said. "He already has the poise."

"Sometimes," Giulia said.

"He's eleven, right? Give him time."

The first two fights broke out on screen. The camera panned back and forth so quickly the images blurred.

Sidney's comments replaced Kanning's. "Nice one, Giulia. You too, Zane. What a bunch of morons." She sat back. "When Jessamine's old enough to go online, I will police her Internet usage like I'm Big Brother himself."

"Same here," Giulia said. "Every time I think about the crazies and creepers I shudder." Everything in her froze. "Hold it a second." She stopped the video, rewound it, stopped again and fast-forwarded. "Now I remember. I couldn't focus enough in the chaos." She pointed to a grinning man in a beige raincoat. "Listen." A high-pitched giggle cut through the yells, chants, and fighting. "He's the craft store creeper. I recognized the giggle."

"The one you got the store staff to toss out the other day?" Sidney leaned forward again. "Why's he at the kid's event?"

Giulia rewound further. "The goth girl with Kord. I'm pretty sure she's the girl he was following at the store."

"Scum bucket," Sidney said.

"Did he go anywhere near her?" Zane asked.

Giulia let the video play out. "Nothing here, and not that I recall. I'm not surprised, though. Too many witnesses." She made a note on a legal pad. "I have to let her know. Her parents, too. Since she's in Kord's YouTube videos, their parents should know each other. I think Kanning mentioned her when he convinced me to take his son as a client." She rubbed her temples. "One more task on the list."

"Want me to handle it?" Sidney said.

Giulia shook her head. "I'm the one who saw him in the craft store and at the soccer field. Eyewitness information is more believable, especially if their daughter is semi-autonomous."

Her email roared. She winced at her screen until she read the subject line. "It's not *The Scoop*. I set up an alert for anything Mardi Gras-party related."

The commercial from the local ABC affiliate opened with stock footage from Mardi Gras in New Orleans. This was followed by photos of children in the Pediatric Cancer Wing of Vandermark Memorial Hospital. Then it switched to the outside of the Jevens House of Kookiness. Underneath all these, the narrator outdid himself.

"Tuesday—Tuesday—Tuesday! The Mardi Gras event of the decade! Bring your friends. Bring your appetite. Bring your wallet to support Children with Cancer. Food, drink, games of chance, music, and dancing until the clock strikes midnight!"

The screen changed to a promotional still of *The Scoop*. Giulia groaned. The narration continued.

"As a special added attraction, *The Scoop* will be at the event! You could appear in a future episode! What are you waiting for? Get your tickets today!"

The promo ended with website addresses for the charity and for buying tickets, plus the date and location of the event on a purple and gold screen.

Giulia planted her forehead on her desk. "If I believed in curses, I'd pay Rowan to lift the one shackling me to *The Scoop*."

Twenty-three

"Speaking of our friendly neighborhood psychics." Giulia picked up the phone and dialed. "Jasper, It's Giulia. Is Rowan free?" She held up a "wait a second" finger at Zane and Sidney. "Hi, Rowan. How are you with possibly haunted objects?"

She hung up a moment later, smiling. "They'll be over as soon as they get their coats on."

Three minutes later the downstairs door screeched and two sets of feet began climbing the steep wooden stairs. Giulia opened the door.

"Welcome to our possibly haunted detective agency. We are not responsible for the actions of any mischievous ghosts."

Tarot Reader Rowan Froelig huffed across the threshold in a fuchsia coat, her many-layered lavender and green dress bursting through at the neck and below the coat's knee-length hem.

"As though you're not keeping any ghosts in line exactly the way you disciplined your high school students all the years you were Sister Latin Something." She struggled free of her sleeves. "This coat is shrinking." She pointed a violet-nailed finger at Sidney. "Don't you dare blame it on my secret stash of Thin Mints."

Sidney's expression of startled innocence caused Zane to snatch Rowan's coat and turn away from the room.

Jasper hung up his own long black coat. "Auntie, don't scare the private eyes. They have ways of unearthing your darkest secrets."

The plump psychic scowled up into her nephew's face. "Sidney knows I'm joking. You, Mister War Hero, ought to have more respect for my age and skills."

He took her hand in his prosthetic one, his original hand having been blown off by an IED when he saved the lives of his fellow soldiers. He raised her hand to his lips. "I abase myself before you."

"As well you should. Giulia, I need a chair. My feet are killing me." She plopped into the first chair by the window and stuck out her legs. The ruffles of her dress fell away to reveal plum patent-leather boots with three-inch heels. "Never choose fashion over comfort, kids. I should be old enough to know better, but I gave in to an urge to relive my youth."

Jasper took the opposite chair. "Yet she nags me to set an example."

"Hush up. Giulia, where's the haunting you promised?"

Giulia opened her messenger bag and set the Whiteboard on the table.

Rowan made a face. "I was hoping for a Chatty Cathy spewing pea soup."

"Nooo, don't make me connect pea soup and hauntings," Sidney said. "I like pea soup."

Rowan patted her hand. "Sorry, sweetie. I forgot you're the wholesome one."

Giulia put her hands on her hips. "What does that make Zane and me?"

Jasper cut in. "Zane is the Singularity and you're the Ghost Tamer. The spirit world bows before your Ruler of Correction."

Zane and Giulia said simultaneously, "I like it."

"Maybe it's time for new business cards." Giulia glanced over at Zane.

"We never did order ones with 'The Power of DI Compels You.'"

Rowan waved a hand at them. "Giulia, explain this contraption, please."

"Ken Kanning's eleven-year-old son—"

"Ken Kanning spawned?" Despair overwhelmed Jasper's voice.

"Check out his YouTube channel," Zane said. "Kord's Kernels with two 'K's."

"I'd rather host a crystal divination party for a classroom of ninth grade girls."

Rowan said without taking her gaze from the Whiteboard, "Word got out that Jasper is a hot babe of the highest caliber. We have a steady clientele of high school girls who all want Tarot readings and crystal jewelry."

"They travel in packs," Jasper said. "And they giggle. All the time."

Giulia failed to repress a smile. "Do you make sure their readings are filled with sweetness and light?

He sent a bitter glance in her direction. "I won't prostitute my skill to such an extent. If the cards indicate negative future events, I frame them in terms of being cyberbullied or getting hooked on K2 or not practicing safe sex."

"You'll be the savior of an entire generation of hormonal teenagers," Zane said.

Rowan said with certainty, "Ten years from now half the kindergarten class of VanderGroot Elementary will be named Jasper."

"God forbid." Jasper turned soulful eyes to Giulia. "Tell us why you called us about this toy."

Giulia summarized the science fair creation. Zane followed up with the soccer field debacle. Giulia finished with the two attempted break-ins.

Rowan took Sidney's hands in her own. "Honey, your beautiful green aura is spiking with slush gray like a porcupine. You know how bad stress is for you. You trust Giulia and Jasper and me. We can handle any ghost in the tri-state area."

Sidney gave her a wan smile. "My learning curve is longer than most."

"Not by a country mile. You ask Jasper about his first precognitive flashes." She whispered a little too loud: "He was five. I had to wash a lot of tighty-whities."

Sidney stifled a giggle.

"Auntie." Jasper's colorless voice said more than a burst of anger would have.

Giulia drew a square in the air like a soccer referee signaling for a video review. Zane saw it and slid into his desk chair and brought up YouTube. Once again, Giulia congratulated herself on hiring a genius.

"Rowan, Jasper, this should explain everything." He played the "socks in the gym bag" video.

Rowan looked from the screen to the Whiteboard and back again. When the segment ended, she said, "Video trickery."

"Magnets or fishing line," Jasper said.

"Exactly what we said." Giulia picked up the Whiteboard. "Before Kanning's son could demonstrate this thing in front of us, the crowd at his event got out of hand."

Jasper took the Whiteboard from Giulia. "I had something like this when I was a kid. Didn't everybody?" He turned it upside down, flipped it back to front, turned it face up again. "This is well made." He rotated the knobs. A few minutes later he showed them all a recognizable Emperor Tarot card.

Zane studied it. "I give up. The only one I can recognize on sight is the naked Adam and Eve one."

Sidney laughed. "Zane, that is the most typical guy thing you've ever said."

Jasper winked at Zane. "This is the Emperor, one of the cards of protection." He turned the Whiteboard back around. "It's staying intact. That pretty much squashes the idea of this thing being haunted. Any ghost with a smidgen of oomph would've erased this card with a vengeance."

Giulia inspected the drawing. "In all seriousness, what if it's haunted by a ghost without an agenda?"

Rowan said, "Pull the other one."

Jasper said, "Every ghost has an agenda. Otherwise they wouldn't be hanging around here."

"Unless they liked playing practical jokes," Zane said.

Sidney groaned. "Don't tell my brothers-in-law. They'll beg us to find ghosts to play tricks with."

Giulia and Rowan shared a glance. "I promise not to discuss any trickster ghosts with your family," Giulia said.

Rowan held out her hands for the Whiteboard. "I don't get a sense of active malevolence from it."

Sidney kept her distance. "That's good, right?"

"It's certainly better than it could be. If this thing really was haunted, it'd be the same as a Ouija board in the hands of amateurs. You know my opinion of Ouija boards."

"Which I share," Giulia said.

Jasper said with a professional gleam in his eye, "Can we bust it open?"

Zane gleamed back. "Can we, please?"

"Not on your lives." Giulia took it out if their reach. "This is client property which we will return intact."

"Adulting is no fun," Zane said.

"Back to the teenagers." Jasper's shoulders slumped.

Rowan heaved herself out of her chair. "They pay the bills." She took one step and winced. "Back to Skechers for my poor feet. Farewell, beautiful boots."

Zane held her coat for her. She favored him with her wide smile.

"You, young man, are a maiden's dream, which has nothing to do with my grandmotherly status." She connected the toggle buttons. "Giulia, don't let down your guard."

Twenty-four

Giulia's cell phone rang at ten p.m. Frank took the sleeping baby from her shoulder and headed upstairs to put him to bed.

"Giulia? It's Rowan. Turn on the little Kanning's YouTube channel right now."

"Rowan, the video won't go stale before office hours tomorrow."

"I know you don't want your home invaded, but the kid is broadcasting live. Did you give him back his toy?"

"Not yet."

"Get rid of it. Is your computer on?"

"A few more seconds. Why are you so insistent about the Whiteboard? You dismissed it this morning." Giulia opened YouTube and clicked Kord's channel. The screen went black. "Darn it. Just a second, Rowan. Something's wrong with my screen."

"No, don't touch it. The little idiot's out in the cemetery with a spirit box."

Giulia turned up the volume. Kord's whisper became audible.

"...Mom said they're called rummage sales and they're a big church thing." As he spoke, a bright, diffused beam of light bobbed up and down.

Rowan said in Giulia's ear, "Camera phones need something to steady them. I'm getting seasick."

Frank slid onto the couch next to Giulia. "Note to self: filming with a smartphone flashlight will not make you the next Steven Spielberg."

Giulia touched her finger to her lips.

From the mostly black screen: "So these rummage sales are full of books nobody wants to read, junky baby toys, and clothes from, like, the 1960s. It's old lady heaven."

A different voice hissed, "Talk softer. There's somebody over in those trees."

"Sorry." Kord's stage whisper dropped to a real whisper. "I made my mom drive me to like two dozen rummage sales until I found, like, the Holy Grail of ghost box makers. It's a RadioShack model 20-125."

The light increased.

"That's not from a smart phone. What's he using for light?" Frank said.

"Tell Frank the kid said he had a pocket spotlight hooked to his phone. Now tell him to hush up."

Giulia relayed both messages. Frank murmured, "I hear and obey."

Kord's whisper continued. "You guys can look up online how to convert a radio into a ghost box. It's stupid easy."

A slim figure stepped into the light and stopped in front of a flower pot wall.

Giulia squinted at the screen. "I thought they were in a cemetery."

"It's the urn garden," Rowan said. "Shhh."

Giulia and Frank shared a confused glance.

Kord said, "My Whiteboard is, um, in for repairs."

Rowan snorted.

"So I wanted to help Shiloh talk to her dad again."

A thin arm waved frantically at Kord.

"Okay, everyone, here we go." The light and video closed in on a camouflage urn.

A plaintive voice said, "Daddy, are you here?"

A burst of static from the radio in her hand.

"Daddy? Can you try again?"

More static. A phrase from a Beatles song. A few random words.

"Shiloh?" Kord said. "Is he here?"

The teenager shook her head.

"Maybe you should tell him how it works?"

"This kid's got it bad," Rowan said.

"We noticed it at the soccer field," Giulia began as Shiloh's voice came through the speaker.

"Daddy, I'm holding a radio Kord altered for me. It can't stay tuned to any single station anymore, it just keeps going up and down the dial past all the songs. You're supposed to pick out bits of song lyrics to talk to me." She touched the radio to the camouflage urn. "I know you can do this, even though the Whiteboard was easier. Please, Daddy? Talk to me?"

Silence. Not even crickets or a car passing in the dark.

Kord stage-whispered, "Maybe he needs something basic to get the hang of it, Shi. Ask him if you should drive to school or take the bus."

"He's not stupid, Kord."

Kord became even more tentative. "I know, but he's dead. Maybe it takes longer to learn things when you're all transparent and stuff."

Giulia laughed. "Rowan, did I tell you about the college professor ghost? He got blackballed in the McCarthy era and kept trying to teach me advanced calculus."

"Math is useful in Tarot."

"Math, yes, but not calculus."

On screen Kord said, "Shi, are you getting anything? I'm cold."

"Grow a pair."

Kord giggled in a much higher register than adult Sidney. "Shi, this is a live feed."

"Shut up. Somebody's creeping on me. See him on the other side of the urn garden?" A hiss. "Don't shine the light on him."

"Should I call my Dad?"

A sharper hiss. "No. I have to talk to Daddy." She shook the radio until its inner workings rattled. "Come on, Daddy. Please use this thing to talk to me."

A police car with wailing sirens filled the pause with the perfect Doppler effect.

"Daddy?"

A pause. The sound of feet crunching in the winter-dry grass. The light swung above the urns and was immediately jerked back to Shiloh.

"Come on, Dad. You can do it."

A longer pause. No crunching footsteps this time.

"Daddy!" Shiloh threw the radio into the grass at her feet and fell sobbing to her knees in the grass.

Rowan made a rude noise. "Teenagers and drama. She's probably in real grief but her overblown gestures are ridiculous."

"Standard operating procedure for some teenagers," Giulia said.

"You're the expert."

The picture bobbled as it came down to Shiloh's level.

"Um, Shi, I'm sorry it didn't work tonight, but we can try again."

"You don't understaaand..."

"Um, well, no, but I don't want you to be sad." A skinny arm in a royal blue ski jacket reached into the picture.

Shiloh batted it away, scrambled to her feet, and ran out of view. Kord turned the camera on himself.

"I guess we'll call it quits for tonight. I'll work on the ghost box some more and we'll try again. Keep checking my feed for the day and time of the new try."

The screen went dark as he yelled, "Hey, Shiloh, you have to drive me home!"

Four Days to Mardi Gras

In the darkness of the closed messenger bag, the round knobs of the Whiteboard began to turn.

Twenty-five

Ken and Kord Kanning knocked on DI's door at 8:01 the next morning. Giulia, in early, opened the door herself. She welcomed them, inured to the spectre of Ken Kanning haunting her with more persistence than any ghost.

"Good morning. I'm putting together your final invoice. If you'll wait I'll have it ready in a few minutes."

Kord held out his hand. "Good morning, Ms. Driscoll. Thank you for your assistance on Wednesday."

Giulia shook his hand. There might still be time to save Kord from becoming a Ken Kanning clone. "You're welcome. You wouldn't be skipping school, would you?"

A happy grin. "Dad called and told the office I had a family emergency. Wait'll I tell my friends they had to go in and I didn't." He shrugged off his backpack. "I brought you something. Can I use your table?"

"Go right ahead."

Kord unzipped the flap and took out an old-fashioned portable radio. "Dad says you're into ghosts. This is a ghost box. It's supposed to help dead people talk to live people. It's kind of rare because RadioShack doesn't make this model anymore."

Giulia kept last night's viewing party to herself. "Thank you, but it's not necessary."

A Ken Kanning Smile appeared on Kord's face. "Wanna trade? The ghost box for my Whiteboard."

"I don't—"

"I really, really, really want my Whiteboard back."

She shook her head. "That's not what I mean. The Whiteboard is yours. We took it on Wednesday because things got out of hand."

Light dawned. "Oh, I get it. Like protective custody."

Giulia got the feeling her status had gone up several notches. "It's in my office. If you'll follow me?"

Kanning and Kord took the client chairs. Giulia freed the Whiteboard from her messenger bag. A few words were scrawled on its screen. Without reading them, she pretended to shake it free of the bag to cover the erasure of whatever Frank had written. What had he been thinking? He knew better than to mess with a client's property. She didn't want to imagine what he'd written.

"Here you go."

Kord snatched it. "Awesome. Thank you. Okay, Dad, your turn."

Before Giulia had time to cringe, Kanning launched. "Giulia, I want to expand the scope of our current contract. Kord and I want you to help establish him as a legitimate investigative reporter."

If Giulia had one thing in common with Ken Kanning, it was the ability to make a quick recovery. She pulled up DI's current caseload. The Mardi Gras project in bold purple letters dominated the spreadsheet.

"Mr. Kanning."

Kord preempted her. "Ms. Driscoll, let me explain why I need outside verification." He pronounced the five-syllable word as though he'd practiced in the van on the way. "My short-term goal is to get accepted into Shady Side Academy. Have you heard about it?"

"It's one of the most exclusive schools in Pittsburgh, and consequently difficult to get into."

"You know it. It's even harder when you live outside the city, like me. So I need a killer résumé."

Giulia's face didn't crack. The young man was conscious of his own charm, but he possessed sincerity his father lacked.

Kord continued. "My long-term goal is a master's in communication from Northwestern or Stanford. Then an internship at a local TV station and right on up to the national stage." He glanced up at his father. "Dad's always fighting to prove his show is real reporting, the same as anything on CNN. He gets legit hate mail. Some people are total morons." He leaned as far across the desk as he could stretch.

"That's why I need you. You're a legit business, you have a license and everything. You, like, testify in court as an expert. If you follow me when I'm working the Whiteboard and write up reports on how I'm doing it all to show how it's an experiment in group psychology and I'm using real research techni—techniques, I'll counter..." His mouth stayed open as he searched for the word.

"Counteract," Giulia supplied.

"Right. You'll counteract any stupid prejudice the Shady Side committee has against Dad's show. See how it can't be only Dad and me on this project?"

Both Kannings knew Giulia had been about to refuse the scope creep request. As Kord explained, his natural enthusiasm sliced through his imitation of his father's varnish. The longer he talked, the more she leaned toward helping him.

Which meant a longer contract with Ken Kanning. Perhaps today was Opposite Day.

She studied the spreadsheet. It could be done if she rearranged this...and worked after she put Finn to bed on this and this...

She opened a comment field and typed in her ideas.

"Mr. Kanning, with some effort we'll be able to squeeze you into our schedule.

Kanning slugged his son's shoulder. "Giulia, Kord and I appreciate your effort."

"You understand this will require an addendum to your original contract."

"Certainly. Always ready to pay for quality work. Remember, Kord, it's all about building relationships within the community."

This was the infallible warning sign of Giulia needing a brain cleanse: she agreed with Kanning's business advice.

Kord turned into a human fireworks display. "Ms. Driscoll, this is going to be so cool. You know about my Whiteboard, but did you know I made the ghost box all by myself? I mean, it's super easy to modify the radio, but when I present my video portfolio to the Shady Side admissions team, they'll totally see how I'll fit right into their para— uh—para—"

"Paradigm," Kanning said.

"Yeah. Paradigm. Not only that: I'm genetically predis—darn it,

Dad, I forgot again."

The Smile became indulgent. "You're predisposed with both the genetics and the aptitude to excel in ways which will increase the reputation of the organization."

With that, Giulia reached her Kanning quota. She checked the calendar. "Kord, are you free for an initial meeting at two or two thirty today?"

Kanning interrupted. "What's wrong with right now? We have the time."

Giulia frosted him. "Mr. Kanning, I will not rearrange our entire schedule for one client."

Kord *meeped*. "Is two thirty okay, Dad?"

Twenty-six

At ten the same morning, the three members of Driscoll Investigations stood before the wrought iron gates at the end of Vernon Jevens' driveway.

"A glimpse into the world of homeowners who can afford MaidPro," Sidney said.

"They can? How do you know?" Zane asked.

Giulia and Sidney shared a look.

"Not being sarcastic here. What's the clue?"

"Zane, do you own a vacuum?" Sidney asked.

"Yeah, why? Oh."

A vintage Mercedes in all its boxy glory parked behind the Nunmobile. Owen Jevens exited the driver's side and unlocked the gate. "You're on time. An excellent practice to cultivate. Good for business."

Their cars followed the Mercedes around the curved driveway and parked at the front door. Owen opened the passenger door for his aunt.

"Oh, my sciatica. Owen, give me your arm." Blossom creaked out of the car wearing the same gray dress.

"Yes, dear aunt."

"Sarcasm is bad for your business deals, dear nephew."

"You're family, Aunt. You get the real me." He turned his toothy smile on Giulia. "Time's a-wasting."

Giulia tried to remember the last time they had a client she liked.

"I presume you have a plan mapped out for Tuesday." He unlocked the front door. "I'd ask to see it, but I know what I'd say if someone wanted the inside scoop on one of my deals ahead of time."

He flung open the door. "Welcome to the family flea market."

They crowded in behind him and his aunt. The hall appeared pitch black after the sunny morning.

"Hold on a second," Owen said, his hand fumbling along the wall. "The switch is right...along...here."

Light flooded the foyer.

Sidney screamed.

Twenty-seven

Blossom cackled at Sidney. "Vernon got you."

"I beg your pardon." Red-faced, Sidney sounded more like her grandmother than herself.

A papier-mâché clown the size of a teenager clung upside down to the newel of a wide staircase. Its glass eyes, aimed directly at the front door, caught and threw back the wall lights. Three four-by-five paintings of human heads in various stages of colorful decay hung on the wall separating the family room from the dining room.

Giulia kept her voice expressionless. "A Halloween fundraiser would've been a good choice, too."

Owen said over his shoulder, "You and Vernon might have gotten along, and that's saying something." He continued into the kitchen and turned on more lights.

Blossom's arthritic hand beckoned them into the dining room. "Owen's better on stairs, so I'll start you on the first floor."

They followed her like ducks but as one stopped before entering the dining room.

"I think I see a table and chairs in there somewhere," Sidney whispered.

"No need to whisper, young woman. The family knows how the house appears to outsiders."

Artwork of varying sizes and styles covered every square inch of wall. Picasso copies. Cats on velvet. Primitive houses, landscapes, flower gardens.

The china cabinet's glass doors ought to have burst from the pressure of three complete sets of dishes: blue flowers, gold edges, and

Christmas wreaths.

Dolls and preserved animals overshadowed it all. Sitting in the corners, perched on the top of the china cabinet, peeking out from among silk ferns, winking at them from chairs and vases and knickknack shelves and lampshades. China dolls. Stuffed dolls. Ceramic poodles, cats, parakeets. Clay primitives of goddesses and gods. Jointed wooden antiques. The red-painted walls augmented the riot of colors.

Blossom made an unladylike noise. "You should see your faces."

Giulia recovered first. "The photos you gave us didn't do it justice."

"That's rich." She raised her voice. "Owen, get down here."

He clattered downstairs at a speed which his age belied. "What's wrong?"

Blossom gave him a look. "Nothing, you old woman. Our detectives say pictures of the house don't do it justice."

Owen's irritation melted into humor. "A precise description. Some rooms are worse than others. Follow me."

Compared to the dining room, the kitchen appeared almost normal. Perhaps because cooking surfaces needed to be free of obstructions, the decorating scheme had been contained to the walls and ceiling.

The breakfast room also reflected Vernon Jevens' affinity for inhuman company. At least one chair in each room held a life-sized occupant. The breakfast room had three plus a butler.

Giulia walked over to one of the seated figures and touched its hand. "It feels like one of those soft baby dolls parents fought over one Christmas in the 1980s."

"Cabbage Patch Dolls," Sidney said. "My older sister had one. I used to hide it from her."

"I once thought you were the sweetest person I'd ever met."

Sidney bridled. "She used to hide glow-in-the-dark monster figurines in my bed." She gazed at the lineup of staring black glass eyes. "These may be worse."

Zane cleared his throat. "Will the house be staying as is for Mardi Gras?"

"What do you think?" Blossom said.

Owen nodded. "The décor is part of the attraction. The charity people lost their collective minds when we brought them here."

Driscoll Investigations shared a glance indicating they were one in heart and mind regarding the décor.

Giulia said, "You're not worried about theft because you have us, correct?"

"Theft of this trash?" Owen asked.

"We'd send a thank you note to anyone who walks off with some of it." Blossom's lips wrinkled into a sneer. "Come on through to the game room."

Giulia decided the most appropriate tchotchke on the entire first floor was the hand-carved "Last chance to RUN!" sign. "I gather you've had a cleaning crew in?"

"Three times, and they cost a fortune," Owen said.

Blossom drew a finger along the edge of a crowded shelf. "You should've seen this place when we finally got the keys. No one had been in here since Vernon kicked off." She showed Owen her clean finger.

He shrugged it off. "My wife used to complain about cleaning the house. If she were still alive, I'd bring her over here to shut her up."

"You try scrubbing floors and cleaning dirty dishes for a week," Blossom said.

"Like you've scrubbed a floor in the last thirty years, you old bag."

"If I had some soap, I'd wash out your mouth with it."

"If you didn't trip over the hem of your throwback dress trying to get to me." Owen turned his back on his aunt and led the procession into the family room.

The bay window's panoramic view of the swimming pool, lawn, and stand of trees at the edge of the property distracted the owners from their bickering. Sidney gulped at the tiger and zebra skins on the floor and the eight-point buck antlers over the fireplace. Giulia touched the elephant trunk lamp stand. *Fake,* she mouthed at Sidney. Perhaps the skins were, too.

This room had its own obsession: bookends minus books. Silver, bronze, ceramic, wood. All carved or glazed or painted and in dozens of different forms. Including, Giulia saw, dolls.

Zane said in Giulia's ear, "At least he doesn't have a wall of those singing fish on plaques."

A pair of shoes from each of the last fifteen decades adorned the fifteen steps. Air Jordans from the 1990s started the parade and Victorian high-button boots finished it at the top.

"Those sneakers are worth three hundred, easy, on eBay," Zane said.

"I'm taking enough pictures to overload my phone," Giulia said. "I didn't know you played basketball."

"I don't, but one of my gaming friends wears anything vintage Jordan."

Giulia took several photos of the staircase from a sense of thoroughness. Vernon Jevens the lover of tricks could have added hidden compartments to the stairs as in the old black and white movie *13 Ghosts*.

"Mr. Jevens, I presume you've checked the stairs and all the furniture with drawers."

Owen said from the top of the stairs, "We explored them all as soon as we got the rights to the house. Not even a hidden piece of paper."

Blossom said from the end of the line, "You'd think any crazy old miser worthy of the name would at least hide a stock certificate or three. Leave it to Vernon to break the mold."

The upstairs rooms continued the decorating scheme. The master bathroom was covered in gingham and mirrors. The master bedroom, patchwork quilts, chairs, curtains. Defying all laws of physics, this floor's art room crammed two rooms' worth of creations into its twelve-by-ten-foot area. The library was the neatest room in the house, if one didn't count shelves overflowing with books as a mess.

Zane murmured after the Jevenses had moved into the hall, "I may develop a doll phobia."

"I'm about to have an allergic reaction to papier-mâché." Giulia shuddered at a one-eyed zombie harlequin.

"What's with the license plate obsession in every single room?" Sidney pointed to three.

"Forty-two in the house so far, by my count," Zane said.

"Some people collect shoes, some people collect clothes," Giulia began.

"And some people collect everything they can get their hands on,"

Sidney said. "Does this family have extra competitive genes? Don't answer that. I was being rhetorical."

The entertainment room did Sidney in. Deer heads loomed over the pool table. Stuffed crows, hawks, blue jays, finches, and cardinals swung from the ceiling on a fishing line. A stuffed child doll riding a tricycle was bolted upside down to the ceiling. Alternating hamsters and guinea pigs had been mounted around the sixty-inch TV so they appeared to be watching the screen.

When everyone was back on the first floor, Owen showed them a closed door off the kitchen. "The basement is locked. It will stay locked for the party. Come out to the deck."

Yesterday's sleet had iced over a foosball table and four rocking chairs. The outdoor kitchen on the arm of the L-shaped deck—grill, sink, bar, refrigerator—also shivered under a crust of ice. A life-sized stuffed shark hung from fishing line over the kitchen's aqua and white tiles.

"The pool's closed and we won't let anyone out here. The weather's supposed to get down into the thirties Tuesday night, so no one will want to extend the party outside."

"All we need is to be sued by the family of some drunk idiot who fell through the pool cover and drowned." Blossom poked a rocking chair. Ice cracked off its arm and fell onto the deck.

Sharp *tinkles* from the ice mingled with Big Ben-style *bongs* in the house.

"I'll get the door," Owen said.

The chair kept rocking. Giulia gave it the side eye.

Twenty-eight

"Mr. Jevens, we can't thank you enough for giving us more time to finalize our plans."

Two women and one man shed their coats in the foyer and emerged wearing identical "Children with Cancer Annual Charity Gala" polo shirts. Their names were embroidered above the slogan: Marcia, Ron, Angie.

Marcia, the woman with gold and purple striped hair, took charge of the house as though it were hers. She handed clipboards to prematurely bald Ron and round glasses with pink tinted lenses Angie.

Owen turned on a personality Giulia hadn't yet seen: offensive patronage.

"Marcia, anything for the cause. We're almost finished giving our detectives a private tour."

The charity staff's heads swiveled as one toward DI. An inveterate hater of being on display, Giulia squashed an impulse to imitate a monkey shaking the bars of a zoo cage.

"Detectives?" Marcia said. "I'm sure we discussed hiring off-duty police to watch ticket sales, bar, and gaming tables."

"We did." Owen's smile didn't reach his eyes. "Driscoll Investigations will be attending as guests of the family."

Marcia backed down. "I see. Well, we don't want to take up more of your valuable time than we absolutely have to. Ron, Angie, let's get to work."

Giulia blocked her path, hand out, and got a quick, firm handshake in return. "I'm Giulia Driscoll. It's a pleasure to meet you. We'd like to shadow your people. When we know your plans for the rooms, we'll be able to avoid accidental interference."

Suspicion and territorialism clouded Marcia's face, but Giulia wore innocence like a saint.

"Makes sense," Marcia said after a moment.

"Thank you. Zane, would you go with Ron and Sidney, would you pair up with Marcia? Giulia moved next to Angie. "Nice to meet you."

Zane and Sidney brought out their phones and took notes. Giulia and Angie headed up to the entertainment room.

"Oh, good," Giulia said. "My assistant isn't a fan of taxidermy."

Angie shuddered. "Neither am I. What's entertaining about dead animals? They're a great decoration for the party, though. If only the Jevenses would let us post pictures of these rooms in the ads. Pictures would bring in even more warm bodies on Tuesday."

She checked off notes about the room dimensions, the door placement, the pool table. "The felt will get ripped, guaranteed. Drunks and accuracy don't mix. It's a good thing the local taxi companies donated rides to the cause for party night."

"Would you think less of me if I admitted I secretly covet the stained glass floor lamps in the family room?" Giulia had already made a mental note to ask the Jevenses if they were for sale after the party.

Angie gave her a conspiratorial smile. "I'm not into breakables, but if no one was looking I'd sneak into the downstairs game room and stuff the Star Wars chess set under my coat. My kids think those movies are the only ones in existence."

Giulia eased into the opening she'd created. "Did you know Vernon Jevens?"

"Nope. I was in charge of sending him an annual thank you note for his contributions, but I never met him. Heard he was a crackpot."

Giulia smiled. "Aren't the rich merely eccentric?"

A short laugh. "You bet. The richer they are, the more eccentric they get to be." She eyed Giulia. "So what's your story?"

Amateur, Giulia thought. "The Jevenses have hired us to watch the partygoers."

"Oh, right, like those department store detectives. You mean they really care if someone pockets a piece of their junk? I bet they don't know half of what's crammed into this place." She flipped over a page on her clipboard. "Done here. Family room's next."

Blossom happened to be tying her orthopedic shoe in the hall near the door. "How are you progressing? Do you need any information from the family?"

Angie became The Perfectly Polite Young Woman. "You're so kind, Mrs. Burd, but we don't want to disturb you. We're finishing all the nitpicky details. Now we're measuring everything to make the best use of the available rooms."

Blossom made a noncommittal sound and closed herself in the bathroom.

"Busybody." The real Angie wrinkled her nose at the closed door.

"How interesting we both knew to keep our voices down." Giulia's voice remained low as they passed the stairway shoe collection on their way to the family room.

Angie became busy writing notes. "She reminds me of my mother-in-law. Her husband died five years ago and left plenty of life insurance. Now she sits at a window all day with high-tech binoculars, spying on everybody."

"Don't judge me too harshly," Giulia said, "but I wouldn't mind putting your mother-in-law on retainer."

Angie laughed. "She'd eat it up. But actually, don't. The woman is constitutionally incapable of keeping anything to herself."

"We live in a fallen world."

"Oh my God, you were taught by nuns. Nobody else on the planet uses that expression." Angie held out a fist and Giulia bumped it. "Do you still have nightmares? We had this one nun in eighth grade homeroom whose face probably would've cracked in half if she smiled." She eyeballed the furniture. "The zydeco band will fit in here if we move the sofas and chairs closer to the tchotchke-filled shelves. The nuns weren't all bitches from hell, if you know what I mean. When I was a senior we had this young nun for sex ed. She was all about practicing safe sex, even though she was required to teach abstinence. There's nothing more useless than preaching 'keep it in your pants' to thirty-eight horny teenagers. If you can believe me, she brought in a wooden penis and used it to show us the right way to put on a condom. We were dying to know if she ditched her habit and went into an adult store to buy it. Nobody had the guts to ask her." She gave a couch a trial push. "Yay. The legs have those smooth moving circle things on them. We used to speculate whether the sex ed. nun had any hands-on experience before she turned herself into a penguin." More writing. "The five-by-eight platform for the band can go in front of the bay window. It'll be dark so no one will gripe about losing the view."

"No," Giulia said.

Angie looked up from the clipboard. "No to the view? The party doesn't start until five p.m."

"No to your previous question."

Angie's eyebrows met over her nose. "What previous...oh, the nun story. Yeah, I suppose not. Poor thing. What a life. Hey, did she teach you too? What year did you graduate?"

Giulia looked around for something black in this hoarder's paradise. She spotted it tucked under one of the end tables: a black blanket with the constellations embroidered in glittery thread. She shook it out and draped it over her head, making sure some silver showed at her hairline.

Angie stared, opened her mouth, closed it, took a step back, then took two steps toward Giulia. "Oh my God. Oh holy mother of Jesus, I don't believe it." Her freckled face glowed with delight. "Please tell me there's a status of Priapus in this flea market so I can take your picture with it for my friends. What did you say your name is now? It was something Latin before, right?"

"Giulia Driscoll."

Angie tugged her phone out of her back pocket. "Our old basketball team gets together once a month for beer and a pickup game. We went to State my senior year, do you remember? No, you don't. You taught hundreds of us teenage doofuses. Please take a selfie with me. My gang is never going to believe this. They're coming to the Mardi Gras party, but I can't spring you on them then. We're both going to be too busy."

Giulia smiled for two joint selfies, one with the starry blanket and one without.

Twenty-nine

Angie craned her neck to see down the hall and lowered her voice anyway. "Have you met Randy?"

"Randy?"

"Their nephew." She drew a diagram of the proposed bandstand as she spoke. "The only Jevens family members still alive are Owen, Blossom, and Randy. Randy is usually their driver and Blossom's human cane. You'd think being third in line for the family fortune he'd be kissing their wrinkled butts."

Giulia gave her an interested look.

"Instead, he knows all their hot buttons and pushes them like an expert. At our very first meeting, he got Blossom so worked up she took a copy of our annual report off Marcia's desk and whacked him over the head with it."

"If only someone had their camera phone ready."

"I know, right? Owen told them to behave and for about two minutes they sat still, like kids in time out. Then they all started arguing about the money Vernon Jevens had left to all the charities. When they left, I told Marcia we'd better hire a referee for future meetings."

Giulia checked the hall herself. "A referee probably wouldn't be good for donor relations."

"Yeah. The Jevenses would spread it all over town, I'd get fired, and I'd have to hustle pickup basketball games for Starbucks money."

"Anything for good coffee. Can you answer a question for me?"

"Would I say no to an ex-nun? Can't you, like, condemn me to hell on the spot?" She poked the tiger skin with her shoe. "I wouldn't be surprised if there's a trap door under one of these rugs opening to a cellar full of people the Jevenses don't like."

"And yet they're letting you use this house."

"I know. We're going to raise more than ten grand on Tuesday. Inconsistent much?"

Giulia made a thoughtful face. "I'd like to implement the trap door idea to inspire certain clients to pay their bills."

Angie's belly laugh was infectious. She clapped her hand over her mouth and checked for lurkers. "No gray dress and big ears in sight. Speaking of which, how many dresses have you seen Blossom wearing?"

"The gray one, but I've only spoken to her twice."

"Five times here, and always the same dress. She's like a human comic strip where the characters wear the same outfit no matter what."

"The Scooby-Doo Gang."

Angie laughed. "You got it. Don't tell anyone, but as a kid I lusted after Daphne's purple mini dress. Hey."

"Yes?"

"I'm gossiping and talking clothes with my former sex ed. teacher who's also a former nun." She swept the chaotic room with a hand. "Considering where we're having this conversation, the effect is a little surreal."

"If I tell you I have a two-month-old at home will I need to find smelling salts?"

"Oh my God, really? That is so cool." Her grin turned wicked. "That means you didn't practice safe sex."

Giulia struck a pose. "Indeed I did. Family planning is part of safe sex."

"Besides, you were a virgin, so—" She slapped her mouth again. "I am such a clod."

"I'm not offended. I did mention it to you a few minutes ago." She smiled.

Angie wilted. "What did you want to ask me? My big mouth will give up anything for you except my bank balance."

Marcia poked her head through the doorway. "Angie, Ron and I are all done. Are you ready?"

"Two minutes."

"We'll meet you in the foyer." The head vanished.

"Quick," Angie said to Giulia. "Marcia will put a stopwatch on us."

Giulia chose her words with care. "Do you think the Jevenses are using dysfunction as a mask for a deeper scheme?"

Angie's continual motion around the room ceased for a moment. "Whoa. You're deep." They finished a final circuit of the room. "It's possible, I guess. They can't be real-life theater of the absurd, right? Ever see Maury Povich or Jerry Springer? I've always been convinced the guests on those shows are actors."

They reached the doorway.

"I've always wondered what it means for humanity if they aren't," Giulia said.

Thirty

When Giulia arrived at the soccer complex at 2:20, Kord was practicing ball control on field two. Between yesterday's sleet and Wednesday's ghost event, field one still looked like a herd of treasure hunters had been mud wrestling for ownership of the Holy Grail. She called Kord over to the bleachers.

"Hi, Ms. Driscoll." He kicked the ball into the bleachers with such force the entire metal structure *twaannged* and sat next to her on the bottom row. "Dad says you're always early, so I am, too."

"It's the polite way to start a business meeting." She looked around. "Did your mother drive you here? I'd like to meet her in calmer circumstances."

"No, Mom got called to work the day shift because somebody didn't show up." His face conveyed ghoulish delight. "She's in charge of everybody who works at the Residence Inn off the Turnpike. She thought I was in the bathroom when her phone rang. Somebody is so toast. I learned some cool new words."

Giulia ignored his glee. If his mother didn't drive him and the goth girl wasn't lurking, only one option remained. "Excuse me a moment."

She walked kitty-corner across the field to the grass-covered ridge separating the soccer complex from the parking lot. Giulia stood five foot five and wore flat, practical winter boots. Despite this, she towered like Avenging Justice over Ken Kanning and Pit Bull as they lay in the wet grass on the parking lot side of the ridge. Only Pit Bull's camera lens showed above the crest.

Kanning grinned up at her. "Hi, Giulia. Gotta record Kord's

progress."

"Mr. Kanning." Giulia clipped each word. "This is a confidential meeting between me and my client."

Pit Bull turned off the camera. Kanning dialed up the grin's wattage. "I'm paying the bill. Doesn't that make me your client?"

Pit Bull said, "Ken, don't do it. Remember the teenage arsonist? You had the kid next door's father sign an appearance contract, but you wouldn't let the father listen in on your interview."

"That was different—"

Giulia inhaled hard enough to close both nostrils. "Mr. Kanning, did you read the last paragraph of the contract you signed?"

Kanning pushed himself off the hill and sat on his heels. The front of his coat and jeans were dark with mud and water. "Sure I read it. A smart businessman never signs without reading every word."

"Then you do recall the final paragraph."

Kanning's mouth opened and closed.

Giulia's neck and shoulder muscles hardened into concrete. "I'll refresh your memory. 'Either party may nullify this agreement with twenty-four hours' notice. Charges incurred will be billed within forty-eight hours and are due and payable in ten business days.'" She straightened her concrete shoulders, increasing the relative difference in their current heights. "Either you and Pit Bull cease recording and remove yourselves to your van immediately, or I will initiate the twenty-four hours' notice."

Pit Bull's expression mirrored Kord's when listening to his mother swear. Kanning went with the classic beached fish look. Giulia waited. Kanning illustrated his ability to adapt to rapid changes by tapping Pit Bull on the shoulder.

"Bull, let's go. Giulia, send Kord to the van when your meeting's done, uh, please."

The Scoop and Driscoll Investigations turned in opposite directions. Kord's eyes were as big and round as dinner plates when she returned to the bleachers.

"Whoa. You got Dad to do what you said." He set his feet flat on the grass and his hands in his lap as though he were at school.

Before they could get down to details, tires screeched on the parking lot's wet asphalt. Giulia jumped up, expecting the speeding beige minivan to T-bone *The Scoop*'s white creeper van.

"Oh, man." Kord stood at her elbow. "I'm dead."

Kord's mother slammed the van into park and leapt out in one movement. She was already yelling as she yanked open *The Scoop*'s driver side door. Giulia enjoyed the tongue-lashing even without making out individual words.

She said to Kord, "Your father didn't tell your mother about the so-called family emergency?"

"No way. He knew she'd have a cow." Kord gulped. "Oh, man, here she comes."

If ever a mother looked like the Wrath of God descending on a sinful world, Kord's mother was it. The mud splashed away from her high-heeled boots like it wanted to get to a safe distance.

"Kord Christopher Kanning, you shameless liar! I came to school to pick you up and they wanted to know if we were okay after the family emergency. I had to go along with your lie rather than tell your teacher I had no idea where my son was." Spit gathered at the corners of her mouth. "You knew I wouldn't agree to let your father take you out of school, but you went with him anyway."

"Mom, I can explain."

"Shut your mouth." Kelly Kanning seemed to see Giulia for the first time. "I don't remember your name."

"Giulia Driscoll."

The fury abated. "I remember you. You rescued this idiot from the drunken crazies the other day. Did I thank you?"

"You did."

Kelly glared down at her son. "At least one of us has manners."

Kord dug the toe of his boot in the mud.

"If I didn't say so the other day, I'm Kelly Kanning. The ex-Mrs. Ken Kanning. What is my son's business with you?"

In an instant Kord turned off "middle schooler in deep trouble" and turned on "Ken Kanning in training."

"Mom, you know my life plans. First I have to get accepted into Shady Side. I told you I need to be better and smarter and cleverer because I don't live in Pittsburgh. My YouTube channel is the first step. Driscoll Investigations is the second step. Impartial ver—verification. This is my future we're talking about."

Kelly's wrath softened but did not abate at her son's earnestness. "So you think skipping middle school is the way to prepare for one of the toughest high schools in the state?"

Kord shot a pleading glance at Giulia, but she wasn't about to help him become another Ken Kanning.

"Fine." Kelly said. "You have ten minutes." Her heels clanked as she climbed to sit on the topmost row.

Giulia and Kord resumed their seats on the bottom row.

"Okay, Ms. Driscoll, here's my plan. Remember how I'm going to use my Whiteboard as the platform for my entrance proposal?" He radiated pride. "Sounds professional, doesn't it? What I want you to do first is check out the messages."

"In what way?" Giulia entered a new note on her phone.

Kord tried to see what she was typing. "You know, follow the people who get an answer, like detectives in the movies do. See if they're a plant or something. If the message comes through on one of my live episodes, I'll give you their IP address and you can check out if the message and the person are the real thing."

Giulia typed. "In what way is this research supposed to benefit you?"

Kord scooted closer. "Don't tell Shiloh this, okay? I staged the whole lucky socks video. I know Dad told you I told him the Whiteboard has a ghost in it, but that's what he calls good copy. I needed Dad to get excited enough to pay attention to me like he does when he's setting up one of his shows."

"I see."

"I think Shiloh really believes the Whiteboard is giving ghost messages from her dad. She's the greatest and so pretty and so nice to me, and I want her to be happy. So I figured out how to make the Whiteboard answer questions."

Giulia said with the same seriousness she gave to all clients, "How are you making the messages appear with correct answers? Your friend doesn't write them."

"You watch my show? Awesome!" Kord became sly. "You wouldn't ask me to show my hand too early, right?"

"Since it's not part of the scope of our contract, I won't press you for details."

Regular Kord returned. "You're cool, Ms. Driscoll. I'm glad you're on my side."

Kelly's heels *clanged* on the benches. "It's time to go."

"Mom, it can't be ten minutes yet."

Giulia turned her phone toward him. "Twelve, actually."

"Shoot. Thanks for the meeting, Ms. Driscoll. Will you send me copies of the reports so I can use them in my presentation?"

Giulia stood. "The reports will go to your father because you're a minor, but I'm sure he'll share them with you. The identifying information will be removed."

"Huh? Why?"

"Without signed releases, using someone's personal information is an invasion of privacy."

His face became studious. "I didn't know that."

Kelly put a hand on her son's shoulder. "There's plenty you don't know yet, young man." She pressed the remote starter on her minivan and began her slog through the mud.

"Okay, Mom." Kord shook Giulia's hand and lowered his voice. "See you at the big Mardi Gras party. The Whiteboard is part of the entertainment."

Three Days to Mardi Gras

The message board's designer had chosen charcoal gray for the background and alien green for the typeface. Every so often a translucent angel or ghost floated across the screen. Comments appeared in fluorescent green type.

Daddy's_Girl: The spirit box was a total bust. Should I cast the same spell on it?

Angels_Watching: No!!! Your father's ghost is connected to the first object you cast the spell on. You never know if a sneaky evil spirit might sense your new spell and follow it to the ghost box.

Daddy's_Girl: I never thought of that.

Friendly_Casper: Can you get a hold of the first object again?

Daddy's_Girl: Yes, but not until Tuesday.

Angels_Watching: You must have patience.

Daddy's_Girl: You guys, there was a creeper at the cemetery! What kind of a weirdo hangs out in cemeteries looking to creep on people in mourning? Gross.

Friendly_Casper: I apologize on behalf of all non-creepy men.

Angels_Watching: Your father is the angel watching over you now. You'll be safe.

Thirty-one

At eleven thirty Saturday morning, Giulia's mother had to be staring down from Heaven in astonishment. Contrary to the habit of a lifetime, Giulia was ignoring the housecleaning and playing with her baby.

"Finn, you're a bad influence." She tickled his tummy and laughed with delight when he giggled.

"Why?" Frank said from behind his camera phone. "Smile, Finn. I'm going to play this at your wedding one day."

Giulia tickled the baby again. "He's a bad influence because it's almost noon on Saturday and the house is a mess. My mother is condemning me from her exalted position in Heaven."

Frank indulged in a minor Irish oath. "The house will survive what you call a mess, which you must be seeing with special glasses, since it looks fine to me. Since your mother condemned you to Hell when you left the convent, who cares what she thinks up in her self-righteous Heaven?"

Giulia blew a raspberry on Finn's belly button. "Your daddy is a smart man."

The doorbell rang.

Giulia looked wildly around the first floor. "This is karma. Visitors on the one Saturday I don't clean."

Frank headed for the door. "We have a baby. If it's a female at the door, she'll see nothing but Finn. If it's a male, he'll be more interested in the gaming closet. Problem solved."

He opened the door. Rowan and Jasper stood on the porch.

Jasper executed a slight bow as he balanced two stacked boxes in his hands. "Rowan and I apologize for barging in on the weekend."

"We bring offerings of food to appease the new mother." Rowan looked past Frank. "I need a baby fix." She draped her fuchsia coat over the nearest chair and enveloped Giulia in a violet chiffon hug. Her pronouncements when she neared Finn in no way resembled the formal pronouncements of her Tarot readings.

"What a little punkin! Look at those cheeks. Look at those eyelashes. Gimme, gimme, gimme."

Giulia placed the baby in Rowan's outstretched arms and Rowan abandoned speech for coos and kisses and nonsense syllables. Finn signified his acceptance of the worship with a *boop* of Rowan's pointed nose.

Rowan melted. "Giulia, he's almost as adorable as my own were when they were babies. Jasper, you'll have to stop me from smuggling him out under my coat."

Her nephew called from the kitchen, "Rowan, I guarantee Giulia will turn into a mama bear if you try."

Frank's laugh from the kitchen was genuine. Giulia's was not.

"Look at his aura! Such a beautiful, warm red with violet glow. Giulia, didn't you tell me he loves excitement? You can see it right here." She glanced over Finn to Giulia. "You still can't see auras? We'll schedule a few sessions."

"Rowan, we'll talk about that later." Giulia didn't want to take even more Saturday time to tell her about the yellow streaks around Haley Comette.

"Don't give me that skeptical look. If you can interact with ghosts, you should be able to see auras. Think how much they'll help your work. You'll be able to see a client's real attitude toward you. You'll be able to see whether someone's lying."

"If she does," Frank called, "I'll drag her along to analyze my suspects."

"There will be no turning of your wife into your servant." Rowan handed Finn back to Giulia. "Come and eat."

Giulia inhaled luxuriously when she entered the kitchen. "Souvlaki. How did you know?" She caught Jasper's eye. "I should know better than to say such things to a clairvoyant." She set the baby in his lounger.

Jasper said, "We have four lamb and four chicken."

Rowan struck a Vanna White pose. "In this box are six different slices of pie from the Garden of Delight."

Giulia said around a mouthful of lamb, "You've more than made up for invading our Saturday with work."

Rowan elbowed Jasper. "See? Your lessons are bearing fruit."

Giulia swallowed. "A good detective recognizes an ulterior motive regardless of its delicious wrapping paper."

Jasper said, "Have you checked the haunted toy's YouTube channel today?"

Giulia batted her eyes at Rowan. "No, because Saturday and Sunday are husband and baby days whenever possible."

"I can't speak to Frank wanting to spend time with a batty old lady, but I'll entertain the baby while you open YouTube." She made a fish mouth at Finn, who giggled. "Babies, I know."

Giulia set her laptop on the kitchen table so they could eat and watch.

Jasper started his second souvlaki. "You can blame me. I subscribed to the kid's YouTube channel and saw an update. He announced he'd be live at noon today. Rowan wanted to see the toy in action."

His aunt *nommed* the baby's toes through their Mardi Gras onesie. "My mother raised me never to visit someone empty handed. You are the cutest little ball of pudge."

Giulia correctly deduced the last sentence was not directed at her.

Rowan waved an authoritative hand at the open laptop. "Bring up the kid's channel."

"Yes, ma'am."

"You keep calling me ma'am and I'll suborn one of your ghosts to spy on you."

"Auntie." Jasper's voice held reproof.

"Don't be such a worrywart." Rowan opened her second souvlaki and snowed it with extra feta. "Giulia knows I'm on her side."

A voice from the laptop interrupted them.

"Remember, guys, leave a question in the comments if you want an answer from our ghostly Whiteboard."

Kord in an Iron Man t-shirt sat shoulder to shoulder with Shiloh in her usual black on black. Kord's room had been cleaned since the last video. Giulia suspected his mother had imposed every possible chore in the house as punishment for skipping school.

"Our next question is from Macho Mike." Kord looked directly into the camera. "Really, dude? Mike's question is: What are next week's Powerball numbers?"

Giulia, Frank, Rowan, and Jasper groaned. Finn made a raspberry.

"Your son has a future in analysis." Jasper shook the tiny hand. "There's too much of Ken Kanning in his kid."

On screen, Kord lectured his viewers about legitimate questions for his invention.

Rowan said, "He's still opening himself up to whack jobs. What's wrong with his father?"

As one, Giulia and Jasper leaned their faces into Rowan's.

"Rhetorical question and you know it. Giulia, you have to protect that kid." She filled her mouth with spiced chicken.

"We are, in a sense." Giulia summarized DI's expanded contract with the Kannings.

Kord's voice from the speaker: "Come on, take a chance. We've shown you the Whiteboard is for real. Challenge us."

Rowan said, "See? No sense of danger. Kids never do at that age. For his eleventh birthday my middle son went parasailing with my second husband. Watching him miss the boat on his landing scared the curl out of my hair. Afterward he was kind enough to tell me they do it on purpose to everyone."

Kord said, "Thanks, Guitar Gracie. The poodle in your avatar is cute. You want to know where your autographed guitar pick is. Who autographed it?" He waited a few seconds and read out loud, "Eddie Van Halen." He looked into the camera. "Totally cool. Okay, Shiloh, please write out the question."

Shiloh propped the Whiteboard on her black-clad knees and wrote.

Giulia interrupted Kord's filler patter. "Yesterday the little con artist told me in so many words his act is a fake. I asked him how he got the answers to appear on the Whiteboard's screen and he wouldn't reveal all his secrets. He claimed he was doing it to make Shiloh happy, but my money is on her being in on it."

"Look." Shiloh turned the Whiteboard to the camera. On the bottom half of its screen similar writing rea: IN DOG BED.

Kord pointed to the camera. "Okay, Guitar Gracie, go check your dog bed and let us know in the comments if the pick is there."

Giulia set down her Coke. "The wiggly writing at the bottom is a little too similar to the wiggly writing at the top."

Finn began to fuss. Frank picked him up and said, "In her defense, my memories of trying to write on one of those toys looked pretty much the same."

Giulia said, "To play devil's advocate, Jasper can create actual art on Kord's science project."

For the first time since Giulia had known Jasper, he looked embarrassed. "I used one to train my prosthetic hand in rehab."

"Someone with similar skills could then make the ghost writing appear unskilled."

On screen, Kord exhorted his viewers not to be scared of this ghost because it wants to help.

Rowan reached for the dessert box. "If she's writing the ghost answers, she has major acting chops. I believed she thought her father was contacting her. Giulia," she lifted the lid, "it's manners to let you and Frank choose the first pieces of pie, but I'd be deliriously happy if you weren't in the mood for peach."

Frank hovered over the box. "When French Silk is a choice, you can have all the peaches you want."

Giulia took Finn from him. "This one needs changing. I'll take any slice not made with rhubarb."

Jasper made a "yuck" face. "My mother always added rhubarb to her strawberry pie. I was twenty years old before I learned to trust a strawberry again."

When Giulia came back downstairs with a better-smelling baby, a slice of pear with cherries graced her place at the table. "Rowan, you're a queen."

"I know. You missed the successful outcome. The guitar pick was in the dog bed under a blanket. The kid is preening and his crush is glowing."

"Kord saw the dog avatar and weighed the odds. Dogs like to keep their toys nearby and if it wasn't the week to wash the dog bed, the pick was more than likely to be there." She took her first bite. "This pie is to die for."

"It's a good racket," Jasper said. "Everyone who plays the lottery thinks their ticket will be the winner. The same hope is guaranteed to increase his subscribers."

Out of nowhere, Kelly Kanning photobombed the camera. "What on earth are you two doing?"

"Mom, we're live," Kord hissed.

"You're what?" She saw the camera and her hands went up to smooth her hair. "Come out into the hall right now."

"Mo-o-o-m."

"Go ahead," Shiloh said in her pale voice. "I'll handle the next question."

Frank and Jasper hooted with laughter. Finn joined them.

"Poor kid," Frank said. "Nobody wants their big moment sabotaged by their mother."

Shiloh, blushing, held up the Whiteboard. "For anybody who joined late, I'll show you we're not using any tricks." She turned the device over. "See? It's one solid piece." She passed her hand over the entire surface. "We're not using wires or magnets."

"Yep, she's in on it," Rowan said.

Shiloh's gaze dropped to a spot below the camera and her eyes moved back and forth before she looked into the lens again. For the first time, color appeared in her face: two red spots high on her cheekbones. "What is it with all the creeps on the internet? Look, morons, I don't want to date you, I don't want to see your junk, and you all talk like disgusting pigs."

Kord popped back into view and whispered in her ear. Then he said into the camera, "Okay, everybody, we're only taking one more question today. Shiloh, anything good in the comments?"

She pointed. He read.

"That's gross. Come on, guys. Act your age."

"Here's one. Mama Cupcake says 'I lost my wedding ring and my husband will kill me. Please help.'" Shiloh looked up into the camera. "Grow a pair, Mama Cupcake. My daddy always said don't be scared of any man."

"Shi," Kord said, "We shouldn't tell her how to live her life."

"You're a guy. You wouldn't understand." She manipulated the Whiteboard's knobs. "I'm writing out the question: 'Where is Mama Cupcake's wedding ring?' See?" She turned it to the screen. The question was written in the same trembling letters. "Now we have to wait."

Kord turned on the Kanning Smile. "While we wait, which won't be long, I want to thank everyone for participating today, and a big thank you to Shiloh's Dad for piercing the veil for us."

"The answer's coming through." Shiloh's eyes followed something on the Whiteboard. "In...the...spice...rack." Shiloh looked into the camera again. "Mama Cupcake, get to the kitchen and come right back before we sign off."

Kord and Shiloh held a whispered conversation for perhaps thirty seconds before he pointed to the screen.

"Here she is and it's all in caps lock: OMG THANK YOU I FORGOT I PUT IT THERE WHEN I MADE COOKIES LAST NIGHT THANK YOU. There's five exclamation points at the end." He grinned with delight. "This has been awesome, guys. We'll be back soon with another Q & A with The Other Side. Check my feed for day and time, and don't forget to hit the subscribe button for automatic notifications."

The video stopped. Rowan thumped her fork onto her napkin. "This will not end well."

Jasper looked at his empty plate with surprise. "Anyone want to split the lemon meringue with me? Giulia, did you say you had a video of how he created the toy?"

"I'll find it."

Frank picked up Finn. "A day off shouldn't be spoiled by a Kanning, even a junior Kanning. Rowan, would you like to meet the lizard?"

Thirty-two

"Finn, you incorrigible dumpling, don't touch the Tarot cards while Aunt Rowan is laying them out for you."

Giulia captured Finn's hands and *nommed* them while Rowan began an abbreviated Celtic Cross layout on a piece of violet silk on the coffee table. From the game closet, Frank and Jasper trash-talked each other in EA Sports' *FIFA*.

Giulia watched as the Sun card upright in the center was covered by the Fool and beneath it, Death. The four of Wands to the left, the nine of Cups above, and the Page of Swords to the right.

Rowan held her hands over the layout and let her eyes unfocus. Giulia was familiar with Rowan's ritual and rocked Finn on her shoulder to keep him quiet. Finn cooperated.

Rowan shook herself. "Reading for little ones is a test of the art. Giulia, honey, I know you're freaking out about the Death card, but I also know you know the reading must be taken as a whole and Death also means new beginnings and playfulness. The Sun is joy, and we combine Death, the Fool, and the rest to reveal a free spirit and love of home." She gathered up the cards. "Also, honey, about the free spirit thing: you should stock up on antacids. This little one—" she tickled Finn's toes and he wriggled— "is going to try every extreme sport known to man. He might even create a new one."

Giulia sighed. "I knew he was going to be an adrenaline junkie. Frank says he'll take him skydiving for his fifth birthday."

Rowan cringed. "Heaven preserve us. Solid ground for me all the way."

A triumphant shout and a wail of anguish came from the gaming closet.

Rowan cocked her head. "Jasper's skills are rusty."

"I foresee twelve school years of struggling with Finn and Frank over homework time versus gaming time."

"You don't need clairvoyance to foresee that."

Frank reentered the family room with hands clasped over his head, congratulating himself.

Jasper followed like Eeyore on a bad day and crouched to look into the baby's eyes. "Finn, you'll have to give me lessons when you get older."

Finn gurgled.

Jasper shook a finger at him. "Don't take his side just because he's your father. Finn reached out and Jasper held the finger still so the baby could grasp it. "You're too young to be trading on your charm, kid." He said to Giulia, "Your husband is cutthroat."

Giulia smiled wickedly. "I didn't think I had to warn you."

Eeyore returned. "Touché."

Rowan wrapped her cards and put them in her coat pocket. "We've invaded your privacy long enough."

Eeyore vanished again. "Giulia, I strongly suggest you destroy the kid's toy."

She temporized. "I returned it to him."

"You could purloin it."

Frank helped Rowan into her coat. "I wouldn't object. To destroying it, I mean."

"There shouldn't be a problem," Giulia said. "Remember, Kord told me he manipulates the Whiteboard himself."

Jasper extricated his finger from Finn's grasp. "Do it anyway."

A brief silence fell. Then Jasper made a cross-eyed raspberry face at Finn and everyone laughed.

When the door closed behind them, Frank turned to Giulia. "See? Rowan didn't notice the un-vacuumed rugs or the dust on the TV."

Giulia raised an eyebrow. "Yes, she did."

Two Days to Mardi Gras

Three voices screamed at each other. The shrill voice rose above the other two, followed by a crash and glass shattering.

A man and woman walked a giant Goldendoodle past the house. They paused and elbowed each other before letting the dog tug them down the sidewalk.

More shouts and breakage came clearly through the windows open a few inches at the top.

A man texting and walking glanced toward the house and hid behind the trunk of a leafless chestnut. The front door opened and a man carrying a briefcase jammed a fedora on his head. A white china coffee cup flew past his ear and bounced on the grass.

A man's high giggle followed the bouncing coffee cup. A woman's screech preceded the shattering of another piece of china. The giggle changed to a curse.

The man behind the tree took a few more pictures and resumed walking when no further crockery missiles appeared.

Thirty-three

The ten o'clock Mass at St. Thomas' church was crowded on the Sunday before Ash Wednesday. Finn Driscoll objected at the top of his two-month-old lungs to the crowd. Or to the old woman doused in Chanel No. 5 behind him. Or to the teenager exuding clouds of Axe body spray in front of him. Or to the length of Father Carlos' sermon. Perhaps to all four at once.

Giulia wasted one long minute trying to quiet him before she bowed to the inevitable and carried him out. Frank followed with their coats and the diaper bag.

Half a minute of fresh air without a sermon restored Finn to his usual smiling self.

Giulia kissed him. "You and your father both love skipping out of church, don't you?"

Frank put his head next to Finn's. "Why, Mom, how can you think these innocent faces would plot any such thing?"

Finn made the fussy sound which preceded his "FOOD NOW" Klaxon.

Giulia looked around. "If we had some privacy, I'd feed him. I should've listened to my gut and brought a bottle."

The Scoop's van screeched into the parking lot.

Giulia said in a hopeless voice, "I shouldn't inaugurate my new life of cursing outside of church, right?"

Frank didn't answer because he was laughing too hard. Finn replied with a rude noise in his diaper. Giulia laughed, too.

Frank said through harder gasps of laughter, "My son is a man of few yet well-placed words."

Ken Kanning and Pit Bull exited the van loaded for bear.

Kanning's voice carried across the intervening cars. "Giulia, we need you."

Pit Bull reached Giulia and Frank first, even carrying his camera. "Cute kid—whoa." He backpedaled.

Giulia said, "Poop happens."

Frank pried her hand off their first-born's back and shook it. "You made a joke."

"Motherhood is mellowing me."

Kanning cut off her last word. "Did you see Kord's live feed yesterday? He's got nutballs coming out of the woodwork."

Frank and Giulia walked to their Camry. *The Scoop* trotted at their heels. Giulia said without turning. "Camera off. Now."

"I know," Pit Bull said. "It's off."

Giulia covered the back seat with the portable changing pad. Kanning kept talking as though she wasn't infinitely more interested in changing her son's diaper.

"They're camping on my kid's front lawn. My ex won't stop screaming at me." He shuddered. "I called the cops, but they don't care about preventing crime. They only want to make an easy arrest after crime happens."

Frank glared at him. Kanning pretended not to see.

Giulia returned her attention to wiping Finn's butt. "Driscoll Investigations is not your personal bodyguard service."

"Not for me. I can handle myself. It's for Kord. He doesn't know about crowd control yet and this isn't the right kind of learning experience. Those paranormal whack jobs need a seasoned professional to handle them properly."

Giulia completed the diapering process. "I repeat: Driscoll Investigations does not offer bodyguard services."

Kanning hovered between Frank and Giulia. "But you rocked it Wednesday when the nut jobs stormed Kord."

Giulia balanced Finn on one arm and stuffed the bag's contents back in any which way. "We were in the right place at the right time."

Kanning moved a step closer to Giulia. "Look, you're already working for me."

Giulia turned to face him. "Have you ever heard of scope creep?"

"I can afford it."

Giulia rocked Finn the least bit. "The question is, can we afford the time?"

"You can't be that busy."

Pit Bull edged closer, poised to leap into the fray. Giulia stepped in before Frank's head exploded like an over-heliumed balloon. *The Scoop* was not going to reduce her to four-letter words; not today.

"Good morning, Mr. Kanning. If you wish to make an appointment to discuss additional services, our office hours are eight thirty to five, Monday through Friday."

Kanning advanced on her. Frank and Pit Bull blocked him. Kanning stalked back to the van. Frank glared at Pit Bull before giving the van a pointed glance. Pit Bull grinned sheepishly at Giulia and followed Kanning.

Giulia turned her back on *The Scoop* and buckled Finn into his carrier. When she straightened, the van had peeled out of the parking lot.

"I wonder," she said as the closing hymn floated through the opened tops of the stained-glass windows, "if Father Carlos will issue a complaint to the station about disturbing the post-Communion meditation."

Frank yanked open the car door. "I'll convince him and volunteer to deliver the complaint personally."

Giulia's fury against Kanning still burned, but her irritation against *The Scoop*'s other half began to dissipate when they were halfway home. "Pit Bull isn't so bad. He's trying to stay on my good side."

Frank took a turn with unnecessary force. "To report every word back to his boss."

Giulia checked Finn's seat belt and tickled his toes until he stopped fussing. "Not all the time. He keeps going back to the old convent to try and capture Florence the Gibson Girl ghost on film."

"What's his obsession with her?"

"He can't get a clear image. He almost hears her or almost sees her and then calls me to try teach him better ghost seeing skills."

Frank took the next corner with less vehemence. "You should charge him."

"When he reaches sixty minutes of phone time I'll remind him of our hourly rate. He's up to forty-nine."

"Then Kanning will badger you for his next special ghost report."

Finn renewed his FEED ME NOW wails. Giulia rubbed his tummy. It didn't help. "Two minutes to home, you bottomless pit." She raised her voice and said to Frank, "I wouldn't bet on it. From what I can tell, Pit Bull's ghost obsession is the single point of friction between them."

Frank hit the garage door opener and coasted into their driveway. "Kanning needs to get more friction than he gives."

Giulia unbuckled herself. "If you come up with a specific idea, I volunteer."

One Day to Mardi Gras

Rustling movement disturbed the chill dark before sunrise. In ones and twos, five shadowy figures approached from the east. Four from the west. Three from the south. No sound from their passage echoed up the street. No sound from adjacent streets broke their stealthy silence.

They converged on a single patch of grass.

Minutes passed.

The sky lightened behind a heavy cloud cover. The light had no effect on the silent and motionless figures.

An alarm clock rang.

Thirty-four

Frank came out of the shower as Giulia finished feeding Finn.

"I'll be in court all day," he said from underneath his towel, his voice vibrating as he rubbed his short red hair.

Giulia patted Finn's back. "I hope to be in the office all day. It'll make a pleasant change." Finn punctuated her sentence with a burp. "Good boy. We have to finalize our Mardi Gras strategy."

"Did you rent our costumes?" The towel came off. His hair stuck out every which way.

"They're on hold. I'll pick them up tomorrow morning." She turned her head toward the window. "Did you hear something?"

Frank wrapped the towel around his waist. "If our incompetent housebreaker is trying again at this hour, I'll laugh in their face." He twitched open the curtains.

A moment of stunned silence preceded a string of Irish profanity. Giulia recognized almost none of it. She crossed to the window with Finn still leaning on the burp cloth.

The chanting began the instant her face appeared in the window.

"We want the Ghost Tamer! Bring out the Ghost Tamer!"

Frank's curses switched to English.

Giulia's phone rang.

"Hello?...Hi." *It's the next-door neighbor,* she mouthed at Frank. "I don't know where they came from...I'm sorry they're bothering your Jack Russells...You bet we're evicting them. I'm calling the police as soon as we hang up...No problem."

She hung up. The phone rang again. Finn grabbed for it. She set him in the bassinet.

"Hello, Mrs. Brandt...No, we don't know what's going on. They're bothering us, too." On cue, Finn began to cry. "The baby's not happy either...We're already taking care of it."

A third ring. Frank answered it while she attended to their outraged offspring.

"Yeah, Pete, we know...We're calling for reinforcements as soon as we get off the phones...We have to get to work, too." He hung up.

Giulia said, "Ken Kanning has interesting ways of getting back at people."

Frank's head snapped around. "Of course. You're right. Why else would these nut cases appear on our lawn the morning after we pissed him off?" He dialed a number. "Keppler? Driscoll. We've got a dozen idiots on our lawn shouting for my wife to come out and show them a ghost...It's not funny. Can you send a couple of cars to scare them off?...The neighbors already called 911? Thought so...No, they look harmless...I don't trust anyone either...Thanks."

He brought the phone to the window. "Evidence time." He snapped several pictures. "I'd get better shots from downstairs, but I don't want them to storm the house. Can you take Finn into the other room so I can get a video with sound?"

Giulia carried the baby into the hall and closed the bedroom door. Frank's "okay" came through a minute later.

"If I show my face again, they may give you a more exciting video."

"No. They may also go berserk."

She rocked the baby as she looked out from an angle which hid her from the outside. "Those aren't the same as the ones at the soccer field last week."

"No overlap at all? Kanning's kid is a nut case magnet."

"Look. They made signs," Giulia said in an awed voice.

"I'm getting more pictures. If they tear up our grass we can nail them on a minor charge."

As the light increased, Giulia made out more details. A woman with blue hair sat cross-legged on a drop cloth with a crystal ball in her lap. A bald man with reptile scales tattooed all over his scalp held an enlarged photograph of the Brown Lady of Raynham Hall. Two women all in black held a banner between them: "Make our great-grandmother speak to us." The only three who weren't calling for her, all men, held up sixteen-by-twenty photos of embalmed bodies in coffins. She counted four vocal women and two other men, all calling for the Ghost Tamer and also holding enlarged photos.

Giulia kissed the top of Finn's head. "If I had no conscience, I could convince all of them I talk to the dead at will and our son's college fund would have a great start."

One of the men without a sign raised a vintage 1980s boom box to his shoulder. The thumping bass of the *Ghostbusters* theme vibrated the window. She began rocking Finn to the beat until Frank poked her.

On their lawn, the men shouted, "Who you gonna call?"

The women shouted back, "Ghostbusters!"

The phone rang. Frank answered. "I know, George...Good. So did we. They should be here any minute..." He laughed. "Don't tempt me."

He tossed the phone on the bed. "George offered to loan us his pit bulls."

"The pit bulls who think they're forty-pound lap dogs?"

"They look ferocious."

"Call him back and tell him to do it. I'll bake him a pie."

The *Ghostbusters* theme looped around to the beginning. The hockey mom across the street came out to her porch and told the squatters her opinion of them in a few succinct words.

Frank cursed again.

"What?" Giulia followed his gaze. A TV news truck stopped on front of the house.

Giulia vibrated with anger. "That clinches it. Ken Kanning's station's truck conveniently arrives to get a scoop." She looked up at the clouds. "Dear weather gods, a sudden thunderstorm would be appreciated."

A reporter and cameraman—not Kanning and Pit Bull—jumped out of the van and ran onto the sidewalk. The singing continued uninterrupted.

"That's Denise down there. The reporter." Finn squeaked and belched. Giulia reminded herself not to grip him tighter as her anger spiked. "Driscoll Investigations is going to invoke the sudden death clause in Kanning's contract the minute I walk into the office."

"An excellent decision." Frank beckoned her to the window. "The cavalry approaches."

Two police cars with sirens on full blast came to a halt on either side of the news van. Four uniformed officers converged on the singing crowd. At the same time, Frank and Giulia's neighbor happened to be walking his giant Rottweiler in front of their house. The singing faltered.

The front doors opened on all houses with sight lines to the Driscolls' lawn. The neighbors appeared on the porches, phones in hand. The reporters closed in on the action.

The squatters backed away from the police. The boom box shut off. The signs and photographs rolled up and disappeared into coat pockets.

The police separated the squatters into sub-groups of twos and threes. The ones with the banner slunk away first. The rest followed, avoiding the Rottweiler. The TV crew packed up before the police reached them.

Giulia said from the window, "Thank them for me, please. I didn't want to go out while the TV camera was there."

"Didn't you say Rowan knows how to cast curses on people?"

She handed Finn to him. "We are not going there."

"Finn, your mother is a spoilsport."

Thirty-five

Giulia slammed DI's door against the wall hard enough to make the frosted glass rattle. Sidney and Zane jumped.

"Sidney, can anger sour my milk?"

Zane stood. "I'm going downstairs for coffee."

Giulia dug into her bag and handed him three dollars. "Extra-large French roast with toffee syrup, please and thank you."

Zane vanished.

Sidney said, "Possibly, but not for long. Want some meditation techniques?"

"I might."

"What happened and is everyone okay?"

Giulia flung her violet coat at the coat rack behind the door. Coat and rack crashed to the floor.

"That was stupid. Yes, we're okay." She righted the rack and hung up everyone's coats.

Zane returned, holding out the cup like an offering. "Is the body fluid talk over?"

Giulia accepted the offering. "Yes. Thank you. I apologize for startling you earlier." She sipped. "Nectar of the gods."

Zane said, "Did I ever tell you I researched the gods when I was a geeky teenager? Each pantheon has its own contender for nectar of the gods. Tequila, pulwe, ale, mead, soma, and of course ambrosia. If only the gods had a brewer who bothered to write down the recipes."

Giulia sipped again. "I'll stick with sugar-drenched caffeine. Zane, may I ask you to drop whatever you're doing and make up the final invoice for Ken Kanning? Please include two hours' time for this morning's event."

He raised his iced coffee to her. "With pleasure."

Sidney hoisted her kale smoothie. "What did he do? I haven't seen you this angry since the pedophile priest."

"My house will be on the six o'clock news."

Zane's voice was meek. "There's no such thing as bad publicity?"

"You may revise your opinion if we're overrun by desperate paranormal junkies." She paced the scrupulously clean floor. "*The Scoop* ambushed us yesterday morning in St. Thomas' parking lot. Kanning wanted to expand the scope of his contract then and there. I refused to rearrange our business hours to suit him."

Her staff waited.

"In an amazing coincidence, two dozen fanatics were camped out on our lawn this morning when we woke up."

"He sent them to your house?" Zane banged the keys. "*Mädane tükk sitta.*"

"I have zero hard evidence."

"You don't need it," Sidney said. "*The Scoop* ought to be used to not getting their way all the time. Why bully you now?"

"Apparently *The Scoop* hasn't heard my one thousand repetitions of 'we are not partners.'" Giulia remembered to sip her still-hot coffee rather than taking a big gulp.

Zane paused his typing. "Are we finally going to inaugurate the 10 percent grief charge? I'd vote for *The Scoop* as the most deserving client."

"I tried to vote for the Bridezilla who argued over every dollar in the prenup." Sidney shuddered.

"Neither eclipse the pedophile priest." Giulia's anger spiked all over again.

"The Church could've afforded it, too." Zane's fingers hovered over the keyboard.

"No," Giulia said at last. "We're an honest company. Ken Kanning is not going to corrupt us."

"Aggravation and harassment are honest," Sidney said.

"I know."

"I can type and listen at the same time," Zane said. "Hint, hint."

Giulia resumed pacing and sipping. "We heard a noise before sunrise. We thought the failed burglar was trying again. Frank opened the bedroom curtains and said something in Irish. Probably what Zane said in Estonian a few minutes ago."

Zane didn't even blush.

When Giulia reached the point in the story of the *Ghostbusters* theme on the boom box, Sidney laughed.

"I'm sorry. I know it isn't funny."

"It definitely isn't. These people know where I live now."

Zane said in a conciliatory voice, "They could've looked you up on the web if they really wanted to."

"I don't publish my home address."

"Ms. D., anyone can be found with a phone number lookup."

Giulia stopped in front of his desk. "You're right. I forgot about the white pages site. And we even have a subscription." She gazed into her coffee. "This is going to be a multiple cup day. Then a news truck from Kanning's TV station showed up before the police did."

"Wasn't that convenient," Sidney said.

"Bingo. If I'd had any doubts about Kanning engineering this stunt, the timely arrival of the news crew silenced them. Too bad for Kanning I know the reporter." She brought out her phone and dialed. "Denise? Giulia. I will owe you two favors if you answer one question...I figured you'd know the question when you saw my Caller ID. I'm 100 percent sure of the answer, but I need confirmation...You know better than that. Why do you think I called your cell instead of your desk?...Thank you. Collect the favors anytime."

Her hand gripped the phone until the edges of her case dug into her fingers. Sidney came over and pried her fingers away.

"Thanks. Ken Kanning called the station at six thirty this morning to report a crowd gathering at my address. Except our alarm rang at six thirty and we didn't notice the crowd until quarter to seven."

The coffee had cooled enough for her to take a large swallow. "The neighbors recorded it all on their phones. If we lived in one of those Homeowner Association communities we'd be receiving a strongly worded letter."

Sidney's nose wrinkled. "HOA neighborhoods are nothing more than the first step along the path to becoming Stepford Wives."

Giulia finished the coffee and looked into the empty cup. "Gone too soon. Zane, is it ready?"

"All set. I wish the total was bigger."

"We live in a fallen world. I seem to be saying that more often, for which I blame Ken Kanning. I will now compose a businesslike email severing our connection with the face of *The Scoop*."

"The invoice is in the shared drive ready for you to attach."

Giulia shook her head. "Thanks, but please print out two copies. He'll be on our doorstep as soon as he can take a break from work. He'll pretend to be pure as the driven snow, then he'll turn on the charm, then he'll use his son's future as his hidden ace because now that I'm a mother I won't be able to resist an underhanded blow to my maternal sensibilities." She considered the process. "I wouldn't mind continuing to help Kord, because he has potential. But since Kord's a minor, he and his father are a package deal."

Zane radiated helpfulness. "If he turns his back on me when he comes in, I'll slap a sticky note on his back with 'Kick Me' in bright pink letters."

"Get thee behind me, Satan."

Zane recoiled, then switched into "Genius at Work" mode. Giulia and Sidney shared a grin. Zane returned to the realm of mortals quicker than usual.

"A phrase co-opted from the Christian Bible to indicate the speaker is being tempted to do something against their principles."

"Zane, you haven't lost your touch." Giulia's grin vanished. "I'll compose the breakup email. Should I have a pint of ice cream delivered to his TV station?"

Sidney made a face. "Shades of high school. My go-to consolation was my mother's homemade pumpkin ice cream. Somehow my breakups always coincided with swim competition season in the fall. I wonder if the guys felt neglected."

"Yes," Zane said.

Giulia looked inquisitive.

"Three of my frat brothers dated girls on the tennis, track, and swim teams." He opened his wallet. "I volunteer to buy a pint of butter pecan to send via our usual delivery service."

Giulia said, "Why butter pecan?"

"It makes me hurl."

Sidney snorted kale smoothie out her nose.

Thirty-six

At eleven thirty, Kanning letter composed and sent and all other business taken care of, Giulia, Sidney, and Zane spread the house blueprints over the table under the window.

Giulia fanned a rainbow of Sharpies in her hands. "Pick a color."

"Green." Sidney plucked it.

"Blue." Zane did the same.

"Red for me." Giulia set the others aside. "Let's plan our attack." She flipped the second-floor page off the far edge of the table. "I want us each to start in one room and move to a different room every twenty minutes or so. The crowd is sure to be fluid." She turned her head toward Sidney. "You snorted."

Another snort. "Good joke."

Giulia replayed her last sentence. "It is?"

Zane struck a pedantic pose. "Fluid crowd is a double entendre. You meant they'd be in continual motion, but they're also going to be continually imbibing alcoholic spirits." He finished with an encouraging expression.

Giulia made a face. "I win the backward student prize of the day."

"Not at all. You win the subtle joke prize. What do you think the prize should be, Sidney? An evil clown doll? I'm sure we can find one at the Jevens place."

"Zane, I'll offer you up to my brothers-in-law the practical jokers if you bring a creepy doll within fifty feet of the office."

Zane favored her with his sweetest smile. "Now I know what to get you for your birthday."

Giulia rapped the table with her marker. "Focus, please. I'll start the night in the family room. Sidney, we'll keep you out of the entertainment room altogether."

"The room with the dead stuffed animals around the TV? Thank you."

"More Christmas ideas. I wonder if Jessamine would enjoy an actual preserved bunny?"

Giulia wrote "G-1" on the family room part of the blueprint. "Zane, you're giving your hidden evil tendencies too much leeway."

"He is, isn't he?" Sidney uncapped her marker. "I'll start in the breakfast room. People will pose for pictures with the stuffed butler and anyone not posing could use the distraction to case the room."

Zane added his initial and the number one. "Downstairs bedroom for me, where they'll drop their coats. An extra-large on a medium man or woman could signal someone planning to take illicit souvenirs."

"Excellent idea." Giulia drew a red arrow from the family room to the first-floor bedroom and added a "G-2." "I'll move from the family room to the bedroom. Sidney, please take the family room second, which gives Zane the breakfast room. Then we'll all move one room to the left." She studied the initials. "More or less. This will give us about an hour of continued arrival scrutiny. We'll have to remember to get snacks and drinks so we blend in. Do it while we're switching rooms so we get maximum time spying on everyone. We'll have to remember to keep covertly spying while we're in line, too." She made a face. "We're earning this money."

Zane looked satisfied. "Now I can add 'casing the joint' to my list of detective skills. Dru Ann will be even more impressed. She loves mystery novels."

"If there's a thief, I hope we catch him right before her eyes," Giulia said. "She might marry you."

Zane mumbled something.

Sidney put her ear an inch from his mouth. "What was that?"

Zane caved. "I said, that's the idea."

"OooOOOooo." Sidney winked at Giulia.

Giulia winked back. "I promise not to tell her of your latent brony tendencies."

"Ms. D.?" Zane turned pale puppy-dog eyes to her.

"Joke. I'd never sabotage your romance and you know it."

He didn't relax. "I'm stressed. I object to stress. You want to see the ring?"

Giulia and Sidney glommed onto his shoulders. "We're women with small children. Romance is no longer a priority in our lives. Of course we want to see the ring."

He showed them a photo of a ruby surrounded by a circle of tiny diamonds. "Rubies mean passion and motivation and enthusiasm. It's the perfect jewel for her. I added the diamonds because they're traditional and the two colors together will glow on her finger."

"We approve," Giulia and Sidney said together.

He relaxed a smidge. "Oh, good. I haven't shown it to my mother or my aunts because they'd be calling me nonstop with nosy advice. My gamer gang wanted me to buy her a Galadriel ring from one of those *Lord of the Rings* replica sites. I told them they were lame." He repocketed the phone. "I've got flop sweat already. Can we go back to tomorrow's battle plan, please?"

"Don't put away your phone." Giulia opened her notes feature. I'd like us to type a list of our paths into our phones to read as we—according to Zane—case the joint."

Zane said, "When I invent an online game called 'Case the Joint' and offer to make you both part of the initial stock offering, you'd better take advantage of it. If you decline, when I sell it to one of the big companies for millions, I will send you a singing telegram on the theme of 'I told you so.'"

They drew arrows and initials from room to room in their chosen colors. After seven minutes the first-floor blueprint sported a rainbow of crosshatching.

"On to the second floor." Giulia and Sidney took the edges of the second-floor page and raised it up and over the first-floor page.

"Wait." Zane pushed all the markers to one side. "Pick it up again." He moved his head in small jerks like a chicken's as he surveyed the schematic. "Put it down again." More chicken jerks. He drew his finger along the right-hand rooms. "Up. Hold it there." He slid his left hand between the thin sheets of paper. "The room outlines on this side of the house don't meet the way they should."

All three bent over the table.

"A hidden room?" Giulia said.

"*The Legend of Hell House,*" Zane said.

"Roddy McDowall, Pamela Franklin, 1973." Giulia's automatic response didn't interfere with her thought processes.

"The what?" Sidney said. "It sounds awful."

Giulia was practically pulling a Nero Wolfe with the way her lips were pursed. When she continued to purse instead of answering, Zane stepped in.

"The usual horror movie types spend a weekend in a haunted mansion. After the main character's fancy machine supposedly evicts any ghosts, surprise: there's a sealed-off room. The evil house owner had his body preserved and hidden so he'd be able to carry out his nefarious plans from the afterlife."

"Ick. Have you ever tried Disney movies?"

Giulia peeled off the top page. "Kitchen, breakfast room, pantry." She repeated the off and on of the top page relative to the bottom. "Entertainment room, master bedroom, master bath." Another off and on. "Master bath, pantry. There it is."

Sidney and Zane leaned in together and clocked heads.

"Ow."

"Ow."

"Sorry."

"Sorry." Zane moved six inches to the right and they bent over again without risking concussion protocol.

"You think it could be a cantilever?" Sidney said.

"The house did resemble four or five Tiny Houses glued together," Zane said.

"Both sides were flat." Giulia wrote in an empty corner. "It's almost a McMansion. They're the definition of cookie cutter."

"My older brother married a social climber." Zane's disgust was evident. "She wanted one of those and he bought it for her. As proof I'm the smarter brother, Dru Ann likes my comfortable and unpretentious house."

Giulia caught Sidney's eye, but said only, "As for this house, Vernon Jevens appears to have had it built to order with the hidden room."

"It's too easy to hope the money our clients are looking for is in there," Sidney said. "I'm glad. I wouldn't want to miss the Mardi Gras party."

"I agree. Only fairy tales have hidden treasure rooms. Still," Giulia said, "unless he wanted to hide something of incredible value, I don't see a purpose to it."

"He stole the Mona Lisa," Sidney said.

"He has the actual *Necronomicon*," Zane said.

"No such thing," Giulia said. "Thanks to you I have an image in my head of a freeze-dried Vernon Jevens."

"Sorry." Zane's voice conveyed the opposite. "From what we've heard, I wouldn't put it past him to have faked his death and be living in his hidden room."

"We need to do the math to get its measurements." Giulia turned her gaze on Zane.

"I hear and obey."

A voice through the door said, "Fast Track Delivery."

"Perfect timing," Sidney said. "My appetite was about to get ruined." She opened the door and took two plastic bags from a man in a ski jacket and a white baseball cap with the Fast Track logo. "I'll get my wallet."

"Tip's included in the delivery fee, ma'am. Have a nice day."

"Sidney?" Giulia said.

"I decided you deserved an antidote to your Ken Kanning morning, so I got lunch for everyone. Zane, shove my keyboard out of the way, would you?"

She set out sandwiches, veggie chips, and bottled water, then opened the keep-cold bag to reveal three bottles of Maine Root root beer and a pint of Fair Trade vanilla ice cream.

"Root beer?" Giulia said

"Don't say it like I've abandoned my principles for a life of chemically sweetened decadence." Sidney held up a bottle with the ingredient label facing out. "Everything in here is 100 percent natural. Next to the Garden of Delight, Whole Foods is paradise on earth. We're having root beer floats for dessert."

"I haven't had one of those since high school," Zane said.

"Me either," Giulia said. "Sidney, this is wonderful."

"It'll be the healthiest I've ever eaten," Zane said.

"Think of it as the start of a new life. Your body will send you love letters." Sidney handed out napkins.

"That's an uncomfortable mental image." He inspected the sandwiches. "What am I eating?"

"Turkey without nitrates or anything artificial, with organic greens, portobello mushrooms, tomatoes, and mustard on whole-grain bread." Her expression dared him to kvetch.

"My nitrate-addicted palate will make the sacrifice for the sake of root beer and ice cream."

As they ate at Sidney's desk, Giulia kept glancing over to the blueprints. "The first question is, do our clients know about the hidden room?"

"Unlikely, or they would've told us about it." Zane extracted a leaf from his sandwich. "Watercress. Nice. I like the hint of pepper."

Giulia crunched a sweet potato chip. "Then again, they might have deliberately omitted mention of the hidden room as some kind of test. Do we tell them?"

"It's outside the scope of our contract," Sidney said. "Mmm, nothing beats Portobellos." She took an appreciative bite.

"Morels," Giulia said. "One day this summer I'll invite you all over and cook them for you. If we don't tell the clients about the room, do we try to get into it ourselves?"

"Depends on its size," Zane said.

"We'll be too busy during the party," Sidney said.

"I agree with both of you, unless the possible thief sneaks in there to look for money." Giulia brightened. "We could mention it in the case summary when we send the bill." She licked mustard off her finger and sent herself an email.

Sidney looked around the desk. "Is everyone finished? Good. It's time to relive our childhoods."

Thirty-seven

Giulia slurped through her bendy straw the last of her melted root beer and ice cream. "Sidney, you were right. My anger has subsided to non-homicidal levels."

Sidney bowed. "A good dessert is actual magic."

"Magic." Giulia snapped her fingers. "Are your costumes set?"

"Ours are," Zane said. "Do you need to know or can we surprise you?"

"As long as you can move freely in it, I like surprises."

"No problem. We tested mine out."

"Ours too," Sidney said.

Giulia gathered the remains of dessert and tossed it in the trash. "Okay, then, let's finish the second floor."

"I'll take the upstairs library after my stint in the family room." Zane initialed it with "Z3a." "We should've thought of this before we numbered the first floor."

"We're flexible," Sidney said. "I'll take the gingham bedroom next." She wrote "G3a."

"Brave woman," Zane said. "If the gods are good, we won't walk in on a couple getting a quickie."

Giulia blinked at him. "From your lips to God's ears." She wrote "G4a" on the master bedroom. "If any of us sees someone exploring too much, send a text and follow them. We'll adjust to cover your current room."

They rainbowed the second floor.

Giulia capped her marker. "Before we spend more time on the hidden room, I want to clarify the master plan."

All the phones opened again.

"First, put your phone on vibrate tomorrow because we'll never hear a text dingle over the party noise. That might be obvious, but we're guaranteed to get distracted by a good costume or grabbing a bite to eat or the band playing a catchy song. We should all check these instructions every so often to counteract the distractions. Shift position in the rooms to see as many angles as possible. Be ready to converge if or when we spot an actual theft. Take as many photos as needed but try not to be obvious."

Zane said, "Pictures will be easier when people get a few drinks in them."

"True." Giulia reread the instructions. "Okay, then, we're as set for tomorrow as we're going to be."

Sidney stretched her back. "How is it two thirty already?"

Jasper opened the door and knocked at the same time. "Are you free?"

"At the moment." Giulia stepped toward her office. "Is it private?"

Jasper put out a hand. "No. You're all involved now. Rowan and I are concerned about the kid's toy."

"Still?"

"Rowan's obsessed with the kid's YouTube archive. We watched the 'Making of' series twice today. Have you?"

"Not more than once."

"Can you pull it up?"

Impressed by Jasper's seriousness, she herded everyone into her office.

Jasper did not push her hand off her mouse and take over. "Start with number three, then number four."

At the end of number four, Giulia scrolled the video back to the two-minute mark.

"What did you see? Zane said.

"It's what I didn't see." She let four play to the end. "Indulge me? I want to watch both again."

Sidney made a face at her. "They're only four minutes long. We can handle it."

Both videos finished. "There's a gap. Kord filmed the Whiteboard's creation step by step until the science fair deadline loomed. Then Shiloh took it home to save him some time with the addition of the powdered aluminum."

Sidney said, "She's older. She'd have a steadier hand with the powder and the soldering iron."

Zane said, "Convenient."

Giulia flapped her hand at everyone. "Wait. Shiloh claimed she cast a spell over the Whiteboard to connect it with her father. She must've done it the night she took it home."

Sidney stepped back from the group. "She thinks the spell made her father's ghost haunt the Whiteboard? Please."

"And after she came to Kord babbling about 'Daddy' talking to her, he figured out how to work the messages to make her think her spell worked. So," Giulia said to Jasper, "why are you and Rowan still bothered by it?"

"We don't necessarily believe the Kanning spawn is faking everything. His method can't be that smooth." Jasper brought out his phone. "See this guy? He and his wife claimed to be automatic writers. He'd go into a 'trance'—" the quotes were apparent when he said the word "—and his wife would ask all the usual questions: Is there a spirit here? What is your name? What can we do for you? And on and on. Then he'd scribble the spirit's 'answers' in big loopy writing."

Zane said, "*The Changeling*, 1980, George C. Scott."

"This is the sound of my eyes rolling," Jasper said. "The movie used automatic writing as a good effect, but I've debunked all the practitioners I've ever seen. It's way too easy to con the suckers with because the supposed evidence is flashy. I showed up at a bunch of the worst offenders' sessions with my trusty phone. Surprise, surprise, the spirit messages were exactly the same at every session."

Giulia said, "Spill, please. Did you cause a dramatic scene?"

A heavy sigh. "I didn't want the news people dragging out the 'War Hero' stuff, so I put together all the videos and sent them into the fraud division anonymously. This was right after I got out of rehab for The Bionic Hand and I was feeling the need to fight for justice." He shrugged. "Sounds hokey. Anyway, they got arrested and a judge ruled they had to repay everyone they'd duped." He closed his phone. "Those two worked for years to perfect their act. The kid can't reach their level in only a few weeks. Therefore, the toy might be haunted." He leaned on Giulia's chair. "Drop the contract."

Giulia smiled. "We've already made out the bill."

The air around Jasper's head ceased to ripple. It had been so faint Giulia hadn't noticed it until it stopped.

She made the choice to process the possible phenomenon later.

"However, Kord and his Whiteboard are one of the attractions at the Mardi Gras party."

Jasper cursed. At least, Giulia figured it for a curse.

"Was that medieval French? I didn't quite catch it."

"I apologize. Yes, medieval French, which I will not translate in polite company. What kind of connection keeps the Kannings clinging to you like a parasite?"

Zane said, "I'll trade you an Estonian curse for your medieval French one."

Jasper's serious face evaporated. "Estonian? Fascinating. You have a deal."

And returned. "Why is a grade-school kid attending an adults-only booze and gambling party?"

"Because *The Scoop* is filming the event. Kord probably convinced Kanning to let him attend as part of his master plan to get video evidence of how he's clever, intelligent, and cool under pressure."

"Ken Kanning is the human equivalent of corn smut."

Giulia and Sidney burst into laughter, without Zane.

"Google it," Jasper said.

Zane tapped several keys and laughed out loud. "If I were the op-ed cartoonist for *The Cottonwood Post-Herald*, I'd illustrate your simile and get it printed in Sunday's edition."

"You could attach it to a comment in the online edition."

Giulia turned reproachful eyes on Jasper.

He raised both hands in surrender. "I retract my unprofessional temptation."

Zane acquiesced. "I'm able to resist only because my drawing skills aren't up to par."

"Jasper," Sidney said, "what do you think will happen with the Whiteboard?"

"Rowan and I aren't sure, which rings every alarm bell in our collection."

The outer door burst open.

"Hi, Ms. Driscoll!"

Thirty-eight

The four of them squeezed through Giulia's door as Kord bounced into the main office. Shiloh plodded behind him, irritation in every line of her body.

Giulia reverted to Sister Mary Regina Coelis. "Kord Kanning, you do not slam the door to a place of business."

His sneakers squealed to a halt. "I thought—I—um—sorry. I got this great idea at school and Shiloh offered to drive me here. I'm not skipping, I swear. We had a half day because of some teacher education thing."

Shiloh spotted Jasper in his usual outfit of indigo jeans, black shirt, and black cord holding his long hair. His silver Celtic infinity knot ear cuff glinted in the sun. Her irritation vanished.

Jasper attempted escape. "Good afternoon, Giulia. I'll head out now. Call us later, please."

Natural pink briefly tinged Shiloh's ghost-pale goth makeup. "Please don't leave because of us."

Kord took over the room. He set the whiteboard on top of the house blueprints. Giulia assimilated Shiloh's discarded irritation.

"It's your turn, Ms. Driscoll. Since you're helping me, I want to use you guys as the dress rehearsal for tomorrow night. The soccer field event sorta went off the rails, so we haven't done an in-person demonstration yet." He turned on the Kanning Smile. "You'll be my guinea pig, right?"

Jasper feigned ignorance. "Guinea pig for what?"

Kord launched. "What you see here is Kord's Whiteboard. I created it for my school's science fair. You may think you've seen something like it in toy stores, but Kord's Whiteboard tops them all."

He picked it up. Giulia took the opportunity to fold the blueprints to one side of the table.

"My Whiteboard is more than a mere drawing toy." Kord rotated the knobs and black squiggles appeared on the drawing surface. "Shiloh added a special touch during its creation. She cast an honest to God magic spell over it and now it connects to The Other Side." He said the words with capital letters.

Jasper included Shiloh in his question to Kord: "May I see it?"

"Who are you anyway?" Kord's question was curious rather than rude.

"I work at the Tarot Shoppe across the street."

"You do? Totally cool. Sure. Here you go." He held it out. Jasper took it with both hands.

Shiloh edged nearer to Jasper. "I'll show you how to work it if you'd like." He set it on the table. She managed to brush her hands over his as she demonstrated the obvious way the knobs turned. The pink reappeared beneath her makeup. "Would you like to ask my dad a question?"

"Your father?" Jasper looked toward the door as though he expected an older man to walk in.

"My dad died last summer. He was mowing the lawn and had a heart attack."

"I'm sorry."

"It was awful. No one understands how I feel about Dad, not even Mom. Even my boyfriend was a total jerk when I explained to him how devastated I was without my dad. I started searching online for websites and discussion boards and things like that for people who were feeling like me. Some of those sites are wacky, you know?"

Kord fidgeted, opened his mouth, then closed it. Shiloh turned slightly so her body blocked out everyone from Jasper.

"One night when I was crying and couldn't sleep I figured I'd try online again. This time I found the most awesome discussion board about contacting ghosts. The people on there finally understood how alone I was."

"Did you meet any of them in person?"

The Whiteboard's knobs began to turn. Giulia raised a finger behind Shiloh's back and pointed. Jasper followed it. Neither changed their facial expressions.

Kord and Zane began to talk computers.

Shiloh gave Jasper a "duh" look. "Everyone knows you can't trust people on the internet. You can't trust me either." She looked pleased with herself. "For my avatar I use a picture of myself from when I was my older sister's bridesmaid. You'd swear I was twenty-one in it."

"A good idea."

The knobs reversed slowly.

"I know, right? No old guys creeping on underage girls for me, thanks."

The knobs re-reversed.

"What did you learn from the board?"

Kord and Zane discovered a mutual interest in rewiring robotic toys.

"They were so helpful," Shiloh's pale face grew serious. "My father will never be able to hug me or kiss me goodnight again, but I remembered something my great-grandmother used to say: Half a loaf is better than none. Well, these website people taught me about casting spells to bring your loved ones back. Not really back, like zombies or gross stuff, but their spirit. You know about spells because you work in the Tarot shop, right?"

"I know something of them," Jasper said.

The Whiteboard's knobs continued their slow-motion twists and turns.

Shiloh the morose goth produced a smile that combined shyness and delight. "There are all kinds of spells. A lot of them are way too nasty. You'd be surprised how evil some people can be."

The knobs paused and began moving again.

"The board members explained all about black magic and white magic and told me what to avoid. This one member, Friendly_Casper, was like my mentor, the way Dad taught me how to drive and how to build a birdhouse. He said his screen name attracted a lot of snarky comments, but he created it because he knows how good ghosts can be." Her eyes sparkled beneath the charcoal gray eyeshadow. "I tried two small spells first, one for luck and one for success."

The knobs ceased turning. Giulia leaned forward a smidge.

Shiloh became excited. "The spells worked. Mom played a scratch-off lottery ticket and won a hundred dollars. The next day I had to take a geometry test. It's my worst subject and I passed it with a ninety-two. When I posted my results to the message board, they said for sure I have spiritual powers. Isn't it wonderful?"

"I'm sure it must be." Jasper leaned to his left a smidge.

"So then Kord needed help with his Whiteboard." She rested a hand on the screen. "I offered to take it home because I'm good with detailing and epoxy and soldering. Right, Kord?"

Kord looked up from the diagram he and Zane were drawing. "Huh?"

Shiloh included Jasper in a glance which conveyed *Aren't young boys silly?* "I was telling how I helped solder the Whiteboard together."

"Oh, yeah, you were great. Building it took longer than I thought and Shiloh's really good with crafts and stuff." He bent his head over the drawing. "After I connect these wires, what do I do with the last row of pins?"

Jasper said, "Can you tell me what you did with the Whiteboard?"

Shiloh picked it up and the screen cleared. Jasper sat back. Giulia returned to making notes in her phone.

"The inside is filled with powdered aluminum, did you know? As I filled it, I recited the spell I learned from the real live witches on the wonderful message board."

Jasper's face expressed polite interest. Shiloh took the interest and ran with it.

"Did you ever try to contact someone who died? They called it a bridging spell and I had to recite it a certain way and truly want the connection with all my heart for the spirit to cross the bridge between the afterlife back to this world." She hugged the toy to her chest. "I didn't know if it worked right away because Kord had to take it to the science fair. When he won first prize he offered me half the money." She leaned closer to Jasper. "He's a sweet kid. I'm pretty sure he has a crush on me. I said I wanted the Whiteboard. He's prouder of it than of anything else he's made, but he gave it to me." She squeezed it tighter. "I waited until I was all alone and asked it if Daddy was here. I watched and watched it but nothing happened." She made a wry face. "I got kind of upset. Then I remembered how these toys work and I wrote on the screen, 'Daddy, are you here?'" A breathy giggle. "He answered me. He really and truly answered me. My daddy came back to me." Her smile changed her entire appearance. "I drove over to Kord's after school the next day and told him all about it." She lowered her voice. "He's like a puppy sometimes. At first he didn't believe me, so I told him to try it for himself."

Like his father, Kord didn't like being out of the spotlight for long. He abandoned Zane and their diagram after Shiloh's last sentence.

"You guys have to subscribe to my YouTube channel." He attempted to shoulder Shiloh out, but a bulldozer wouldn't have budged Shiloh from her place next to Jasper the Dreamy.

Also like his father, Kord knew how to make a virtue of necessity. He pried the Whiteboard from Shiloh and displayed its clear surface.

"You gotta admit Shi's story sounded seriously wacky. But I knew she wouldn't mess with me, so I figured a test would make a great live cast. It'd be cool if it worked because of ghosts and stuff, and cool if it didn't because I would've played it up like I was a super-analytical researcher. Sorry, Shi," he said over his shoulder, "but you know I have to be the best ever to get into Shady Side."

"Kord, sometimes you're a pain in the butt."

Kord's face crumpled, but only for a moment. As though he was the focus of Pit Bull's camera, he became a showman again. "Right. So I remembered how I lost my favorite pair of socks. You can watch the whole thing on my YouTube channel. Shi is a magician. She got her dad's ghost into my Whiteboard." He tipped a wink at Giulia.

A song by the Red Hot Chili Peppers began to play from Kord's jeans. He tugged a cell phone out of his pocket and became eleven years old again.

"It's Mom." He made a face. "Hi, Mom...Okay...Okay, I got it. Bye." Eyeroll. "Shi, we gotta go. Ms. Driscoll, can you ask a question real quick? Maybe Shi's dad will answer real quick, too."

Giulia's eyes flicked to the Whiteboard. The air around it shimmered. To the window. Clouds had moved in, which meant the shimmer wasn't reflected sunlight. A frown pinched Jasper's forehead.

In desperation Giulia said, "Where did I leave Sidney and Zane's last two pens?"

Kord wrote out the question.

They waited in silence.

An ambulance siren wailed past the closed windows.

Sidney coughed.

Kord's sneaker tapped the floor.

The knobs moved.

Everyone inhaled.

Kord read out loud, "Middle...desk...drawer."

Giulia spun on her heel and went to her office. The sound of the wooden drawer opening was much louder than usual. Five pens rolled forward from to the back of the shallow drawer. She held them up, mouth quirked.

Kord high-fived Shiloh. "Awesome. My dad says we'll be the hit of the party tomorrow night." He stuffed the Whiteboard into his backpack. "We really gotta go. Mom's been on my case something wicked ever since the soccer field mess."

"It was nice to meet you," Shiloh said to Jasper.

"My pleasure." He held out his prosthetic right hand. She flinched, then grasped it while staring into his eyes.

Kord tugged her free arm. "Shi, come on."

Jasper released her hand and she moved for the first time since discovering Jasper's existence.

"See you tomorrow, Ms. Driscoll." Kord bounded down the stairs sounding like his entire class had come to visit.

Shiloh followed with a last backward glance at Jasper.

Thirty-nine

"Protect her," Giulia said.

"Who?" Sidney said.

"Yes," Jasper said.

"Protect who?" Zane said.

"I couldn't take a picture," Giulia said. "It would've been too obvious."

"I was too busy being fangirled," Jasper said in a resigned voice.

"You were indeed." Giulia pulled a piece of paper from the printer tray. "While Shiloh was explaining her foray into witchcraft to Jasper, the Whiteboard's knobs began to turn on their own."

She took the unused black Sharpie and drew a rectangle on the paper.

Sidney choked off an inappropriate word.

"Sorry, Sidney." Giulia imitated the Whiteboard's wiggly writing. To Jasper she said, "It drew slowly, like this, yes?"

"Snails crawling," Jasper said. Unlike the answer to your question later."

Zane leapt from his chair. "What did it say?"

Giulia finished the connected letters.

"Protect her," Zane read. "I get it now."

Jasper said to Giulia, "What else?"

Giulia groped for words. "It..." She made futile motions with her hands over the paper. "It...shimmered, the way asphalt does on a sunny day." She looked out the window. "The sun had already gone behind the clouds when I saw the shimmer."

Zane leaned back and looked her up and down. "Ms. D., you're like a video game character."

Giulia raised an eyebrow. "Thank you, I think."

Sidney gave a strained chuckle. "Are you dressing as Lara Croft tomorrow?"

"No, no, no," Zane said. "Lara Croft is all wrong. Ms. D. is Green Lantern."

"I'd prefer to be a Super Saiyan."

Zane made large gestures around Giulia while saying "*Whoosh-whoosh-shoosh.*"

Jasper laughed. "Life needs to imitate anime more."

Giulia didn't laugh. "It didn't feel bad. Bad evil. The Whiteboard."

"How did it feel?" Jasper said.

"I don't...neutral. No, weak." She rubbed her fingers. "Yes, weak."

"Color?" Jasper said.

"Just the shimmer. Maybe a few silver-colored flakes?"

"Now I want a shot of tequila." Zane made a note in his phone.

"Not during working hours," Giulia murmured.

"Perish the thought." To Jasper, Zane said, "Is the shimmer the same as an aura?"

"Possibly," Jasper cocked his head at Giulia. "Yours has a strong overlay of dark, muddy yellow. You're stressed."

"You think?" Giulia snapped and immediately berated herself. "Sorry."

Sidney's laugh this time was real. "Every time I think you're turning into Miss Cleo, you become yourself again."

"The fake Jamaican psychic hotline woman? Please." Giulia turned to Jasper. "Let's put aside the question of me seeing what might have been an aura. What do bright silver flecks mean?"

Jasper said without hesitation. "Not setting aside anything, if Miss Electra Complex's protective dad is inhabiting the toy, you saw the correct color."

"That's good, right?" Sidney said. "I mean, the color."

Everyone stared at Sidney, who bristled.

"What? It's part of the job."

"Yes, it's good," Jasper said. "Silver means nurturing. It seems Shiloh's father responded to her extreme need."

Giulia said, "What happens if I take your advice and destroy the

Whiteboard?"

"His spirit will return to its rightful place."

Jasper spoke with such certainty Giulia didn't question him. She foresaw a long, joint session with Father Carlos and Father Pat soon.

"Something good may come out of this mess if I'm driven to extremes."

"Not for Shiloh," Zane said.

"I'm going to have to talk to her mother." Giulia made a note in her phone. "First the creeper and now the ghost." She finished the note. "Her mother may not believe me about the ghost."

"Stick with the creeper," Sidney said. "If this dad's ghost thing is real, it doesn't seem to be threatening."

Jasper put his phone on speaker. "Rowan? Developments. The toy is haunted by the teenager's dad, but he appears to be benevolent."

"Good." Rowan's voice came through the speaker. "What did you see?"

"Me? A faint glow. Giulia may have seen its aura."

Rowan crowed. "Are we on speaker? Giulia, I told you so."

"Rowan," Giulia said, "I'm stressed."

Jasper said, "She is. You should see her colors."

Rowan said, "Sidney, sweetie, it's chamomile smoothie time. Jasper, Sidney's stressed, too. Am I right?"

"As always."

His aunt made an unladylike noise. "Why are you kissing my ample butt?"

The door chimes of the Tarot Shoppe tinkled. Rowan whispered, "Drat. My three o'clock's early." She raised her voice. "Good afternoon, Jacinta. I'll be with you in a few minutes."

A moment later a door closed. "All right, I'm in the main reading room now. Giulia, didn't you say the little Kanning was doing it all himself?"

"He told me he was."

"Jasper, we have a newbie ghost feeling its way through the communication process."

Giulia said, "So after the first message Shiloh received in her own house, Kord manufactured the rest of the messages while the ghost worked through a crash course on How to Communicate with Your

Not-Yet-Dead Relatives." She chewed her bottom lip. "It—he—Shiloh's father is a quick learner to master the technique just in time to give us a personal message during the brief window the Whiteboard was here."

Jasper and Rowan said almost in sync: "Not us. You."

Forty

Giulia massaged her forehead. "Why me? Don't answer. The question was rhetorical."

"A better question is, protect her from what?" All lightheartedness left Rowan's voice.

"I know," Giulia said. She summarized the craft store and soccer field incidents.

Rowan's reply was R-rated.

"Shiloh didn't recognize me today," Giulia said, "but I blame that on Jasper the Magnificent."

Rowan snorted. "It's too bad Daddy's ghost has so little force."

"I know. I'll have to tell her and her mother. He hasn't done anything actionable yet, curse the luck."

"Darn it, it's one minute to three," Rowan said. "I have to go. Jasper, don't forget."

"I won't." He ended the call. "She means convincing you to drop the case."

Giulia shook her head. "She should've known better. Besides, I can't throw a goofy eleven-year-old to the wolves. Now if it were Ken Kanning and a pack of wolves..." She let the image blossom in everyone's minds.

"Too bad the only wolves in town are the tame ones in the zoo." Sidney stood. "Giulia, I won't weigh in on the ghost thing, but you're right. We can't leave either one of them unprotected just because Kanning is an idiot for bringing them to the party tomorrow."

"It's guaranteed *The Scoop* will only be thinking about their show." Zane poked his keyboard. "We're talking a couple of hundred people drinking and dancing and losing money at the roulette wheel."

Jasper drummed his prosthetic fingers on the table. "The gamblers will flock to the kid and demand the ghost give them winning numbers before they place their bets." Metal against the wooden table sounded like BB shots. He frowned at his hand and set it flat on the surface. "Sorry. All right. I agree. Both kids need to be protected tomorrow night."

"If it'll make you and Rowan feel better," Giulia said, "off-duty police will be guarding the booze and gambling areas."

"If I'd thought things through, I would've realized they'd be there. At least you'll have backup." He transferred the frown to Giulia. "If the spirit inhabiting the toy really is the teenager's father, your main worry will be him going rogue if he senses someone attacking his daughter."

"Wait." Giulia said. "Jasper, is the daddy ghost the reason we didn't get an evil vibe from the Whiteboard?"

"Probably. I was on the alert for anger or hate or malevolence. Weak and protective never blipped on my radar." A wry smile. "If only my information was more specific."

Zane said, "Then you could share next week's winning lottery numbers with us."

Jasper gave him the stink eye. "You know it doesn't work that way. If I could get specific precognitive flashes, I'd be out rescuing people from danger like Superman." He glanced over his shoulder. "Think I'd look good in a cape?"

"A black one," Sidney said. "Shiloh could be your sidekick."

Jasper shuddered. "God forbid."

Forty-one

Ken Kanning pushed past Jasper in the doorway as though Jasper wasn't there. He waved the final invoice under Giulia's nose.

"What the hell is this?"

Sidney placed her hand on her desk phone. Zane moved behind Kanning in the optimal position to throw him out.

Giulia crossed her arms. "It's our final invoice."

"It can't be. We had a deal."

"Which did not include sending a vocal group of crazies from to my lawn at six thirty this morning."

"I had nothing to do with that!"

"A telephone call to your news station at six fifteen with the news of the exact group of people making a disturbance on my lawn indicates otherwise."

"You can't pin that on me. I'll sue you to keep our contract. I'll force you—"

His next word turned into a squawk as Zane picked him up by the collar and belt and hustled him into the hall.

"Wait!" He pushed against the closing door. Zane pushed harder. Kanning stuck a hand in the gap and made the peace sign. "Five minutes."

Giulia nodded and Zane stopped applying counter-pressure so fast Kanning tripped over the threshold and caught the corner of a desk before he face-planted on the floor.

Before Kanning opened his mouth again, Giulia held up her phone in stop watch mode. "You have two minutes starting now." She pressed Start.

"Okay, look, you ticked me off yesterday, I admit it." The wheedling smile of a kid caught breaking a rule appeared on his face. "You have to admit sending the ghostly types was a great idea. Besides, it's your own fault for not negotiating with me yesterday."

Zane reached for his collar and Kanning backed against the wall, hands up. "Okay, okay, no victim blaming, I get it. Look, this isn't about me, it's about Kord. What can I do to make you tear up this invoice?"

Giulia hadn't changed her position. "Can you make all those people forget my home address?"

"Well, no, but they're harmless types. Besides, it's good for business, right?"

She clicked off the stopwatch. "Good day, Mr. Kanning. The invoice is payable in ten business days."

"No. Wait. You have to protect Kord. I don't care if you hate my guts, but don't take it out on my son. His future is at stake here. You know some people think I'm a carnival barker. What if some of those people run the fancy school he wants to get into?" He finally took a breath. "Mardi Gras is tomorrow. Show up for this one event. Just this one and I'll make up a bunch of phony restraining orders and contact every single person who came to your house this morning. I'll get one of my friends to dress up like a cop and give the phony papers to them. They're really harmless nut cases. They'll fall for it."

Giulia considered the idea, knowing that the real result of this morning's incident would be a home security system regardless of Kanning's schemes.

"Please," Kanning said.

Giulia also considered how many times she could hold this over Kanning's head in the future. Not only invading her neighborhood, but falsifying legal documents. She didn't even spare a thought for how the old, innocent Giulia would think about such actions. Protecting her family was paramount.

"You are correct in one thing. It's not fair to Kord. Tomorrow night will complete our contract. Good day, Mr. Kanning."

Forty-two

Half an hour after Kanning left they finalized the last piece of their party strategy. Pictures of the now multicolored map resided in their phones.

"They'll make it easy to keep to our plan. We're bound to get distracted multiple times by the music or the costumes or strangers wanting to chat."

"Or by a possessed doll shouting Latin curses in a squeaky voice," Zane said.

Sidney threw a marker at him.

The door opened on Owen Jevens, solo. He advanced on Giulia.

"Good. You're here. I want fifteen minutes of your time."

Giulia contemplated asking Zane to wire the doorknob to give certain visitors a mild electric shock.

"Good afternoon, Mr. Jevens. We are quite busy, but I will be able to give you a few minutes."

He began to speak while her office door was still closing. "I'm sure you've discovered who has the most at stake in this business. Blossom's going to kick off within the next couple of years. Her pickled liver's giving her the first sign of jaundice. Did you get a good look at her eyes? Of course you did. You're a detective. My nephew has sponged off the family long enough. By age thirty-five a Jevens should have established his place in the corporate world. You're going to help me help him do it."

From her chair, Giulia watched him pace the length of the room, gesticulating and stabbing a finger at invisible auditors. He ended by crowding the side of her desk too close for her preference.

"It's easy and there's more money in it for you. Who doesn't want more money? Here's how we're going to make this work. When you find the thief tomorrow—because there will be a thief, Vernon was an SOB and he hated all of us—you're not going to turn everything you find over to our little triumvirate. You're going to—"

Giulia's office door opened.

"Owen, you disgusting excuse for a human being." Blossom's long hem tripped her on the threshold. A younger man in a tan coat steadied her.

Giulia made a mental note to check the lease for rules on guard dogs. A Miniature Pinscher might generate fewer personal injury lawsuits than a shock-wired doorknob.

Owen's momentary embarrassment had passed. "Blossom, what are you doing here?"

"I don't trust you, dear nephew-in-law. When you left the house oh so quietly half an hour ago, RJ and I decided to go for a little drive. And look what we found: our dear relative cutting a secret deal with our detective."

Giulia put on her best poker face. She'd seen Tan Coat before. Once in a craft store and once on a soccer field. If she ever cursed, she would've indulged in Frank's favorite two-word Irish expression.

Owen played the stern businessman. "Blossom, don't leap to conclusions like you always do. I was only having a quick meeting with our detective about the plans for tomorrow night."

Blossom plumped herself into the nearest client chair. "In a pig's eye. You're trying to cut us out of our share of the hidden money. Well we're here to make sure our detective—emphasis on 'our'—adheres to our contract." Another emphasis as Blossom's eyes shot daggers at Giulia.

Giulia's voice became more businesslike than Owen's. "Mr. Jevens, Ms. Burd, Mr.—?"

The third man said, "Randy Jevens, but everyone calls me RJ."

"Mr. Jevens. Please be assured that Driscoll Investigations will adhere to the contract as signed by all parties."

"Not by me," RJ said, "but Auntie Blossom wouldn't sign anything to my disadvantage." He pinched her wrinkled cheek. "I'm her favorite."

"Silly boy." Blossom softened for a nanosecond. To Giulia, back to her usual self: "I expected no less." To Owen: "You might as well give it up. We're not leaving here until you do."

The standoff lasted eleven seconds by the clock over the door. RJ watched the show with a delighted grin on his face.

Owen blinked first, but his smooth delivery didn't falter. "Thank you for your time, Ms. Driscoll. On behalf of the family, I approve of your strategy. We'll see you tomorrow evening."

RJ gave his arm to Blossom and the Jevenses processed out. Giulia closed and locked the door and dropped into Zane's client chair.

"Zane, did you recognize him?"

"The guy in the raincoat? No. Why?"

"Soccer field. Giggler."

"Holy shit."

"Yes."

Sidney looked from one to the other. "Who is he?"

"He's the guy following Shiloh."

"Holy—uh, at least we know who it is?"

"Now to prove it. Can anyone think of a way other than watching him at the party?"

"Ugh." Sidney grimaced. "No, unfortunately."

"I can take him," Zane said.

"Good," Giulia said. "I'll tell Pit Bull to use up a lot of film on him. Pit Bull's a decent guy even though he works for Kanning. We'll get video evidence."

"Maybe we should've hired a few temps," Sidney said.

"What we really need is a guard dog."

"Oh, no, no." Sidney said. "A guard goose. Aunt Genevieve bought Mom and Dad a pair for Christmas. They have the nastiest tempers of any animal I've ever seen."

"Worse than Belle the alpaca when a man dares to come near her?"

"Definitely. Every time we invade their space they honk and scream and chase us with their wings spread out like they're a prehistoric monster." Sidney stretched out her arms, screeched, and flapped.

"I never have my phone when I need it," Zane said.

Sidney squawked at him.

"Geese need a lot of space." Giulia gestured at their two small offices.

"They're poop factories, too." Zane made a gagging face.

"There's probably a regulation prohibiting farm animals within city limits." Giulia sighed. "It was a good idea while it lasted."

Sidney reverted to her human self. "What we really need is more non-dysfunctional clients." She held up her fluorescent pink Prenup folder. "Starting with fewer micromanaging brides and suspicious in-laws."

"Think how boring your days would be," Giulia said.

Forty-three

Giulia rang the doorbell of a brown condo at the end of a row of alternating white, gray, and brown condos. The development had attracted a clientele of like-minded gardeners. Every front lawn had raised beds for flowers and vegetables.

A bulgy woman in hot pink spandex and matching running shoes jogged up next to Giulia.

"Hi. Are you the detective? I'm Mary Maclay." Impossible to tell what her voice sounded like through all the panting. "I timed my run to meet you here. Come on in."

Shiloh's mother unlocked the door and led Giulia down a short hall into a galley kitchen with a breakfast bar. Shiloh's colors might range from dark gray to black, but her mother embraced everything bright. The kitchen sported canary yellow walls, leaf-green chairs, cherry-red toaster and coffee maker, and willow-blue patterned floors.

"May I offer you a glass of water?"

"Thank you, yes." Giulia hung her violet coat on the back of a green chair. The effect wasn't optimal.

Shiloh's mother set a flowered glass before Giulia and dropped to the floor. "Go ahead and talk. I need my post-run stretches or my hamstrings seize up. Sucks to get old." She spread her bright pink legs in a wide V and folded her torso over each leg in turn. "So—" *grunt* "—what did you want to see me about?"

Much too friendly with a total stranger who also happened to be a PI.

Giulia eased into her prepared opening. "Last week I was in the old craft store downtown. Your daughter was also there."

The pink thighs slapped together. The jaunty façade crumbled. The hands clutched each other.

"Oh, God, what did she steal? Are you the store detective? Has the owner called the police?" She burst into tears, exactly like a cliché.

Giulia added together several facts fast and got a more three-dimensional Shiloh as a result.

"Ms. Maclay."

"Dammit, I'm a professional and now look at me." She lumbered to her feet and wiped her face on a yellow checked dish towel. After several deep breaths she dropped the towel in the sink, poured herself a glass of water, and drank half of it. "I apologize." She sat next to Giulia. "Please tell me what my daughter has done this time."

Giulia infused a little warmth into her voice. "I think you've misunderstood me."

Without the false geniality, Mary's voice was strained and tired. "Not that you care, but my husband died six months ago and Shiloh hasn't been handling it well. Acting out, pretending she's a goth, even buying a stupid, noisy crow." She tipped her chair onto its back legs and aimed her voice into the room behind. "Fried crow for dinner!"

A squawk and the sound of flapping feathers came from the other room.

"I hate that bird." Her chair *thunked* on the floor. "You've heard of an Oedipus complex? Its opposite is an Electra complex. Shiloh and Lewis were the poster children for it."

Giulia said only, "Shoplifting was part of her acting out?"

Mary's round shoulders slumped. "A $140 pair of Doc Martens. Little Miss Goth Girl thought nobody would notice if she tried them on and walked out in them."

"The store pressed charges."

"Do you blame them? She got six months' probation and one hundred hours of community service. They kept her in the holding center overnight. I thought the experience scared her straight, if you know what I mean."

Giulia said, "I can relieve you of one fear. Shiloh didn't steal anything from the craft store."

Mary Maclay melted. A second later she firmed up again. "What do you mean, 'one fear?' What else did she do?"

"Your daughter hasn't done anything illegal as far as we know. I'm here for another reason."

"Who hired you? Are you working for the parole board? Is she ditching her community service?"

The pet crow must have been a sensitive bird. It picked up on the anxiety flooding the condo and began squawking and flapping enough for three crows.

Giulia radiated calm. "Let me explain. I was in the downtown craft store next to the Dahlia dress shop."

"Dahlia? Oh, no."

"Ms. Maclay, please. Your daughter was in the craft store engrossed in deciding on a purchase. I noticed an older man at the end of the same aisle. When she changed aisles, so did he. I followed them. When she went to the cash registers, the man planted himself by a front display and kept watching her. I came up to the second cash register and alerted the cashier. Two minutes later, the staff escorted him out." She gauged Mary's stress level and ripped off the bandage. "While I didn't know her then, I recognized her when I saw her at the soccer field with Kord on Wednesday. Also at the soccer field was the man who'd been watching her."

Mary gripped the edge of the counter. "How can you be sure?"

"He had a particular, high-pitched giggle. I heard it in the craft store and again on the soccer field. Developments in one of our current cases confirmed my suspicions." She braced herself for the reaction to her next words. "I believe this man is stalking your daughter."

Mary's short, straight hair stood on end.

Giulia projected superhuman levels of calm. "We're tracking him in addition to our current casework. Can you give me the details of her browsing history? We don't think he appeared at the soccer field because he's following Kord on YouTube."

"She shared her passwords with my husband. I don't know them."

Giulia said the unethical: "There are ways to discover passwords."

Mary leaped to her feet, rattling the chair. "Come with me."

The crow cackled as they passed its cage on the way to the stairs.

"Shut up, you creepy freeloader." To Giulia, she said, "Is this connected with Kord's science project?"

"How much do you know about Kord's Whiteboard?"

"More than any human being needs to know." She grasped the railing and took the stairs two at a time. "Shiloh's been babysitting Kord since his parents divorced when he was six." A *grunt* as her legs stretched. "He's a good kid and a smart one. He also has a massive crush on Shiloh."

"I noticed." Giulia's shorter legs followed one stair at a time.

"Its hard not to." She reached the second floor. "I've been hoping his endless enthusiasm for everything would be contagious enough to shake Shiloh out of her funk. It's like she's been reading *Goth for Dummies*, if such a book existed."

"Are you aware she and Kord are attending the Mardi Gras party tomorrow night?"

"What?" She spun on one sneakered heel.

Giulia gained the second floor.

"Kord convinced me to become an objective observer for his Whiteboard experiments. He needs professional credibility for his presentation to the administrators of Shady Side Academy."

Mary recrossed her arms. "Shady Side Academy is another subject I've heard too much about."

Giulia pushed against her barrier. "Today Shiloh drove Kord to my office and he told me both he and Shiloh were attending the party. He wanted to use my staff as his dry run."

"That conniving little brat." Mary massaged her neck with one hand. "I've been the recipient of his charm, too. He wouldn't have to use it on Shiloh. She'd leap at the chance to attend an adult party." She switched hands. "My only consolation is the teenage years don't last forever. I drink too much as it is." Her hands clenched at her sides. "I heard *The Scoop* is chronicling the party. Why isn't Ken Kanning chauffeuring his son himself?"

Before Giulia answered, Mary said, "Why am I asking you? You're not privy to his inmost thoughts."

"Thank God for small favors." They both laughed.

Mary led Giulia past a bathroom to the second door on their left. "If I had any qualms about invading my daughter's privacy, they're gone. She's forfeited it herself." She opened the door.

If there was a book called *Goth for Dummies*, Giulia might be looking at the result of its step-by-step house decorating chapter. Black curtains. Gray walls. Throw rug the color of blackberries. Black bedspread, lamp, computer desk, bookshelf. A framed ten-by-twelve photograph of a smiling middle-aged man was the only color in the room.

"That's my husband." Mary's mouth crooked.

"I'm sorry."

"Thanks. It was a shock. He'd gained weight and stopped working out. Last September he insisted on tilling over all the gardens in our row for the winter. It was a wicked hot day and he wore one of those stupid baseball caps with holders and straws on either side for beer." She turned away from the picture. "A hot, humid day and he was drinking beer instead of water. He collapsed in front of our house. The ER doctors said he was dead before he hit the ground." She straightened the bedspread. "I'm getting used to it. This is the second time I've told the story without blubbering like an idiot."

Giulia listened with one ear as she studied the room for a hint of personality beneath the clichés. "Your daughter's high school offers Greek?" She indicated a Greek-English dictionary on the shelf.

Mary huffed. "No. she's teaching herself. Ask me why."

Never one to refuse the gift of an easy opening, Giulia said, "Why?"

"Electra." Mary tipped out three books. "Aeschylus, Sophocles, Euripides. English translations of them all, in every edition available. Also Eugene O'Neill and Jean Giraudoux. Thank God for the AbeBooks website, or she'd be broke." She turned on the laptop. "It's all yours. Shiloh's watching Kord until six. His mother's working late."

The password cursor blinked. Giulia channeled her inner Zane. "How did your husband spell his name?"

"L-E-W-I-S."

Giulia tried the name in order. In reverse order. Swapping out letters with numbers, with capitals, with special characters. She could already hear Zane's disappointment.

"Does Shiloh have a boyfriend?" She turned the chair toward Mary.

"Not anymore." Mary pushed the books back into line. "She dumped him because he didn't sympathize enough with her ongoing angst." She punched a pillow sham. "You must think I'm heartless. I'm not, honestly. I made her see a shrink three months ago. She wouldn't open her mouth for the entire fifty-minute appointment." Mary glared at the bookshelf. "I'm trying everything to get her back to the way she used to be. I don't want this to be her new normal."

Giulia spun the chair to face the keyboard again and typed "Electra." When that didn't work, she lower-cased the initial "e," turned each "e" into a "3," and changed the "t" into a "4." Before she gave up and called Zane, she stood and ran her fingers over the book spines. The answer was here. She knew it.

"One of these things is not like the others," she murmured. Her fingers touched a faded dust jacket. She threw herself back into the chair and typed "Elektra."

Nothing.

"That has to be it." She tried "El3ktra." The login screen changed to a stylized Greek vase.

"We're in."

Forty-four

Shiloh's mother hung over Giulia's left shoulder as Giulia opened her daughter's bookmarks.

"It looks so average. The school website, homework help sites, games." Mary leaned in. "She still plays *Super Mario Galaxy*? I didn't know. We used to play it together, all three of us, from different rooms." She let out a long breath. "No porn."

Giulia's cheeks burned but she said to ease the tension, "Porn gives people an unrealistic idea of how quickly a plumber will come to your house."

Mary laughed. "I'm stealing that for my next girl's night out."

"It's not mine. I saw it on Twitter."

"Then it's fair game."

Giulia opened Shiloh's browsing history. Kord's YouTube channel, Facebook, Instagram, AbeBooks, the library, manga scan sites. The list filled the screen and kept going.

"Jackpot. She hasn't cleared her history in months. Let's see. Merriam-Webster. YouTube channels on how to build toys. Sites for plastics and powdered aluminum." She glanced up at Mary. "Most related to building the Whiteboard."

"To be expected." She peered at the screen. "No dating sites?"

"None I can see." She kept scrolling and swallowed a chuckle. "You were almost right. Back in October she accessed multiple YouTube channels about the basics of goth."

Mary groaned. "My daughter used to have brains. I understand they return after the teenage years."

"So I'm told." She read the next entries and stiffened. Three

YouTube videos in a row on how to pick a lock with a nail file.

"What's the matter?" Mary leaned in. "Lock picking? Oh, yeah, she told me a friend lost the key to his locker padlock and didn't want the school to use the cutters on it, so she learned how to pick locks for her."

A complete set of bullet points materialized in Giulia's head:

Giulia had taken the Whiteboard the day of the attempted break-ins.

Shiloh had already shown her obsession for the Whiteboard.

Shiloh's version of acting out was to steal.

All Giulia had to do was compare Shiloh on the soccer field video to the thief in the security footage.

Priorities:

1. The Whiteboard ghost and the possibility of it going south

2. RJ the creeper and Shiloh at the party

3. Shiloh the budding criminal

Saving Shiloh from the ghost and/or creeper is paramount. The break-in attempts can be handled on Wednesday.

Giulia pushed everything about the break-ins aside and continued searching for ghost sites.

"Here's what we're looking for. SeeYourAngels dot net, LadySolana dot net." Giulia didn't look forward to browsing her website again. "ThirdEyeOpen dot net."

"What is all that?"

"Websites about contacting the dead."

"What a bunch of horseshit."

Giulia wondered if Florence would make a house call. A visit from a snarky, chain-smoking, Gibson Girl ghost might change Mary's mind.

"Perhaps, but these sites are geared to attract True Believers." She swiveled to face Mary again. "What else do you know about the Whiteboard?"

Mary sat on the bed. "What do you mean? I know it won first prize at the science fair and Kord offered Shiloh half the money. He's a good kid. Shiloh wanted the Whiteboard instead. She had a similar toy when she was little. I thought it was nostalgia."

Giulia girded her loins. "Shiloh told us she cast a spell on the Whiteboard to bring her father's ghost into it."

Mary simply stared.

"She then had us ask a question of the spirit and wrote it out on the Whiteboard. A minute later, the knobs turned on their own and answered our question."

Mary exploded. "Are you kidding? What kind of bullshit is this? Who's been feeding my daughter these disgusting lies? Are you involved in it? Did you and Kord put her up to this—this—" She slammed her hands on the computer desk hard enough to rattle everything on it. "No wonder she's acting crazy." She pushed her face right up against Giulia's. "If you've endangered my daughter's mental health, I'll sue your ass into Hell and back. I'll—"

"Ms. Maclay." Sister Mary Regina Coelis cut through the rant. Shiloh's mother choked on her next word, gulped, and shut up.

"Perhaps you didn't hear what I said. We didn't connect your daughter to the stalker in the craft store until after the soccer field incident. The first time we saw the Whiteboard was at the soccer field. Therefore we could not possibly have known how it was created until two hours ago when she and Kord came to our office to demonstrate it."

All Giulia's work to discover how Shiloh was being targeted would be ruined if she told this frantic mother her husband's ghost did indeed inhabit the Whiteboard. She held her ground and waited for Mary to get hold of herself.

Which, to her credit, she did in less than a minute.

"I beg your pardon, Ms. Driscoll. I'd like to blame my outburst on PMS and make it a girl bonding moment, but the truth is, between my husband's death and my daughter's—" she gestured around the room "—everything, I'm on a short fuse."

Having recently recovered from everything pregnancy did to one's equilibrium, Giulia relinquished her own anger.

"Who wouldn't be? Let's see where Shiloh's been spending her time."

ThirdEyeOpen was chock full of infallible methods to open your chakras, see auras, and generally increase positive influences in day-to-day life. Shiloh didn't stay long there. Lady Solana's discussion board showed promise, but drilling down revealed what appeared to be shills pushing members to schedule fee-based services. In one discussion it was personal house cleansings. In another, it was past life regressions. In a third, Ouija Board sessions. Shiloh was smart enough to recognize the game and bailed within two weeks.

Giulia muttered excoriations at Lady Solana.

"Something wrong?"

"Sorry. Lady Solana and I have had unpleasant encounters."

"I know who came out on top."

Giulia allowed herself a modest smile and clicked on SeeYourAngels.

"Good God." Mary took a step away from the laptop. "It looks like a Halloween store puked on the screen. Who in their right mind uses neon green for a discussion board font?"

Giulia clicked on the Community tab. A screen full of glowing green letters threatened to create a monster headache. The floating images and irregular moans didn't help.

"Let's skip this one." Mary leaned back in. "Is that God the Creator from the Sistine Chapel ceiling pointing at the board rules?"

"It is. Somehow I doubt the Vatican has given permission for its use." Giulia read thread titles. A moment later she no longer cared about the eye-wracking color scheme.

They took turns reading titles aloud.

"What's wrong with my spirit box?"

"Can somebody check this spell?"

"I made contact with my grandmother and she's still trying to run my life."

"Please help me contact my dad, posted by Daddy's_Girl."

Mary caught her breath. Giulia clicked.

"That empty-headed little idiot." Mary's finger stabbed at the screen. "Look at her in fancy makeup pretending she's legal. I will ground her until she really is legal."

Giulia scrolled without responding. "Listen to this: Please, everybody, I need a guaranteed spell to bring my dad's spirit back over. I have a special solution all prepared, but I have to be one thousand percent certain it'll work."

"Special solution? What is she taking about?"

If auras existed, and if she was seeing Mary's, Giulia decided the shades of red and orange burning at the edges of her vision meant

Mary was about to reenact Mount Etna versus Pompeii.

"I don't know." Giulia scrolled. "Here's a follow-up: It worked! It worked! Thank you!!!" The teacher in her cringed at the multiple exclamation points. "I talked to my daddy! He talked to me, for real! You were right!!!" She scrolled farther. "Seven different people congratulated her. Four of the seven asked for details but she became coy again."

Mount Etna erupted. "Those pieces of shit! Only scumbags lie to a vulnerable teenager. What kind of sick bastards are on this website?"

Giulia spared a moment of thanks she didn't have to lie to Mary about whether the Whiteboard was haunted.

Still ranting, Mary opened her phone. "Little Miss Goth is about to get an unpleasant surprise." Her thumbs moved on the keypad fast enough to blur. "One ticket...electronic, not will call...twenty-five bucks? Hell, it's a tax write-off...Good thing I know my Discover card number by heart...There. Wait a few seconds..." A *ding* came from the phone. The smile on her face was less than charitable as she turned her screen toward Giulia. "The Children with Cancer Foundation is twenty-five dollars richer and I'm going to a party tomorrow night."

Giulia wondered how much trouble this wrinkle was going to make for them. "The local costume stores are picked pretty thin."

"I've sewn my own clothes for decades. All I need is a trip to the fabric store. Clytemnestra would be an appropriate choice, don't you think? Or should I go as Agamemnon?"

As long as Mary the Vengeful didn't get in their way, Giulia didn't care. "Do you mind if I keep looking for a few minutes? I want to narrow down the stalker's potential avatars."

Mount Etna subsided. "I almost forgot. You're sure he's on there?"

"Not 100 percent yet, but it's logical. She didn't stay long on the other two sites, and this is the only other one in her history. See this post by Angels_Watching, full of sympathy and encouragement? Or this one by Haunt_Me, hinting that spells aren't foolproof? Or this one by Friendly_Casper encouraging her to go to the cemetery often and alone, to strengthen the connection? None of them have photograph avatars." She right-clicked their usernames one at a time and brought up their personal information in separate tabs.

Angels_Watching had filled out every section, including pictures of her six cats. Haunt_Me had done likewise, substituting a rifle collection for the cats. Friendly_Casper had entered the minimum. Only an illustration of the classic cartoon character.

"I need to study these." Giulia took pictures of the tabs with her phone and shut down the computer. "Thank you for letting me look at these here. It made gathering information much easier."

Mary stood with Giulia. "No, thank you. I hope Ken Kanning will be near his son and my daughter when I surprise her tomorrow night. The expression on her face should make good copy for his show."

Forty-five

"Zane I need your genius." Giulia wrote the website address and two of the screen names on a phone message slip. "I'm 93 percent positive the giggler is stalking Shiloh through this site. I have three possibles. You're faster at this than I am, so please work on these two while I take the third."

Zane held out a fist. "Wonder Twin powers, activate." Giulia bumped it with her own.

"I knew there was a cartoon I wanted to show Jessamine." Sidney typed into her phone. "My sisters and I were massive fans of *Justice League* when we were kids."

"Anything's better than Barney the Dinosaur," Zane said.

Sidney and Giulia made gagging noises.

"Giulia, do you need me?" Sidney said. "I have to finish the final details for Olivier's birthday surprise."

"You're free to go as long as you take video of the surprise for us."

Sidney pulled on her coat. "I will, but I can only show it to us, which is so annoying. I can't upload it to YouTube because I don't want him to look unprofessional."

More than an hour after Sidney left, Zane and Giulia compared notes.

"Angels_Watching is so sweet she makes my teeth ache," Zane said. "I tracked her to two other message boards. One belonged to her church." He turned over one sheet of paper. "She cleans the church, runs the rummage sale, and is a star member of Meals on Wheels."

Giulia whistled. "If I get to Heaven, I'll be assigned a much lower level than she will."

"You should try Asatru. No class distinctions allowed after death. Feast in your god's Great Hall until you're reincarnated."

"It's tempting. What about Haunt_Me?"

"This one could be an actual witch. Probably a female. She gave Shiloh the spell to lure her father's ghost into the whiteboard." He picked up the second paper. "Do we know any witches?"

"Rowan is the closest."

"She's not the right kind of witch. We should get a second opinion on the spell."

"Let me ask her." She dialed the Tarot Shoppe. "Jasper? Giulia. Is Rowan free? Thanks...Rowan? Giulia. We need to check the authenticity of a spell...No, not for me. For the Whiteboard...Let me write this down...thanks...I promise to tell you all about the Whiteboard's performance at the party, but not until Wednesday afternoon. I'm sleeping in."

"Success?" Zane said.

"I have a name and address, which will have to be acted upon tonight." She grimaced. "Even though Finn needs his mother."

"And his mother needs him?"

"In the worst way, so this may be the shortest meeting in the history of new motherhood."

"What about Friendly_Casper?"

Giulia made a gagging face. "To reuse a word, he gives me the creeps. He's not overt or vulgar. He must know he'd get reported to the site admins. His syntax screams 'predator' after the most cursory analysis."

"Enough to bring in the cops?"

"I'll need to read more of it in relation to Shiloh. I'll have to check the messages on Kord's YouTube channel as well. I don't look forward to the experience."

"Another reason why you make the big bucks."

Forty-six

Giulia discovered an unexpected result from combining motherhood and the private investigation business: resentment at evening time away from Finn. The longer the drive stretched to the Pittsburgh witch's address, the hotter her rancor burned. Twenty minutes each way, plus interview time. Waiting at home was a pudgy two-month-old who smiled toothlessly at her whenever she picked him up. And all for a side job bringing no income to DI.

She forced herself to picture Shiloh: inexperienced, angry, desperate, and too obsessed with her grief to recognize the stalker signs.

"Shiloh, I hope you appreciate this."

She turned onto a narrow city street lined on both sides with aging three-story houses. The ground floors on most had been converted to storefronts: PC repair, doggy day care, yarn, fabrics, yoga, used books, cupcakes.

A hand-lettered sign above the door she sought read: "The Tea Cozy." A window filled with mason jars of colorful herbal teas sparkled in the thin March sunshine. They looked so tempting, Giulia almost wished she didn't hate herbal tea.

Instead of chimes, the Wicked Witch of the West cackled when Giulia opened the door. A tall, thin blonde in a green long-sleeved knit dress was arranging boxes of sachets. She said without looking over her shoulder, "We close at seven."

"I'm sure we won't need more than seventeen minutes." Giulia kept a smile in her voice. "Rowan Froelig says if you can't vet a spell it isn't worth bothering with."

The blonde turned around. "You're the ghost detective." She clapped silver-manicured hands. "We've all been hearing rumors about you. I'm thrilled to meet you in person."

Giulia's years of working with a living, breathing Christmas elf stood her in good stead. She was in the presence of Sidney-level perkiness.

"I'm pleased to meet you, too. How do you know Rowan?"

"Please sit." She indicated two armchairs in the corner by the window. "Rowan and her blazing hot nephew crashed our Beltane gathering last year. They'd seen scandal and danger and he'd driven her to five possible locations until they found us."

Giulia grinned at her own memories. "Was it one of her 'drop everything and listen to me' Tarot readings?"

A laugh like wind chimes. "You know how she works. They were right, of course. An expelled member was hiding in the woods with an AR-15." A graceful shiver. "What is past is past. We haven't introduced ourselves. I'm Holly Spring."

"Giulia Driscoll."

"It's been a slow day. I think I'll close a little early." She reached a long arm to the "Open" sign hanging in the door and flipped it to "Closed." "Would you like some tea?"

"Thank you, but I have to get home to my baby as soon as we're finished." Being forced out of courtesy to drink herbal tea would take her aura—if such things existed—to new heights of stress colors.

"A baby! How old is he—or she? My twins turned eleven last month." She indicated two framed school pictures of a tall, thin, blonde girl and a nearly identical boy.

Giulia shared the latest picture of Finn and they swapped stories of their children's adorableness.

"You have a drive to get back to yours," Holly said, "and I promised to teach mine how to bake a King Cake for tomorrow. Tell me about this spell."

Giulia gave her the essentials.

Holly *tsk*ed. "The internet causes more trouble than it's worth, sometimes. Did you bring a copy?"

Giulia handed her phone to Holly, with the website screencap open. The witch read, frowned, read further, and chewed the corner of her bottom lip. "I'd never put those two herbs together. On their own they're quite powerful, but combined..." More lip chewing. "The steps for casting the circle are correct, and simple enough for a novice to understand. Whoever wrote this wasn't out to harm the girl." She looked over the phone at Giulia. "The teenager cast this spell?"

"So she says." Giulia explained Kord's claim to be creating the messages himself, even though the Whiteboard appeared to create a message on its own while in their office. "Kord was at the opposite end of the room. It's possible he rigged up magnets inside the Whiteboard powerful enough to be manipulated at that distance."

"A signal of some kind, perhaps." Holly's foot beat a rhythm on the floor. "We bought the twins miniature radio-controlled airplanes for their birthday. Those little toys send powerful signals. I can easily picture a tech whiz hacking them."

"Radio controls." Giulia was so going to rag on Zane—gently—for not thinking of it himself.

"It's not too plausible, to be honest. A ghost camping out in the toy makes more sense."

"If I owned the Whiteboard, I'd have no qualms about taking a hammer to it to see if it has hidden technology."

Giulia expected Holly to agree.

"I don't recommend such an action," she said instead. "If the spell worked as promised and a ghost is trapped inside, breaking it open may startle the ghost."

Giulia made a face. "I don't like the way you said 'startle.'"

Holly didn't soften. "You have more experience with ghosts than I do. I understand they're not necessarily stable."

"Erratic." Giulia rubbed her temples. "Yes, that was a deliberate understatement. A convent in downtown Cottonwood has a resident chain-smoking Gibson Girl. So much fun, right? Except I watched her open mouth turn into a pit of hell." She smiled. "My new motto is 'There's not enough coffee in the world.'"

"Substitute 'herbal tea' for 'coffee' and I'm right there with you." She returned Giulia's phone. "My professional opinion is the daughter's intense emotions amplified the spell enough to guarantee success."

"Guarantee?"

Holly opened her hands. "Eighty-five to 95 percent worth."

Giulia slid the phone into her messenger bag. "You've confirmed our misgivings. I'll proceed with more caution."

"Can you convince her to give you the object?"

"Not at this point. She and Kord are bringing it to the big Mardi Gras charity bash tomorrow."

Holly started. "At the Jevens house? No, no, no. This is a bad idea. He collected haunted artifacts."

Giulia braced herself. "I know he did, but why is it a bad idea? Please be specific."

"My fellow witches who work with spirits have talked about a situation like this. The new object could be a trigger for the existing objects." She held up a hand. "No, 'could be' is weak. The new object most likely will be a trigger. You've seen *Ghostbusters*? Think of the scene where the grid is powered down and every entity they've captured during the movie breaks loose. There's the potential for that kind of chaos on a house-wide scale instead of a city-wide scale."

Giulia banged her head on the back of the chair. "Six months ago I thought ghosts were nothing more than clever special effects in horror movies."

"They're not like Sadako from *Ringu*, are they?"

Giulia responded to her concern. "No, they're not all volcanoes of vengeance. Most are mischievous or sad or frightened. I'm also sorry to report that mansplainers don't lose the tendency after death."

"Why am I not surprised?" Holly stood and opened a drawer in an antique tallboy.

"Have you ever encountered a ghost?" Giulia gathered her bag and stood. She needed a major Finn and Frank antidote to this news of a potential otherworldly explosion.

"Yes, thanks to our coven leader. She traveled to the UK for an IT conference—her day job—and made a side trip to Wales to visit the location of her family's ancestral cottage." Holly took out several different boxes and a square of muslin. "An ugly apartment building stood on the spot, something like twenty stories of peeling brick face and a parking lot which left only a few square feet of actual grass from the original lot." The muslin received a generous pinch of something spiky. "She didn't want to waste an opportunity to connect with the past, so she cast a circle in the tiny patch of grass." Dried red berries, green leaves, and two different delicate white flowers joined the spiky greens. "Her great-great-grandmother appeared almost before she finished casting."

"Not an angry ghost, I hope?" Giulia smelled cloves and rosemary.

Another wind-chime laugh. "Let's call her crotchety. She informed her great-great-granddaughter of her intent to travel, as in, back to the States with her."

Giulia returned the laugh. "I had a grandmother who could've been her twin."

"You understand then." Holly added a drop of amber liquid to the herbs and the air was filled with the scent of woods, honeycomb, and lemon. "She's a big help to us at our gatherings. She taught my daughter to knit. My daughter has the Sight, too. A good thing for her crafting skills, because I'm hopeless with knitting needles." She brought the corners of the muslin together and tied the little bag with a white ribbon. "This is for you."

Giulia held up a hand. "Thank you, but—"

"No arguing. You're not dealing with a crotchety old woman ghost. You're not sure exactly what you're up against, correct?"

"I want to say I'm only up against an overprotective father, but now that I'm a mother I wouldn't guarantee the safety of anyone who threatened my baby."

"Same here. Don't lose sight of the possible haunted objects in the Jevens house. You're in unmapped territory until you discover what or who is squatting in the objects." She placed the sachet in Giulia's hand. "This contains everything I have on hand to safeguard against spiritual attack: boneset, yellow gentian, coriander, cloves, rosemary, and a few drops of frankincense to bind it together. Keep it in your pocket when you're in the Jevens house."

Even thinking fast, she couldn't come up with a polite refusal. "I'm familiar with cloves and rosemary in the kitchen and frankincense from church."

"Oh, you're Catholic? So is my husband. Every time I use frankincense he says it gives him altar boy nightmares." She closed Giulia's fingers around the sachet. "When I went to my pastor—he was Church of the Nazarene—and told him I had a vision from Brigid as the

Physician, I was sure he was going to skin me alive." Even her shudder was perky.

Giulia remembered how her brother-in-law, Father Pat, had reacted when he learned about her consultations with Rowan and Jasper. Those were several tense minutes. "But he didn't?"

A brilliant smile. "He didn't. We scheduled several meetings and he told me about his own vision that led him to his path."

If Giulia wasn't itching to get home, she would've suffered through a cup of herbal tea and swapped stories. "Thank you. I'm getting used to many new rituals. I appreciate your help."

"Any time. A connection of Rowan's is always welcome. Next time I'll brew one of my signature tea blends for us."

On her way home, Giulia stopped at Starbucks to wash out the phantom taste of herbal tea.

Forty-seven

Giulia arrived back home twenty minutes from the Tea Cozy on the dot. A delighted Finn was in her arms thirty-five seconds later.

Frank sniffed. "Why do you smell like Church?"

Finn sneezed.

"I wish you hadn't talked me into changing our Mardi Gras outfits." She raised her voice over Finn's "I'm hungry" siren-level wail. "I left a bottle for him in the fridge."

"We were playing *Halo*. He was fine until you came home." When Finn settled into feeding position, Frank said, "Why don't you like the costume switch anymore? What's wrong with Freddy and Daphne from *Scooby-Doo*?"

"After tonight's encounter, going as a priest and a nun would've been even more incongruous."

Frank sat in the opposite chair. "You said you'd never put on a veil again,"

"Not me. You."

Finn protested Giulia's lack of attention. She resettled him and stroked his thick red hair. "This may be one of the oddest conversations I've ever had."

Frank climbed over the coffee table and put his arm around her. "I never want to see you put on a veil again either."

"Scooby-Doo it is then. Could you fire up my laptop? I have a hunch and it needs either to turn into a fact or waft out of my brain."

She handed Finn over to his father to burp and logged into the DI network.

"Friendly_Casper?" Frank said and Finn belched. "Good

commentary, son. He's either a middle-schooler who lied about his age on the registration form or a predator."

Giulia said while typing, "Have we been married long enough to think alike?"

"Blame the detective business. We all think in the same patterns." A different rude noise emanated from his first-born. "Whoa. You dig deeper while I perform cleanup."

Giulia made an assenting sound as she cross-checked Casper's entries on SeeYourAngels against comments on Kord's Whiteboard videos.

Frank returned in a cloud of baby powder. "There may have been a minor explosion."

Giulia glanced up. "An adult male should not be bested by an inanimate object. You have powder in your hair."

"I'm helping you get into the ghostly mood." He read the dual windows on her screen. "Casper on one and Friendly_Casper on the other? The man has no imagination."

"He's also a Jevens."

"He's your client?"

"One of the three, RJ. What concerns me is he's overconfident because he's gotten away with this before. He gives off gross vibes in person, too. Watch."

She played the relevant clips from the soccer field debacle.

"He wears a flasher raincoat? Overconfident much?" He set Finn between them on the couch and gave his index fingers for the baby to hold. "Can you nail him yet?"

"No. I don't have enough. I've warned her mother, who'll be at the Mardi Gras party. We're going to have to be in more than six different places at once, but I'm also going to email Pit Bull tonight. Since Kanning will have the camera trained on Kord as often as possible, I'm going to have him watch for RJ to make a move on Shiloh when the party is loud and crowded."

"I'll do what I can, too."

Giulia kissed him, then turned all her attention to Finn. "Don't you let your grandma and grandpa spoil you too much tomorrow."

Finn smiled.

Mardi Gras

The Zydeco band leader cursed. The stage hand cursed. The trombone played *wah-wah-wah* on a descending scale.

The stage hand cursed the trombone player and rerouted the wiring for the third time. "Everything worked fine until we got into this freak show of a house."

In the *L*-shaped corner of the main hallway, one of the roulette operators arranged an armful of handcrafted dolls between the two wheels.

"Mascots," he said. "They'll bring the players luck."

Forty-eight

Frank parked the Camry half a block from the Jevens house's wrought iron gates. Zane pulled in behind them, Sidney behind him.

The weather approved of the Children with Cancer Foundation's efforts to make money tonight. The skies were clear at last and the temperature hovered around forty-five degrees.

Giulia's legs in her purple tights didn't approve of anything below sixty degrees. She'd altered the thin Daphne mini-dress to add pockets, but all the Scooby-Doo Gang costumes were designed for indoor parties. Even the lime green scarf didn't keep her neck warm.

Frank pocketed the car keys and adjusted his Fred Jones orange ascot and gleaming white pants. "You should wear miniskirts more often."

Giulia pulled her purple headband over her ears. "As long as I don't have to wear anything on my head. No veil flashbacks for me tonight." She tucked a stray brown curl beneath the long orange wig.

Sidney stood on her truck's running board. "Why did we both pick tiny skirts to wear in early March?" She tugged her ultra-short pleated Sailor Moon skirt down a millimeter. "These tall pink boots are paper thin, too."

Her husband Olivier knocked his blue foam wig over one ear as he exited the truck. "A Super Saiyan's hair should be immune to door frame attacks." He slipped his white gauntlets off his hands as he straightened it.

Frank said with a critical air, "You were born to wear a blue Spandex jumpsuit and white boots. When are we going to discuss the psychological implications of Vegeta, a character whose road rage personality is the polar opposite of your own?"

"The licensed psychologist of the group is off duty for the night."
He spread his arms. "If only this suit granted me the power of flight."

"Jessamine would love it," Sidney said.

"So would Finn." Giulia untangled Sidney's ankle-length blonde
ponytails. "I can see it now: within a week, we'll get hired to subdue a
ghost who will offer to levitate our children in exchange for not being
booted to the next level of the afterlife."

Sidney's wig swirled around her body with the force of her denial.
"I plan to enjoy stopping plain, ordinary crime and nothing else this
evening."

Zane stuck his head over his Chevy Cruze's doorframe. "Wait a
minute. I thought you were dressing as a priest and a nun."

"Too obvious," Frank said.

Olivier shook a finger at him. "You didn't have the spine to dress
as a nun."

"Spinal fortitude had nothing to do with it. I can't chase a living
criminal in a long dress."

Giulia assumed a dejected pose. "I couldn't argue with his logic."

"Well, my evening is ruined," Sidney said.

Zane exited the car completely and everyone broke into applause.
Baggy blue pants and a matching long-skirted coat draped his tall, thin
frame. A row of large gold buttons ran from his neck to his wide black
belt. An oversized silver star emblazoned the left side of his chest. A tall
helmet with another star in a circle crowned his head and an old-
fashioned nightstick hung from a holster attached to the belt.

"What are you?" Sidney said.

"Ms. D.?"

"I knew I forgot something." Giulia circled Zane. "You are a
Keystone Kop from the old Mack Sennett comedies. Who sewed this?
It's not a mass-market costume. What I forgot was to tell you to please
drop the 'Ms. D.' I've been meaning to mention it since I came back
from maternity leave."

Zane beamed. "Thanks, Ms.—Giulia. Here, let me introduce you."
He opened the passenger door and handed out a tall, beautiful woman
wearing an ostrich feather in a beaded headband. The rest of the
costume became visible as she walked around the front of the car: a

four-tier ivory lace dress that reached to the tops of her silver heels, a lace shrug lined with silver-tipped fur, and a long row of rhinestones on a silver chain around her neck.

"Everyone, this is Dru Ann." Zane completed the round of introductions.

"No, she's not," Giulia said. "This is Mabel Normand. Your costume is amazing. My sewing skills aren't one-tenth that good."

"Thank you." Dru Ann said in a low, soft voice.

"All right, I give up." Sidney said. "Someone email me the movie titles."

"Which you'll watch in our endless hours of spare time." Olivier said to Zane and Dru Ann, "We'll catch them in fifteen-minute segments."

"They're silent," Zane said. "Lots of repetition and one-sentence plots. It's all about the comedy. Good for short stints in between taking care of little kids."

"The perfect choice for parents of small children." Olivier gathered Sidney's ponytails and handed the ends to her.

"Okay, Driscoll Investigations and deputies," Giulia said. "Final check. Cell phones on silent?"

Six hands slid six phones out of pockets and in again.

"Wallets and other valuables locked away so we're not distracted by potential pickpockets?"

"Ma'am, yes ma'am." Zane said.

"What's in your other pocket?" Sidney pointed. "It's bulging."

Giulia took out a flask. "Holy water, just in case. It helps to have a priest in the family."

Dru Ann glanced from Giulia to Zane.

"I promised you surprises." He tucked her hand in his arm. "Police escort ready."

Forty-nine

Purple, gold, and green luminaries lined both sides of the curving driveway. The windows along the front of the house were cracked a few inches at the top, allowing the bands warming up to entertain the guests as they arrived. Strings of miniature lights in the same three colors illuminated the landscaping and outlined the house itself. Jester hats crowned the old-fashioned street lamps flanking the gates and the front steps, their bright white glow giving partygoers actual light to ascend and descend by.

Giulia rang the doorbell. Its Big Ben chimes pushed back against a trumpet solo from within. Cinderella answered the door. The button on her ball gown marred the costume's effect: a Children with Cancer logo and "Marcia" above it in gold script.

Little Red Riding Hood stood next in line: her button read "Angie." Instead of a basket of goodies, she held an electronic reader. "May I see your tickets, please?"

Giulia held out hers to be scanned.

"Please leave your coats in the room at the end of the welcome line."

Beep after *beep* from the scanner followed her as she moved down the receiving line to Rich Uncle Pennybags from the Monopoly game.

"Welcome to the Jevens Castle." Owen's hearty bonhomie was more out of character than the outfit of a fictional financier.

"Good evening, Mr. Jevens."

His green money bag dropped to the floor without a sound. Giulia guessed it contained pillow stuffing. "Ms. Driscoll? I didn't recognize you. Marvelous. We expect great things from you tonight. Blossom, didn't we watch this cartoon show with RJ when he was a kid?"

The Queen of Hearts looked down her long nose at Giulia. An unsuccessful attempt, as Giulia in lavender pumps topped her by a good four inches.

"Off with her head!" Blossom cackled. "I enjoy saying that. Your outfit is too cute for a professional detective. So is your companion's. I expect you to justify our trust in you."

Behind them, Owen complimented Zane and Dru Ann, but Sidney and Olivier had to explain their costumes. Giulia pasted on Polite Smile Number Two and reached the last person in line. Green velvet tailcoat, checkered green trousers, emerald patterned vest, curly white wig and handlebar mustache. A thin cane with a large emerald crystal hung over one arm.

"*The Wizard of Oz*, I presume?"

"Pay no attention to the man behind the, uh," he ducked behind Blossom, "the man behind the Queen of Hearts." He giggled. "It doesn't have the right ring to it. I'm RJ. We met the other day in your office." He held out a thick hand. Giulia shook it, remembering how he stalked Shiloh, but refrained from giving it the special self-defense pivot guaranteed to break a wrist.

"So," boomed Owen, "what's your strategy?"

Giulia wrenched her mouth into Polite Smile Number Two again before she turned around. "Mr. Jevens, I'm sure you're aware we'll be able to work more freely if no one, including the family, knows too many details."

Another loud laugh. "If you insist. Go ahead and implement your strategy. I care about results anyway, not how you achieve them."

Blossom added, "Make sure you leave the thief in one piece so we can have a crack at him."

RJ squeezed her. "I like the way you think, Auntie."

She coughed and yelped and pushed him away. "Don't crush my ribs, you hulk."

Owen stepped out of the line and beckoned to Giulia. "I want to show you something before the crowds arrive."

He led her into the kitchen. A half-dozen people from three different local restaurants scurried between the counters and the large central island, setting out trays of barbecue, kabobs, sliders, walking tacos, fruit cups, miniature cheesecakes, and cupcakes. Towers of disposable plates swayed next to buckets of utensils and stacks of napkins. One of the supposedly possessed dolls sat enthroned on the island, casting covetous glass eyes on the desserts.

Sidney and Zane dodged a tray of prepared sliders on their way in. "The Significant Others are exploring the dining room," Sidney said.

Owen talked over her. "Remember when I mentioned my father left too much of our money to crackpot ghost hunters? Here's one reason why: somebody convinced him this doll was haunted." He flicked one of its moving eyelids. "How somebody so smart could be so gullible is beyond me. We decided at the last minute these things would make good entertainment. *The Scoop* is going to use them for random scares throughout the night. It'll make for an interesting program."

Giulia hadn't had to rely on her Polite Smile arsenal to this extent in a while. She favored Owen with yet another Number Two. "May we see the rooms in which the items are dispersed? We don't want to be distracted from the job you hired us for by an artificially induced scream."

He laughed. "An artificial scream. That's a good one. Come with me."

They snaked through the caterers and down the hall to the game room. The distressed wood table had been moved to the center of the room and the doll house now covered the table's inlaid chess board. Owen opened its hinged front.

"It came with dolls and furniture. Five will get you ten some drunk millennial will try to relive her childhood with it tonight. I hope I'm in here when *The Scoop* does its thing."

At this point, Giulia was seriously considering whether switching DI to an all ghost, all the time agency would be an improvement over living clients.

Sidney whispered in her ear, "I know that look. Humans are still better than ghosts."

As they entered the family room, a feedback screech assaulted their ears. The accordion player cursed and saw Owen. "Sorry." The trumpet player jiggled the connections.

The Victorian mourning doll had been posed on the mantlepiece like Mae West on a chaise lounge waiting for her maid to peel her a grape.

"This doll's supposed to be haunted too," Owen said to the band. "Maybe she doesn't like Zydeco."

The drummer laughed. The accordion player cursed again. The trumpet player produced a small red velvet packet. "Gris gris bag, man. I'm protected."

Giulia touched the witch's protection sachet in her pocket beneath the holy water flask. Regardless of her opinion of such charms, a ghost who believed in its power would make her work easier.

They processed upstairs as three clocks chimed four forty-five. The doors officially opened at five, so the house was still their own. Owen went straight to the master bedroom. Sidney braked in the doorway, heels hitting Zane's boots.

The antique wedding dress floated above the bed, suspended from the ceiling by fishing wire at shoulders, wrists, waist, and train.

"The placement is effective, "Giulia said, "but aren't you worried someone may damage it?"

"Come on, you've seen *Beetlejuice*, right? You're young enough. I hadn't, but when RJ showed me the part where the ghosts get conjured into their wedding clothes I knew we had to do it with this dress. It's not fancy enough or old enough to make it worthwhile trying to sell, so I don't care if the drunks play around with it. Besides," he elbowed Giulia, "I've got you and your people to keep an eye on things."

With studied patience, Giulia said, "You hired us to catch a potential thief, not to guard antiques."

Owen laughed yet again. "I know. I know. You're right. I like your stick-to-it-ive-ness. Blossom thinks this thing is worth saving, but she'd only wear it if she dyed it gray first. Come into the library."

Zane held Giulia and Sidney back. "Drunk?" he whispered.

"Must be," Sidney said.

"Drunk or sober, I'll be happy to see the back of him," Giulia said.

An eye-level shelf had been cleared of books. The haunted Bible leaned against the wall with a desk lamp under-lighting it like it was a villain in a cheap horror movie. The peeling gilt on the title and the frayed binding added to the effect.

"I wanted to hollow it out and put in one of those snakes that spring out at you, but my lawyer says the book's worth money."

No one commented.

"Well, I thought it was funny. Come back downstairs for the last one."

He opened the door to the first-floor bathroom. "This is the real thing. Any drunk breaks this, I break their head."

The three-foot tall mirror dominated the small bathroom. No mean feat, as seven mirrors of varying sizes hung on the antique rose papered walls. Owen had placed it so the person entering the room confronted themselves.

"What's the urban legend about mirrors?" He turned to Giulia.

"If someone stands in front of it and repeats 'Bloody Mary' three times—"

"Right. Some dead witch shows up and kills you." He closed in on the mirror until his nose touched the glass. "Bloody Mary, Bloody Mary, Bloody Mary."

Giulia caught herself holding her breath.

Owen's laugh echoed in the small room. "Maybe the ghost is getting her hair done. When we sell this, we'll repeat 'It's not haunted, despite what we were told' over and over. People will get into a cage match for it." He pushed past them into the hall. "Now you've seen all the haunted objects. Keep an eye on the mirror and the doll in the family room, if you can. They're the priciest ones."

"We'll do our best."

The doorbell rang. Cinderella/Marcia shouted, "Curtain up!"

Driscoll Investigations ducked into the dining room.

"He might be on something," Sidney said.

"I still vote for drunk," Zane said. "If he keeps it up, he'll be on the floor by ten o'clock."

"Not our problem," Giulia said. "Neither are any of the antiques. We're sticking to the plan."

Many voices filled the front hall.

"Showtime," Giulia said.

Zane and Dru Ann took up their first position in the downstairs bedroom. Sidney and Olivier retraced their steps to the kitchen to get to the breakfast room. Giulia and Frank turned left at the kitchen, stopped at one of the two pop-up bars at which Frank purchased plain Cokes for both of them, and continued past the mirrored bathroom and the roulette table into the family room.

The band might not have solved the sound problem, because they weren't playing at deafness level.

Frank indicated the décor. "You could've given me fair warning."

She shammed innocence. "And spoil the surprise?"

He zeroed in on the mourning doll. "I'll never watch one of the Chucky movies again."

"Good catch. It's supposed to be possessed."

An Irish curse. "You're not kidding."

"Correct. I'm not."

Her husband dragged his eyes away from the lounging doll. "I'm going to explore the house."

"The other haunted objects are in the library, master bedroom, game room, and kitchen."

"Hooray. A scavenger hunt."

Giulia poked her head into the hall after he left. The line at the front door must have begun to form right after they arrived because the house was filling up fast. The ambient noise of conversation plus eating plus gambling leapt to new heights with every passing minute.

She returned her attention to the room, in particular the bay window. By positioning herself at one side, she could see two-thirds of the room in it. Five fifteen in early March was enough time after sunset to turn the window into a mirror.

Marie Antoinette and King Louis XVI strolled in, sipping martinis. Kurt Cobain—complete with bloody head wound—and Courtney Love followed. The band vamped the opening bars of "Smells Like Teen Spirit," an odd choice for accordion and trumpet.

"Whoa, Dude, I have to be way more hammered to hear that." Cobain raised his beer in salute nonetheless.

Cheers and groans from the roulette area. From the front hall, shouts of friends outside seeing other friends inside. A group of five dressed as characters from *Bob's Burgers* entered the family room. Giulia moved away from the window and wandered the room's perimeter, sipping her Coke. Han Solo passed her, eating barbecue on a bun. Giulia's mouth watered. Miss Marple and Hercule Poirot entered and went straight to the glassed-in bookshelf. Giulia strolled toward them.

"Encyclopedias? In this day and age?" Poirot said.

"Perhaps they're hollow and contain fabulous jewels." Miss Marple tried the bookcase door without success.

Cobain joined them. "Booze. My dad had flasks hidden in three huge books in the den when I was a kid. Volumes of collected sermons from like the 1800s. Who'd want to open those, right?"

"Could be a gun," Poirot said.

"Too hard to get to when you need it." Courtney Love cupped her hands around her face and pressed her nose to the glass. "Can't tell from out here if the encyclopedias are hiding anything. Whoever did it, did a good job."

Poirot said to Marple, "If they auction off the house's contents, we should bid on this bookcase with contents as is."

Sidney and Olivier joined the group at the bookcase. "Nothing," she said quietly to Giulia as they passed each other.

Kurt Cobain bonded with Vegeta immediately. Within a minute they were debating the merits of Majin Buu versus Frieza as the more effective villain. Sidney turned her back on the mourning doll and joined The Powerpuff Girls inspecting the handmade knickknacks tucked into every available niche.

Giulia retraced her steps to the front of the house in the manner of Billy in the *Family Circus* cartoon strip. Around the gambling audience to the end of the roulette table, backtrack three steps because the space wasn't wide enough for Daphne and an advancing Mr. Potato Head, squeeze through the three-deep crowd at the bar, angle across the hall and behind the reception line.

The party was a gift to pickpockets, something Giulia should've realized as she was bumped and brushed and squeezed by a dozen strangers. More than half the crush were taking photos or video with their phones. Everyone within her range of vision had followed the DI plan for the night: cell phone cases with slots for cash, credit cards, and ID. Too bad for one type of thief tonight.

"Ms. Driscoll! Hey, Ms. Driscoll!" Kord Kanning squeezed through Captains Kirk and Picard. He muttered a quick "'Scuse me" to Uhura and Counselor Troi and screeched to a halt at Giulia's toes. "I totally recognized you even in your Scooby-Doo girl detective costume. Maybe I should be a detective, too. Like my outfit? Shiloh told me it'd make me look mysterious. Dad's finding us a spot right in the middle of things. I wanted us by the gamblers, but Shi says we should set up by the bar. She says the bar will be in a, what do you call it, a—"

"A high traffic area." Shiloh materialized behind Kord. "Is Jasper here, Ms. Driscoll?"

"Not that I know of."

Shiloh's clothes had been upgraded from the usual black jeans, sneakers, and long-sleeved t-shirts. The jeans and sneakers remained, but the addition of a black velvet tail coat and a mulberry burnout velvet t-shirt to her goth makeup and hair gave her a mysterious, bohemian air.

Kord's adoration for Shiloh had never been more apparent than in his clothing tonight. Black jeans, a button-down black shirt, a crimson tie with a shadowed paisley pattern of skulls, and a black fedora tilted a few degrees to the right. Without goth makeup subjugating his bright brown hair and eyes, the effect was Justin Bieber-esque.

Giulia drew on every shred of manners within herself not to comment. For the first time in her life, Ken Kanning came to her rescue.

"You're all set up, Kord." He said to Giulia, "Excuse me, miss. We have to set up these two as part of tonight's entertainment. If you'd like to ask a question of Kord's Whiteboard—"

He stopped when his son laughed at him. "Dad, you dork. This is Ms. Driscoll. Good thing you're not the detective here."

Never at a loss for more than ten seconds, Kanning crooked one finger over his shoulder. Pit Bull loomed over the group, camera running. Kanning the father became Kanning the voice of *The Scoop*.

"Tonight's costumes are so much more than what you take off the shelf on Halloween, Scoopers. Daphne of *Scooby-Doo* fame here is none other than Cottonwood's loveliest sleuth, Giulia Driscoll. Would you believe I didn't recognize her?"

Giulia fluffed her wig for the camera. "Jeepers, gang, we have a mystery on our hands."

Behind the camera, Pit Bull gave her a thumbs up. Ken Kanning wore his usual show makeup, but Pit Bull had transformed his entire head into a multi-colored sugar skull.

"Kill it, Bull." Kanning turned his back on Giulia. "Kord, let's go."

"See you later, Ms. Driscoll." Kord bounced past her. "Five bucks to ask Shi's dad a question! Tell everybody you see, okay?"

Shiloh followed in silence. Pit Bull pointed to the camera and to Shiloh. Giulia nodded and put all things Kanning out of her mind as she took up her position in the downstairs bedroom.

Fortunately for any guests who might wonder why Daphne was hovering in one room, the bedroom's Southwest theme gave her plenty of kitsch to explore. She removed a banjo from its wall hooks and tuned it. When guests tossed coats onto the growing mountain of wool, leather, and padded nylon, they saw a cartoon character picking her way through "Turkey in the Straw."

"Don't give up your day job."

"Are we going to square dance?"

Giulia feigned total concentration. People were more interested in the party than in an amateur musician and left. No one entering the room in the next twenty minutes shrugged out of a coat twice the appropriate size. Only three costumes raised her suspicions: a clown with baggy pants held up by fat suspenders, a Big Bad Wolf in a too-large nightgown, and a couple dressed as salt and pepper shakers with wide tunics.

Sidney entered the room finishing a chicken kabob. "Locally

sourced free-range chickens and local hydroponic veggies," she said to Giulia's inquiring look. "I know the restaurant."

"I expected no less." Giulia rehung the banjo and flexed her fingers. "Plaid clown pants, salt and pepper shakers, Big Bad Wolf dressed as Grandma."

"Got it. We were right about the butler selfies. Look for a grim reaper with a Marilyn Monroe wig and Santa Claus complete with sack."

"Counting on us assuming no one would be that obvious?" Giulia stood and stretched.

"My thoughts exactly."

Giulia was halfway to the kitchen when a woman screamed.

Fifty-one

A few heads turned toward the scream, but the majority kept eating, drinking, and gambling. Giulia fought her way through the lines at the bar to a tight circle of onlookers around Kord and Shiloh. Galadriel from *The Lord of the Rings* was on the floor at the foot of the ornate love seat Kanning had chosen for his son's performance, wrinkling her glittery dress. *The Scoop*'s camera lens was zoomed to its maximum setting toward her face.

"He's a witch!" She pointed at Kord with a shaking finger.

Her audience laughed.

"Someone find a duck and a big set of scales," one man said.

"What?" another man said.

"*Monty Python and the Holy Grail.* Don't you watch the classics?"

Ken Kanning snapped his fingers.

The action released Kord from his deer in the headlights pose. "I guess this is proof our ghost answered this lady's question." He turned on the Kanning grin. "Let me read it to them, Shi."

Shiloh passed him the Whiteboard.

"The question was, what was my father's childhood nickname for me? The answer was Pattycake." He said to Galadriel, "Is your name Patty?"

Galadriel impersonated a beached fish for a few seconds. "My middle name is. I stopped using it years ago. No one knows it."

"Our ghost knows it because he's in contact with every other ghost there is." Kord switched to carnival barker mode. "There you have it, folks. Five bucks well spent, and remember, all the money goes to helping kids with cancer. Who's next?"

Galadriel got to her feet and pushed her way to the front of the bar. "Whiskey. Neat." She slapped a ten-dollar bill on the clear plastic counter and threw back the liquor like Humphrey Bogart mooning over Ingrid Bergman in *Casablanca*.

The roulette wheel operator called over, "Can we spin?"

The off-duty cop dressed as a London bobby returned to his position overseeing the gambling. "Go ahead."

Giulia continued through the kitchen into the breakfast room, snagging a slider on the way. Every seat at the table was occupied. Another seven people were checking out the bookshelves. Rizzo and Sandy from *Grease* had pulled the stuffed butler off his stand and were jitterbugging with it.

The Scoop ran in on Giulia's heels. All she had to do was keep behind and to the left of Pit Bull to perform her job without interference.

Three minutes later, *The Scoop* moved on to fresh fodder. Shaggy holding a stuffed Scooby-Doo under one arm and a beer in his other hand yelled, "Daphne!" and made her pose for selfies. It took her six minutes to get rid of him.

When she could give the room her complete attention again, a different set of characters sat eating at the table. The butler was back on his stand, and Don Quixote was intent on one of the bookshelves.

Too intent. Giulia began at the end of the row of bookshelves and moved along the row of five until she was next to Don Quixote. Vernon Jevens also collected detective stories, so Giulia plucked out *The Maltese Falcon* and channeled her inner Sidney.

"Oh, I love this book. Everybody's seen the Bogart version, but have you seen the 1931 version with Ricardo Cortez in the Bogart role?" She turned a few pages. "Honestly, he was so much better as Perry Mason. What do you think?"

Don Quixote turned his bearded face toward her. "If I wanted conversation, I would have brought my parrot."

Giulia pretended to be embarrassed. She stumbled through a generic apology and returned the book. With a flustered air, she adjusted her wig and tripped on the throw rug as she moved to the sideboard against the other wall.

She picked up the first antique cup and saucer set her hands touched. Under the guise of getting a better look at it, she approached the hanging lamp over the table. By a convenient coincidence, this position also kept Don Quixote in view.

Glinda the Good Witch of the North was at the table examining a different cup. Dorothy Gale had taken apart a matryoshka doll and was comparing the different faces on each piece. The three of them studied their choice of objects intently and without conversation. As Giulia's real object of study was Dismissive Don Quixote, the setup was ideal.

The tilter at windmills read his book for the next twelve minutes. In that time, Giulia took a picture of the cup with her phone, volunteered to take a picture of the Oz characters with the butler, and noted everyone else entering. Most of them concentrated on their food. One began an extended phone conversation with "Jill" who wasn't going to meet him at the party and wouldn't change her mind.

Don Quixote put away the book and left. In three more minutes the population of the room turned over and Giulia beelined for the book: *The Definitive History of Classic Comics*. The spine opened at, of course, *Don Quixote*. The artist had allowed plenty of room for large paragraphs of dialogue. Giulia skimmed it and concluded twelve minutes was a reasonable amount of time to finish.

One attendee eliminated out of two hundred plus. She tried not to think about becoming desperate enough to ask Shiloh's ghost for assistance.

No. She would never put herself in a Kanning's power. She took a miniature chocolate cheesecake as she passed through the kitchen. For an instant she thought she saw a cloud of roiling energy surround the supposedly haunted doll. She shook herself and continued to her next stop. This place was getting to her.

Fifty-two

As Giulia slipped into the dining room to check her phone, The Phantom of the Opera slipped a jade Fu Dog with ruby eyes into his cloak.

Giulia snapped a picture and grasped his wrist. "Come with me, please."

"What? Who are you? Let me go." The Phantom must have let his gym membership lapse, because Giulia dragged him into the hall with ease.

"Officer!"

The crowd parted for the bobby guarding the door receipts. "What's the trouble, Miss?"

Owen and Blossom left the dwindling receiving line and joined them.

"I caught this man stealing an object from the dining room as I was checking messages. Here's a picture of the incident."

Phone technology being what it was, they all saw the Fu Dog in the Phantom's hand. Its ruby eyes caught the light as its feet disappeared into the cloak.

The Phantom quit making excuses and cursed Giulia. Nothing so colorful as Frank's extensive cache of Irish curses; the Phantom went straight for vulgarity. Owen complimented her, the cop read the Phantom his rights, and the Fu Dog now weighted Blossom's purse.

Giulia checked her phone: seventeen minutes lost to this distraction.

More screams, this time from the family room. Not the Whiteboard, then. She pushed her way to the room. The screams changed to voices cheering someone on.

RJ joined her, swinging his cane in a narrow arc next to his hip. "Early for a drunk fight. I'll separate them."

Pit Bull materialized from somewhere near the front of the house, Ken Kanning a step in front of him.

Zane came through the door, dragging Doctor Frankenstein in a lab coat drenched in dark beer. Harley Quinn followed them. The collar of her black and red shirt was ripped from neck to shoulder.

Zane threw the Doctor at the feet of the roulette bobby. "This waste of skin tried to force himself on Harley here. When she refused and tried to push him off, he became aggressive, as you can see."

Harley Quinn stepped up. "Bastard ripped my costume trying to cop a feel. My friend tried to pry him off me but couldn't. Then my white knight here hauled him off me like it was nothing and clocked him in the jaw."

She-Ra strode up to the group. "I was coming into the room when Harley was yelling 'No' and 'Stop.' Would a recording of the event help throw him in jail?"

At Zane's feet, Doctor Frankenstein began to breathe heavily and twitch.

"It would, ma'am." The bobby's face betrayed nothing.

Giulia joined them to watch thirty seconds of pure justice. Doctor Frankenstein pawed Harley's shoulder. The band finished a song as he grabbed her, and comparative silence fell. Holding her beer out of his reach, she said "No." He grabbed her again. "Come on, baby, you're too hot to resist." "Stop," she shouted. Teen Titan Starfire pushed ineffectually at the Doctor's grabby hands. He shouldered Starfire away and got a handful of Harley's shirt. She threw her beer over him. He shouted "Bitch!" and clawed her breast. Zane's Keystone Kop uniform filled the screen for two seconds: One, and he jerked the Doctor vertical. Two, and he walloped the Doctor in the sweet spot on the jaw. Zane took a step back and the Doctor slumped to the floor at his feet. Applause replaced the music. Before the video ended, Giulia caught a glimpse of Dru Ann watching with admiration and approval.

"The hell?" Doctor Frankenstein put a hand to his jaw and worked it gingerly back and forth.

The bobby heaved him to his feet. "Your name, sir?"

"Stan. Stan Schrack."

"Stan Schrack, you are under arrest..." He listed several charges and read him his rights.

The Doctor blustered and struggled without effect. The bobby hustled him out the front door, Harley Quinn and Starfire at the procession's end. The gauntlet cheered Harley and remarked on the size of the Doctor's ineffectual manhood. The bar's attendant bobby adjusted his position so he could keep one eye on the bar and the other on the gambling.

Pit Bull lowered the camera. "Arrest footage. Not bad. I need a drink."

"One." Kanning said. "I'll be in the bathroom."

"Yes, Dad." Pit Bull winked at Giulia.

Sidney came up to Giulia and Zane. "You're getting all the excitement."

"Not me," Giulia said. "Zane. I arrived for the denouement."

Zane looked around. "Where's Dru Ann? I was so intent on stopping Frankenstein I didn't think about her."

"I'm not a fragile flower." Dru Ann joined the group. "You don't have to keep me under your wing at all times." She kissed Zane's cheek. "You're a hero."

Zane's answering grin may have veered toward "goopy." He and Dru Ann returned to the family room. Giulia realized the band had resumed playing during the drama. Sidney's white boots took a left turn into the art room. Frank and Olivier detached themselves from the TV mounted on a stand behind the bar.

"Honey, we owe Sidney and Olivier dinner."

Giulia eyed her husband. His innocent expression should've worked like a charm in his Fred Jones costume.

"Why?"

"The Lakers hit more three-pointers than the Cavs."

"Olivier, does he need to make an appointment with you to get to the roots of his gambling habit?"

"Habit?" Moral outrage didn't go with the Freddy costume.

Olivier, looking smug as Vegeta should, put a comforting arm around Frank. "My hours are flexible. I'm sure we can work out a schedule which suits your on-duty hours."

"*Póg mo thóin,*" Frank said with a toothy grin.

"Do I want to know what you said?" Olivier's smugness faltered.

"You do not." Giulia tugged Frank's ascot. "We're professionals here, darling husband."

"The chances anyone here understands Irish are less than 1 percent." He eased the ascot out of her grasp and flattened out the wrinkles.

"Olivier," Giulia said, "I'm always happy to have you and Sidney and Jessamine over for supper. Perhaps I'll save a plate of leftovers for Frank. Now I'm getting back to work."

"Yes, dear. Whatever you say, dear." Frank's voice followed her partway down the hall to the game room.

Owen's prediction about the dollhouse was on its way to fulfillment. Seven women surrounded it squealing like little girls.

"Look at this detail." Wonder Woman held out a miniature grandfather clock.

"This doll's hair feels like the real thing." Princess Buttercup stroked the hair with her fingertips.

"Stand back, I figured out the hinge." With a harsh *click,* the dollhouse split in the middle as Cleopatra swung open its sides.

"Ooooh, my." Seven voices sighed in ecstasy.

"The wallpaper is coming down." Jessica Rabbit slid a nail under a peeling strip.

"It's a haunted dollhouse. It's supposed to be peeling." Catwoman reached in and touched a silvered mirror.

"If only the attic has a ghost." Wilma Flintstone, taller than the others, stood on tiptoe and looked down into the attic.

"No. I don't like scary things." Betty Rubble turned big eyes up to Wilma, who smiled.

"Okay, little sister. No ghosts, just for you."

Giulia put her back against the bookshelf of board games and took in the room. The women played with the dolls and furniture as though they'd reverted to grade school. If the dollhouse turned out to be haunted, their enjoyment could go south in a heartbeat. She clenched her teeth and made another mental note to have a Serious Talk with Rowan. Then she unfocused her eyes and stared at the dollhouse.

The air swirled as though someone blew smoke into the mix. The swirls increased, ballooned, overlapped each other. They reminded Giulia of a flock of starlings gliding and swooping and dancing against a blue summer sky. As soon as the image coalesced in her head, the swirls separated into a globe over each woman's head. Reds, oranges, yellows—bright, happy colors, the colors of favorite childhood toys.

If Giulia could've spared time for introspection, she would've wondered at the skills she never in a thousand years knew were lurking within herself. Mother and wife and successful professional skills were plenty. She hadn't asked for all these extra layers.

But she didn't have time. She threw aside the shaky ground of seeing auras, for real, forget about prevarication, and texted Rowan.

Auras. What do red, yellow, and orange mean?

A reply vibrated five seconds later. *Together?*

No. Separate. Five people enjoying themselves.

Fifteen seconds this time as the three bouncy dots indicated Rowan was typing. *Happiness, peace, excitement, as long as the colors aren't muddy or shot through with black or gray.*

Correct. Clear colors. Thank you.

You're seeing auras that clearly. Wonderful!

Giulia drew on her inner stores of patience. *We Have To Talk.*

Rowan replied with a string of laughing emojis.

Giulia put away her phone. She needed a month of uninterrupted thirty-six-hour days to process all this. With effort she shut out the women's colors and concentrated on the dollhouse.

"Hey, Daphne, sorry. We didn't mean to hog the fun." Cleopatra opened a space for Giulia.

She joined them. "No problem. The party's going on for a while."

"Yeah, but we'll be too sloshed to appreciate this later." Wilma bumped Betty's shoulder. "The taxi company and the Uber drivers won't be complaining about who's stealing who's business tonight."

Giulia held the little grandfather clock for a moment before Buttercup switched it for the doll with human hair. She marveled at the workmanship and rubbed a braid between her fingers. She reached in and touched the walls, the floors, the fireplaces, the attic.

Nothing. The timid ghost in Kord's Whiteboard gave off stronger energy. Haley Comette and her Society were getting played by her so-called psychic.

Wilma set a baby doll in a highchair. "Nostalgia accomplished. Who's up for tequila?"

Betty straightened her back. "I vote for getting stupid on adult beverages."

Wonder Woman hooked her arms around both sisters. "My Lasso of Truth is unnecessary to determine your honest desire for this adventure. To the bar!"

Giulia wandered with apparent aimlessness over to the bench seat beneath the window. The life-sized stuffed doll in it wore brown shorts with matching embroidered suspenders, white shirt and knee socks, and a small-brimmed fedora with a white feather in the band. His hands held a full-sized accordion, the instrument's weight squashing the stuffing in his legs.

She sat next to the doll and played a C chord on the accordion. No sound, as expected. More women came to rhapsodize over the dollhouse. She was about to give up and slip into the bathroom when the salt and pepper couple came in. The woman gravitated to the dollhouse, the man to the shelves of games.

Giulia continued to play soundless chords on the accordion. The man called the woman over.

"You have to see this dollhouse, honey." She left it with reluctance.

"Whatever. I found it." He reached into the topmost shelf and brought down a battered cardboard box.

"That sneaky SOB." The salt shaker touched the faded lettering on the lid. "He swore he wasn't the winning bidder."

The pepper shaker lifted the lid. "He stuffed it up here like it wasn't worth anything. He wasn't just sneaky. He was vindictive." Pepper unfolded a game board. "The 1935 Edition with the single early patent. I'd wipe our savings for this."

"He knew you would." Salt looked around the room. "Let's get something to eat. We can look at it again before we leave."

Pepper returned it to the shelf and they left the room. Giulia opened a board game auction site and typed in the phrase Pepper used. Then she texted Zane: *1st fl game room now.* Sidney had wiry athletic strength, but Zane had bulk and height. When she stepped into the hall, RJ the giggling creeper was still the only Jevens in sight, one eye on Shiloh surrounded by Whiteboard questioners. She tapped him on the arm.

"Mr, Jevens? May I speak to you a moment?"

He started. "Who are you? Oh, the detective." She had his full attention then. "You found something? Come on, we'll keep it between you and me. I'll make it worth your while."

Giulia didn't even bother to paste on one of the Polite Smiles. "Mr. Jevens, we're working for the entire family and all discoveries will be communicated to the entire family."

The dollhouse women left after Giulia and RJ reentered. Giulia closed the door, but the doorknob turned in her hand. Half a thought said "ghost" and the sensible half said "Zane." The sensible half won.

"What's up, Ms. D.?"

"I need your height, please. Mr. Jevens, two people were in here a few minutes ago with prior knowledge of a purchase made by Vernon. Zane, would you bring down the yellowed Monopoly box on the top shelf?"

Zane placed it on the bench next to the stuffed accordion player. "This is old."

"Old and valuable. I found one of the few still available on an auction site." She turned her screen to Zane.

"Whoa." Zane regarded the aging box with new respect.

RJ reached for her phone. She moved it out of his reach.

"Sorry." He squinted at the screen. "Are you shitting me? No, you're not. Sorry again. My great-uncle was a shifty SOB." He opened the door and shouted into the crowd, "Owen!" Waited a few seconds and shouted again.

"Coming." Owen's new boisterous voice cut through the crowd and band noise. He jogged into the game room, stuffed moneybag bouncing against his thigh. When RJ closed the door, Owen regarded the room with a puzzled expression.

"Our late and unlamented patriarch left us a present." RJ pointed to the Monopoly box. "And our sleuth just earned us back her advance."

Zane glanced at Giulia and looked away quickly.

"Give him the skinny, Detective."

Giulia, wondering if anyone else on the planet still used "skinny" for "details," showed Owen the website on her phone and repeated the salt and pepper shakers' conversation.

Owen the businessman didn't waste time in profanity. He picked up the Monopoly box with care and took a key ring strung with tiny keys out of his pocket. He inserted one into the glass trophy case behind the dollhouse. "RJ."

His nephew lifted the wood-framed glass lid. Owen tipped the box on its end and slid it behind a messy stack of *National Geographic* magazines. He stepped back and looked into the case from all sides, then pushed two oil paintings against the sides of the magazines.

"Close it," he said to RJ. Then he locked the case and pocketed the key ring. "Excellent work, Ms. Driscoll. RJ, I'd appreciate it if you'd take the time to check the rest of the games on the shelf."

RJ grumbled but got to work. Owen took control of the doorknob.

"Ms. Driscoll, I'm surprised at your discovery. What're the chances for more of the same around the house?"

"Low," Giulia said. "The auction site had only a few games and the bids weren't high. As a way to secrete wealth, they're too bulky and too easily damaged."

"Like a jigsaw puzzle with a missing piece, you mean?"

"In a way."

"You're the professional." He opened the door and the roar of party noise rushed in.

Giulia led Zane into the dining room where they affected interest in the sculptured figures on a triangular corner shelf.

"Maybe we should initiate a condescending client percentage on their bill." Zane pitched his voice so only she could hear it.

"One day we'll be pushed over the edge." She picked up a miniature Venus de Milo. "I meant what I said in there. The game was a one-off. If Vernon hid something in the house, it won't be so obvious."

"I agree. Is it too much to hope Vernon hid stacks of money in the cushions of the love seat Kord Kanning's enthroned on?"

"If anyone tries to take Kord's spot, *The Scoop* will do our sleuthing for us." She eyed Zane. "I wouldn't like that. Would you?"

"Hell no. Sorry."

"*The Scoop* does drive one to profanity." She checked her phone.

"The salt and pepper shakers destroyed my schedule. I'm at the end of my shift in the game room."

"I'm starting mine. Sidney's upstairs in the library."

"Let's hope I didn't miss an essential clue in there. I'm due in the library, then entertainment room. If you and I have nightmares of stuffed guinea pigs attacking us, I really will add an upcharge to the bill."

Fifty-three

Giulia's luck was in: the downstairs bathroom was unoccupied. Her plan had been to finish as soon as possible and get back to work. She admired the antique rose wallpaper as she washed her hands and did the best she could with her wig's flyaways. Two of the seven mirrors were mounted so she could see both sides of herself at once.

The supposedly haunted mirror hung on the wall facing the door, and she had to face it to toss the paper towel in the waste basket. A fetid miasma *whooshed* at her from the glass.

One of Frank's Irish curses almost passed her lips. The center of the glass clouded into a humanlike silhouette with odd spiky bits.

No.

She unscrewed the flask and flung drops of Holy Water from her fingertips. They sizzled on the mirror. The stink evaporated. The glass cleared.

She screwed the cap on with unsteady fingers and opened the voice memo function on her phone. "Note: We need a separate ghost fee schedule. It must have a percentage contingency scale for spirits ranging from neutral to aggressive."

She straightened her shoulders, took a few deep breaths, and opened the door.

"Perfect timing." Julius Caesar ran inside.

Giulia hovered until she heard the water in the sink turn off. She moved a few paces away to watch. Caesar came out adjusting his toga. A normal bathroom visit.

Frank came over to her. "What?"

She smiled up at him. "Is there a target on my purple back?"

He looked behind her. "No." He faced her. "Why?"

"One of Vernon's collection of six possibly haunted items is haunted for real."

"What?"

"Don't spill beer on me, please. The large mirror in this bathroom has an occupant, but a splash of Holy Water stash did the trick. The guy who used it after me experienced nothing unusual. I waited to see him exit."

Frank indulged in a lengthy Irish sentence.

"I don't recognize some of that. Has your grandfather been giving you extra lessons?" A horrifying thought came to Giulia. "I'd like to put in a request for Finn's first words not to be Irish curses, please and thank you."

Frank didn't reply. When she took his face between her hands, he didn't meet her eyes.

She hung her head against his chest. "We are going to receive so many letters from our son's teachers. I'm going back to work."

"Wait. You're serious? Jevens really did collect a ghost?"

Giulia snapped to attention. "I am not in the habit of lying."

"I know you're not. Dammit. Please don't do anything reckless."

"I'll do my best."

Yet another scream from the front of the house sent her plowing through the crush in the main hall. Two identical Black Widows squealed and embraced and chattered in the foyer. Giulia breathed and continued to the stairs, surprised there hadn't been more costume duplicates. At least these women enjoyed the fun of it. All the party needed was a costume-ripping catfight.

Her phone buzzed with a text from Sidney. *Library? TS is interfering.*

Something by Spyrogyra floated down the upstairs hall from the jazz trio in the entertainment room. Giulia hung a left at the top of the stairs. In the library, Pit Bull's camera focused on the antique Bible. Ken Kanning was in Sidney's face as he narrated.

"Scoopers, I'm sure you'd like to hear what one of the intrepid members of Driscoll Investigations has to say about this ancient Bible. According to the Jevens family, it's harboring a being from the Other Side."

"Mr. Kanning." Giulia infused enough ice into the words to make the furnace kick in.

If only Ken Kanning weren't always in *Scoop* mode. He spun around and snapped his fingers. Pit Bull swung the camera 180 degrees.

"*The Scoop* is always happy to see the lovely Giulia Driscoll, Cottonwood's premier ghost hunter. Perhaps she'll lay hands on the Bible and contact the spirit inhabiting it."

Giulia repeated to herself, *He's filming me. Be professional.* She replied without one of the Polite Smiles. "Mr. Kanning, I'm sure the Children with Cancer staff would be thrilled to promote the work they do in the community. Wouldn't *The Scoop* benefit from a little charity work as well? Everyone likes to see local celebrities using their fame to help a good cause." It took great restraint not to bat her eyes at him.

Pit Bull's lips with their painted-on Sugar Skull teeth distorted in a smile. Kanning took three seconds to regroup and turned to the camera. "Scoopers, my mother always told me to listen to the nuns. She was right, and so is Cottonwood's favorite detecting ex-nun. *The Scoop* is off to interview the director of the Children with Cancer foundation." He made a throat-slashing gesture and Pit Bull lowered the camera.

Giulia stepped aside to clear the doorway. Kanning opened his mouth but walked past her without saying anything.

In the hallway Tarzan said to Jane next to him, "That was *The Scoop*. I heard they were going to be here. Come on, let's try to get them to film us."

"They're welcome to every moment of my potential *Scoop* time," Giulia said to Sidney. "Are you okay?"

"Yeah. Remember how I once said it'd be cool to get on a *Scoop* episode? I take it back." She finger-combed her long blonde ponytails. "I kept worrying my wig was ratty or my makeup was smeared, or some other mess happened to make me look horrible on screen."

"It's because he always appears perfect. He has the same effect on me. Where are you headed next?"

"Master bedroom. Olivier said he and Frank were going to find the biggest doll in the house to stuff in the wedding dress, then hide and make spooky sounds when people came in."

Giulia sighed. "Are all men twelve years old at heart?"

"Yes, and we don't need my husband's psych degree to confirm it." She flipped her ponytails into position. "If they try anything, I'll whack them with the nearest velvet painting."

"An excellent idea."

The upstairs was perhaps half as crowded as the first floor. Giulia peered out a window at the surrounding backyard. The lights must have been the motion sensor kind, because everything was black. Good. One less area to patrol.

Without *The Scoop* to interfere, Giulia tried the dollhouse aura discovery method on the Bible.

Nothing.

Good.

Two harmless antiques to one. She liked these odds.

Fifty-four

Knowing the Bible was untenanted turned Giulia's library duty into the equivalent of a coffee break. Scrooge and Marley wandered in, looked around, and wandered out. Giulia paged through a collection of *Calvin and Hobbes* cartoons with her feet propped on a leather ottoman. In the entire twenty minutes only eight partygoers wandered in. Of the eight, only three stayed for more than five minutes.

Two of the three who stayed were interested more in the knickknacks than the books. Like every other room, stuffed or carved or crafted dolls and animals occupied every possible niche.

An idea unfurled in Giulia's mind.

The jazz trio played extended versions of the "The Pink Panther Theme" and "The Girl from Ipanema" during her stint, making it the best twenty minutes of the entire evening. At the end of her time, she texted Sidney and Zane: *Meet on the back porch to report?*

The downstairs surge toward the roulette table, bar, and kitchen was explained by the Zydeco band on break. Giulia opened the sliding door to the back porch as Sidney and Zane arrived. The livable temperatures when they arrived were long gone. The porch's motion sensor illuminated the clouds of breath issuing from their mouths.

"Quick meeting." Giulia rubbed her arms. "Sidney, remember Salt and Pepper? They were after a valuable board game. They didn't get it. Also, you two, stay out of the downstairs bathroom. The mirror is bad."

"Cool," Zane said.

"Not cool," Sidney said. "Not cool at all."

"Except for *The Scoop*," Sidney said, "my rooms have been boring. The only suspicious types I encountered were looking for a private place to fool around."

"Another drunk would make my night," Zane said. "This engagement ring is burning a hole in my pocket. I want to propose right after I throw another idiot at the feet of the cops."

"May your wish be fulfilled," Giulia said. "Good Heavens, it's freezing out here. Before we beg for hot coffee, would you take special note of anyone paying too much attention to the dolls and animals? Speaking of, I'm overdue for my shift in Dead Hamster Central."

They dived back into the overheated family room as the band returned to the makeshift stage. Zydeco was growing on Giulia.

"Give me country western any day," Sidney muttered. "The stuffed butler in the breakfast room is looking better and better."

Giulia, famished, detoured toward the kitchen with Sidney. *The Scoop* was filming as Kord handed a stack of fives to Giulia's former student, Little Red Riding Hood, who was as radiant as Shiloh.

"Kord, you're the best. We'll make sure you're thanked on our website when we total up the intake from tonight."

Giulia returned Kord's wave as...something...hit her. She turned her head both ways, but she happened to be standing in a niche created by the bar and the kitchen entrance. She narrowed her eyes on the air surrounding the Whiteboard.

Extremely not good.

Fifty-five

Not daring to let anything eerie slide, Giulia positioned herself behind the fancy love seat shared by the Whiteboard operators. "How's the connection going with your dad, Shiloh?"

"Fantastic." Shiloh beamed. "He's giving us answers so fast tonight. It's like he's inspired by the energy of the party."

"Nothing unusual?" Giulia said, hoping to hear "no."

"Well, a few times he—oh, shit."

Mary Maclay as Clytemnestra approached the dual throne. She wore a blood-red gown with an ornate gold necklace and matching crown. A long black wig cascaded over her shoulders. Instead of a Greek tragedy mask, she'd painted gold highlights on her face.

Giulia recognized greatness. Shiloh's mother wasn't costumed, she was transformed. Her bearing was regal with an undercurrent of vengeance. The crowd made way for her.

"Hello, Little Miss Underage Liar at an adults-only party."

A passable companion to Giulia's Sister Mary Regina Coelis voice. She wouldn't want to be a guilty teenager on its receiving end.

"Mom, I can explain."

"I'm not interested in one word from you, missy. Let's go."

"But, Mom—"

Kanning slithered next to Clytemnestra. "Scoopers, we may have a clear first prize winner of tonight's costume contest." Pit Bull let the camera take in the costume top to toe before advancing for a close-up of the face paint.

Then he stepped back again. Agamemnon in victorious regalia stepped up to stand at Clytemnestra's side. Red robe with gold sash, gilt spear and high headpiece, and similar gold highlights in place of a tragedy mask.

In one of those inexplicable lulls in group conversation, Giulia heard Kord's tiny echo of Shiloh's "Oh shit."

Party conversation resumed, but not from Ken Kanning. He stared at Agamemnon and only a kick from Pit Bull broke his paralysis.

"Kelly? What are you doing here?"

Agamemnon's voice was as regal as her attire. "One of us has to be the responsible parent. Kord, we're leaving."

"But, Mom—"

Panic bloomed in Kanning's eyes. But, as always, only for a moment. Cinderella, licking cheesecake from her fingertips, appeared as a true *deus ex machina*. Kanning dragged her into the shot.

"Marcia, one moment of your time for our fans, please. Scoopers, allow me to introduce you to the driving force behind tonight's charity ball: Cinderella, also known as Marcia, the director of the Children with Cancer Foundation."

Giulia should've known Kanning wouldn't take her hint in the library about interviewing Marcia. He'd probably been in the family room scaring people with the mourning doll.

Mary and Kelly descended upon their offspring. Kanning was half a step behind.

"And here are tonight's youngest volunteers for this worthwhile charity: my son Kord and his friend Shiloh. For only five dollars, anyone can ask a question of Kord's magical Whiteboard. Marcia, how much have they contributed to helping sick children so far?"

Marcia was a student of the "never be caught off guard" school. She took in the situation and composed herself with a smile. "They're one of our best attractions, *Scoop* fans. We've collected eighty-five dollars from them in only two hours. Think of how happy the hospitalized children will be when they learn kids their own age are using their free time to help find a cure."

At Pit Bull's elbow, Giulia silently applauded. Clytemnestra and Agamemnon stared at each other. As though they were synchronized, they placed their hands on their children's shoulders.

"We're proud of our kids," they said together.

"So is everyone." Marcia turned her smile on the Greek

characters. "Thank you on behalf of the Children with Cancer foundation for allowing your children to break curfew on a school night."

Pit Bull stopped filming. Marcia scurried to the bar and took the receipts the bartender had totaled. The bobby stationed by the roulette table opened a portable safe for her to stow away the cash.

Agamemnon stalked up to Kanning. She kept her voice low, but her body language spoke for her. Back at the loveseat, Kord was trying to disappear under the cushion. Shiloh reverted to stubborn teenager as Clytemnestra conveyed her displeasure with her daughter's irresponsible choices.

Giulia spent only a second being amused at the situation. As soon as the thrum of dozens of conversations created white noise, she returned all her attention to the Whiteboard. Kord's protective hand on it didn't interfere with her ability to confirm what she'd thought she'd seen earlier. The sense of the Whiteboard's rather weak inhabitant was amplified. Muddy reds and browns undulated within a dirty fog now overlaying the pale green and slow pulse she'd sensed in the office.

If Ken Kanning hadn't used the Foundation's director to sabotage his ex-wife's attempt to take Kord home, Giulia could've intercepted Shiloh's mother and helped to get the kids out of here, preferably leaving the Whiteboard behind. She could've found Frank and taken the thing to the shed in the backyard where there must be a shovel or axe or hammer. The next day she would've informed the Kannings there'd been an accident with the Whiteboard, and at Saturday confession she would've performed the penance Father Carlos meted out with relief.

Now she had to figure out another way to get the Whiteboard away from those kids, from Pit Bull's camera, and especially from Kanning in *The Scoop* mode.

She walked to the kitchen and asked the espresso attendant for a double shot.

Fifty-six

Caffeine had little effect on Giulia, but the strong, hot, bitter half-cup stung her tongue and kicked her brain into a higher gear.

She took her place in the upstairs entertainment room. The jazz trio was playing danceable music. Half a dozen couples swayed in the narrow space between the band's platform and the pool table. Two Power Rangers were playing pool. Sometime between DI's pre-party walk through and now, the eight-point buck heads had acquired gold and purple streamers. They kept wanting to stream into the pool players' faces at a crucial shot.

The stuffed birds dangling from the ceiling had also acquired decorations from someone with a well-developed sense of organization. The crows and blue jays wore purple beads. The hawks and finches gold. The cardinals green, looking more Christmassy than Fat Tuesday-esque. The upside-down child doll riding the tricycle bolted to the ceiling had been given a complete change of clothes. Now a miniature Harlequin stared at everyone entering the room.

Giulia was glad she didn't have a clown or doll phobia. She looked toward the TV and was even more glad she didn't skeeve taxidermied animals. Sidney would've needed therapy from her husband had she been assigned this room.

The hamsters wore tiny jester hats or tiaras. The guinea pigs wore crowns or bow ties. At first glance it added to the festivity. The closer Giulia came to the preserved conga line, the more it creeped her out. The way they'd been positioned to appear to be watching the TV screen made it worse.

Someone had taped together several sheets of notebook paper on either side of the TV. Magic markers hanging from twisted rubber bands were tacked to the papers next to outlines of the stuffed animals' heads.

A single sheet above the TV read: CONTEST! Name the dead animals! Best five names win a shot of tequila!

Giulia stopped reading when the handwriting wobbled like Kord's Whiteboard ghost's and the names all became vulgar synonyms for body parts or sex. She hoped Marcia and her staff had hired an extra set of off-duty police officers to perform Breathalyzer tests on every departing guest. And had the taxi companies on standby.

The jazz ballad ended. Rhett Butler and Scarlett O'Hara came over to the TV with Ashley Wilkes and Melanie Hamilton. Scarlett and Melanie touched the nearest hamsters.

"Ew. Gross." Scarlett was out of character.

"Why would anyone do such a thing?" Melanie wasn't.

Ashley took one of the miniature jester hats and perched it on his slicked-back hair. Scarlett and Melanie giggled and took pictures. Rhett and Ashley joined them in divesting the animals and posing with the spoils.

The jazz trio shifted into "Sing Sing Sing." Giulia clenched teeth and fists. One alto sax, one double bass, and one drummer could not do justice to this piece of music.

Rhett and Ashley stood on chairs and pushed all the birds in the direction of the preserved animals.

Melanie said, "Someone call Alfred Hitchcock."

Scarlett said, "He's dead."

Rhett said, "The kid downstairs says he has a ghost in some contraption or other. Let's ask his ghost to bring up Hitchcock's ghost."

"There's no such thing as ghosts." Rhett stepped off the chair.

Ashley grabbed a jay and a cardinal and aimed them at Melanie. The fishing lines snapped and the birds dive-bombed like the ones in the movie. Scarlett and Melanie screamed. The birds crashed into the wall next to the TV, fell, and bounced behind the DVD case.

With a flurry of panicked curses, all three couples hightailed it out of the entertainment room. The remaining audience applauded their exit. Giulia got on her knees and reached behind the case to retrieve the birds.

"Ruh-roh, Daphne." A thin man in a furry one-piece Scooby-Doo costume put his paws on one end of the DVD case.

"Zoinks, Scoob." A taller, thinner man in a green tunic and brown pants grasped the other side. Together they moved the case out far enough for Giulia to retrieve both birds.

"Thanks, guys. I wish I had some Scooby Snax for you."

"Like, no prob," Shaggy said. "We just chowed down on about a dozen of those groovy barbecue sliders."

"Right, ro roblem," Scooby said. "Rum re-rul reed roo rearn rheir ralcohol rimits."

Shaggy and Scooby found chairs and began to video the band. Giulia looked for a place to set the birds. In a house without an inch of knickknack-free space, she settled on rearranging several dolls positioned so their glass eyes caught the lights. They looked almost alive. So did the birds, which made her notice one of the cardinal's eyes had popped out.

"Sing Sing Sing" finally finished and segued into "Minnie the Moocher." Also not meant for a trio, but everyone in the room sang along, so it didn't matter.

Giulia crouched by the DVD shelf and patted the carpet behind it. Stretch—stretch—her middle finger touched something round—one more stretch and she tapped it toward her palm and covered it.

Only when she scooted out did she realize her mini dress had pushed itself nearly to her hips. She yanked it down and glanced around the room. Everyone was singing the second chorus and paying no attention to her. She picked up the cardinal to see if the pointed end of the black bead could be pushed back in.

One side had a scrape. Glass beads didn't scrape. Paint scraped. She set down the bird and enlarged the gash with her fingernail. It glittered white beneath the paint.

She removed an eye from the blue jay. When she used her thumbnail on it, it sparkled green.

Keeping to casual movements, she approached the preserved creatures around the TV. "Minnie the Moocher" still had everyone's attention. She plucked an eye from the bottommost guinea pig. It sparkled blue when she removed a sliver of paint.

She left the room with the three eyes in her pocket. In the hall she texted Sidney and Zane: *Anyone seem too interested in the dolls or animals?*

Sidney: *One drunk kept talking to dolls in dining room.*

Zane: *No.*

Giulia: *Glue yourselves to anyone too much into them.*

She went off-script into the upstairs art room. Too much art and not enough floor space made the room uncomfortable for more than three people at once. Giulia was one. A 1920s gangster in the loudest red zoot suit ever created was number two. A 1970s disco dancer in shimmering polyester and platform shoes was number three. The gangster was flipping through classic vinyl album covers. The disco dancer was inspecting a lighted Dickensian Christmas village.

She went downstairs. Shiloh detached herself from the Whiteboard and went into the kitchen. RJ approached her. Giulia detoured toward them, but RJ sat next to Kord and began a smiling conversation.

Giulia continued toward her original objective: the dining room with its hundreds of dolls. Three other people occupied it at the moment: Blossom Burd giving the history of a ceramic poodle to Raggedy Ann, and the green-haired clown with plaid pants from her first shift in the downstairs bedroom. Giulia held her phone in an inconspicuous position and began recording.

The clown was interested in dolls with glass eyes. All sizes of dolls; he didn't discriminate. Giulia made an irritated noise and crouched to fuss with her shoe buckle. She took the shoe off and poked at the plastic square. The clown moved on. She sat with her back to the doorway and replayed the video. The clown had picked up and admired several dolls. Certain ones he returned intact. Others he replaced so their heads faced away from observers.

Giulia checked the latter dolls. All their eyes had been removed.

She texted everyone: *Clown with plaid pants and green hair taking eyes from dolls. Eyes are jewels. Stop him.*

Fifty-seven

Giulia tried to run after the clown. The crowded hallway and even more crowded rooms made it impossible. There hadn't been this many people an hour ago. Marcia/Cinderella was counting receipts with an ecstatic face. The bobby guarding the money was so close he might have been Velcroed to her ball gown.

Giulia texted, *Clown to family room. Converge.*

So many people to plow through. The roulette players and watchers alone were probably breaking a maximum occupancy rule. Giulia lost count of how many times she said "Excuse me" before she reached the family room.

The Zydeco band was playing something with a repeating line of "Don't mess with my toot-toot" and most of the audience was singing along. Someone had opened the sliding glass doors to the deck and the room was cooling down.

Sidney, Olivier, and Frank were already there. Zane and Dru Ann arrived on Giulia's heels.

The song ended. "Okay, everybody." The accordion player raised his voice over the applause. "Let's have some dance floor here. Come on, push back a good ten feet. It's time to dance your feet off, get thirsty, and buy more drinks to support the Children with Cancer Foundation."

The band played the opening bars of a song several times. The crowd pushed back, back, back until the last row bumped into the couches. When the space was about eight feet square, the drummer crashed the cymbals and started a fast beat.

"Are you ready to dance?"

"Yes!"

"I can't hear you!"

"Yes!"

"Here comes 'Go Daddy-O' from our favorite, Big Bad Voodoo Daddy!"

Cheers and applause. Six couples jumped onto the makeshift dance floor. The drums played a driving beat.

The plaid clown passed the mourning doll for a shelf of classic clown dolls. Krusty the Clown with a beer in each hand threw an arm around the shoulders of Plaid Clown.

"Brothers in arms! We make a great team. Hey, somebody get our picture with all these miniatures."

Charlie Chaplin removed a phone from Krusty's pocket and took several pictures while the two clowns mugged for the camera. As soon as the shoot finished, Plaid Clown returned to the shelf of classics.

Giulia stared into the glass door bookcase with her phone hidden under her arm and recording. Plaid Clown's reflection in the glass showed him using the same trick he'd used in the dining room. The clowns had already been picked up and tossed back any which way, so the next person who stopped to see the collection wouldn't think much of antiques missing a few eyes.

Plaid Clown pocketed the eyes of Bozo and Emmett Kelly before moving on to the stuffed finches on the shelf above.

Giulia texted Frank. *Get the bobby from the roulette table.*

When they arrived, Giulia took her eyes off the suspect long enough to explain who she was and what was happening.

The bobby brought a hand down on Plaid Clown's shoulder as the clown inspected a bright-eyed stuffed sugar glider.

"What's all this then?" in a passable British accent.

The clown jumped, clapped a hand where a pocket would be in a pair of regular pants, and looked over his shoulder. When he saw the bobby costume, he gave a weak smile.

"It's a fair cop," in a worse British accent.

Charlie Chaplin laughed. So did Olivier and Dru Ann. Plaid Clown eased out from under the bobby's hand and sauntered toward the doorway. When his floppy shoes touched the threshold, he made a break for it. He shoved super heroes and cartoon characters out of his way. Drinks and food went flying.

Zane gave chase. One hand on his tall helmet, he waved his foam nightstick in circles in the air, shouting "Stop, thief!"

People at a safe distance laughed and applauded.

"Get him, copper!" from a bewigged judge.

"Don't let the fuzz win!" from a flowered hippie.

Zane closed the distance between them. Characters who'd lost ten- or fifteen-dollar drinks drowned out the pro-clown comments with cheers for Zane. The clown hit a roadblock of Disney princesses at the bar and dived into the bathroom. The door slammed and locked.

More boos and cheers. The roulette wheel spun. The entire DI contingent joined Zane.

"Anyone have a store card they don't want?" Giulia said. "I can pop the lock."

A terrified scream came from the bathroom. The door burst open. Plaid Clown leaped into Zane's arms.

"Help! Get it away! It's after me!"

Zane locked one arm around the clown's neck and twisted a plaid right arm up behind his back.

The clown returned to the present. "Leggo, you fake cop. Help! Police! Real police!"

Owen advanced on them, Blossom hobbling behind.

"What's going on here?" Owen spoke to the group but looked to Giulia.

She herded everyone into the bathroom, especially the bobby, and closed the door. Groans and more boos from the audience.

The clown squirmed and fought. "No! There's something in the mirror! Don't let it get me!"

The bobby took hold of his other arm. Giulia glanced at the antique mirror. So did the clown. Nothing happened.

"It attacked me! It did! It's waiting to catch us off-guard. It'll kill us all!"

Giulia held out the sugar glider. "Mr. Jevens, please look at the eyes in this animal."

"Yes, glass eyes. So what? All the dead animals in this house have them."

Giulia removed the eye and scraped off the paint with her

thumbnail. The exposed streak shone red.

Blossom snatched it. Owen snatched it from Bossom. "I'll be—"

His choice of profanity inspired Giulia to reach for the soap. Sidney stopped her, so she took out her phone.

"I have video of this man removing eyes from dolls and preserved animals in different rooms. His actions when we discovered him in the family room lead me to believe he's hidden them in the pants he's wearing beneath his costume."

Plaid Clown tried to kick down the door. "You can't touch me. I have rights."

Owen advanced on him. "The hell I can't. This is my house." He grabbed the clown pants and yanked down. The oversized buttons popped off and *pinged* against the untenanted mirrors. Owen's hands dived into the clown's tennis shorts and came out with two fistfuls of black cabochon cut beads in various sizes.

He handed a larger bead to Blossom. "You have nails. Use them."

Blossom clawed at the black paint until the round top of the bead was clear. She held it up to the marquee lights on the nearest mirror. Its hidden facets sparkled and glittered white.

Owen indulged in more profanity. Blossom aimed a slap at his mouth with her paint-speckled nails as he puffed out Uncle Pennybags' chest like an offended peacock.

"Officer, this man has in his possession thousands of dollars of jewels belonging to me. This detective has evidence. I demand his immediate arrest."

The bobby unhooked his real—not costume—handcuffs from his belt.

Plaid Clown snatched the handcuffs and lunged for Owen. "You're not pinning all this on me. Listen, you cops, he knew about the jewels. He hired me to steal as many as I could tonight using the party as cover. He promised me 20 percent of the profits." With every "He" the handcuffs smashed Owen's face. Owen tried to block the blows but the clown ducked under his arms.

Frank and the bobby dragged the clown back. A bloody tooth fell to the floor. More blood followed. Owen felt his nose and gave vent to a wet curse. The mirrors reflected no longer sharply dressed Uncle Pennybags with a broken nose, two split lips, and one missing incisor.

Blossom beat feebly on her brother-in-law's chest with her wrinkled fists. "You cheat! You thief! You stole our inheritance!" Her Red Queen headgear fell off.

Frank showed his detective badge to the bobby and took charge of Owen. The bobby took the pantsless clown. Zane helped Blossom restore her costume.

Giulia opened the door. *The Scoop*'s camera light flooded them.

A collective gasp came from the packed hall followed by the indistinguishable buzz of multiple conversations.

Ken Kanning's voice cut through the buzz. "Scoopers, we promised you a fantastic show and we always deliver. We won't disturb our favorite detective in the course of her duties, but it looks to me as though a crime has been stopped in its tracks." He stuck the microphone into Owen's bleeding face. "Mr. Jevens, can you tell us what happened? Who attacked you? Is this half-naked clown the culprit? Our Scoopers want to know."

Owen spat into the microphone and a second bloody tooth bounced off its foam surface.

Blossom obliged the Scoopers with a furious recap. Plaid Clown treated the Scoopers to a profanity-laced rant on the perfidy of Owen Jevens.

Pit Bull grinned behind the viewfinder. Giulia didn't envy him the heavy editing in his future.

Kings and queens, knights and Disney princesses, superheroes and action figures burst into laughter and applause. Several of them clapped Zane on the back.

"RJ!" Owen shouted, spewing blood on a cowboy. "RJ, you sponge, where are you?"

The Children with Cancer staff escorted two uniformed officers into the mix. Giulia and the bobby explained the situation.

"This is my house and I have a right to everything in it." Blood from Owen's nose and mouth landed on the uniformed cops as he spoke.

Frank turned a smile of delight on Giulia. "Wait for it."

The uniformed officer cuffed Owen and read him his rights.

"What are you charging me with? I'm the one being robbed."

The officer added assault to the list of charges. Giulia saw the light. "Body fluids. They can carry HIV and STDs and are now considered assault." The light fizzled out. "We're never going to see the rest of our money."

Ken Kanning claimed the spotlight. "Scoopers, we're breaking away from party fun to bring you the arrest of the head of the Jevens family. Yes, you heard it right. We're not exactly sure what happened. Something about a clown stealing hidden valuables, but the clown may have been in the pay of one of the Jevenses to the detriment of the others." He pushed between a ketchup and mustard bottle pair mugging for the camera. "Get out of the way, we're filming real news here. Scoopers, we're heading outside now as Owen Jevens is being taken into custody. Remember, you saw it on *The Scoop* first."

Blossom stood in the doorway and shouted, "Off with his head!" to even more applause.

Giulia nursed a forlorn hope that *The Scoop* would follow the police to the station.

A tentative tap on her shoulder broke her reverie.

"Have you seen Kord?"

Fifty-eight

Shiloh held a dripping can of pop in each hand. Her skin was beginning to absorb her white makeup and her eyes looked tired and hollow.

Giulia looked over Shiloh's shoulder at the vacant love seat. "Bathroom?"

Shiloh shook her head. "He took a pee break half an hour ago. We got thirsty from talking so much, and everybody wanted to see what was going on with the clown, so I volunteered to get drinks." She hoisted the pop cans. "He said he'd stay here and have people take numbers like in a deli for when I came back."

"He's probably following his father."

The teenager indulged in the Eyeroll of Death. "God, he is such a dweeb sometimes." She set the cans on the floor next to the loveseat and weaved through the crowded hallway.

Giulia stood on her tiptoes. No one from DI was in sight. She sent a group text: *Where is everyone?*

From Sidney: *Family Room.*

From Frank: *Playing pool.*

Nothing from Zane. Giulia didn't text again lest she interrupt Zane mid-proposal. She fought her way to the family room. Sidney and Olivier were dancing. The song ended within a minute and she made her way onto the dance floor.

"The Jevenses are gone. We're through working for the night."

"Did Zane propose?" Sidney said.

"He didn't answer the group text."

"OooOOOoooh. Want to spy on him?"

"Honey," Olivier said.

"Oh, all right. I'll be an adult." She brightened. "Let's see if there's any cupcakes left."

Giulia walked with her. "I like this idea."

Olivier wedged them into the hall past the roulette table. Even more characters squeezed into the gambling corner now. The dealer never altered or rushed his cadence. The roars of success and groans of loss reached deafening levels.

Shiloh leaped at Giulia when they reached the bar. "I can't find Kord anywhere. He's not in either of the bathrooms. He's not in the kitchen or the dining room. He's not outside. Mr. Kanning says he hasn't seen him either." She took a breath. "You have to help me find him. He has the Whiteboard."

The bartender reached out and tapped Giulia's arm. "If you're looking for the kid with the haunted toy, he went off with somebody dressed like the Wizard of Oz. The kid was bouncing like Tigger. Said he was going to talk to the ghost all by himself."

Shiloh went nuclear. "He's got my daddy! He stole my daddy!" She clutched Giulia. "You have to get him back—you have to—"

Giulia broke her hold. "Stop it."

Shiloh inhaled and burst into tears. "You don't understaaand..."

Giulia dragged her to the love seat. "What exactly don't I understand?"

Clytemnestra appeared in the kitchen doorway. "I know that whine. Shiloh, what's going on?"

"Kord's—" *sniff* "—gone and he has the Whiteboard—" *sniff* "—and it's really mine—" *sniff* "—and I have to have it back. I have to!" More sobs.

Agamemnon joined them, sipping a dark beer. "What's the problem?"

Shades of high school parent-teacher conferences. A teenager with issues and two hovering parents. And no veil on Giulia's head to command authority.

The real issue clicked. The giggling creeper had taken eleven-year-old Kord someplace private.

Fifty-nine

Giulia whipped out her phone and texted everyone again. *Bar. Now. Hurry.*

Agamemnon scanned the love seat and bar area. "Where's Kord?"

Clytemnestra got in her daughter's face. "Shiloh Amanda Maclay, stop sniveling and act your age. What's the matter?"

Zane and Dru Ann came running—as much as anyone could run in this fire hazard-sized crowd. Frank was one step behind them. Sidney got stuck by the roulette table with an identical Sailor Moon who shoved her phone into Olivier's hands and insisted on multiple pictures.

Giulia gave Zane and Dru Ann ten seconds by her phone clock to stare into each other's eyes with goopy smiles on their faces. Sidney and Olivier had extricated themselves when the time expired.

"Zane," Giulia said, "do we congratulate you?"

In an absent voice: "You bet."

Dru Ann nudged him.

"What, hon?"

Dru Ann gave a pointed look in Giulia's direction.

Zane came back to Earth. "Giulia? Did you say something?"

"Never mind. We have the answer. Congratulations, you two. Dru Ann, I'll ask to ogle your ring later. Right now we have a problem. Kord and his Whiteboard are missing. We don't know for how long. The bartender says RJ took him away for a private session."

"It's my whiteboard." Shiloh confronted Giulia. "He gave it to me because Daddy's ghost is in it."

Clytemnestra interrupted. "Dear God, you're still going on about that? Ms. Driscoll, I apologize."

"Shut up!" Shiloh shoved her mother onto the love seat. Tears had carved flesh-colored streaks into her white makeup. Her mascara hadn't run, but her smeared eyeshadow had turned her into a raccoon. The effect would've been humorous if Shiloh hadn't been enacting the Tragic Muse. "You don't care about Daddy. I do. I always cared more than you. You didn't bring him back. I did. Kord's not going to keep him from me."

By the tension in Clytemnestra's body, only their presence in a public place filled with cell phones prevented her from slapping her daughter's face.

Agamemnon did an end run around this family drama to push her own to the forefront of Giulia's attention. "What's up?"

Knowing the thunderstorm she was about to cause, Giulia gave a truthful answer anyway. "The person who took Kord for a private session has been stalking Shiloh online and in person. We've been waiting for him to make a move on Shiloh to nab him."

Kelly Kanning went nuclear. "Why are you standing here? We have to find him." She cupped her hands around her mouth and shouted, "Ken Kanning!"

"Who?" several voices replied.

"The Scoop!"

A dozen gloved and ringed hands pointed to the roulette table. All the DI heads turned to see Kanning and Pit Bull filming Samurai Jack cashing in on a massive jackpot. Agamemnon removed her helmet and waved it over her head. Kanning finished his narration and noticed the movement. His moment of deflation said more than his mouth usually did.

He came over, Pit Bull in tow. "What is it, Kelly? I'm working." He glanced at the love seat, where Shiloh and her mother were still at bay. "Where's Kord?"

Shiloh ran up to Kanning. "He has the Whiteboard but it's mine! He has to give it back!"

Kanning ignored her. "Giulia, where's my son?"

Giulia ignored the implied accusation of negligence. "Fan out," she said to DI and partners.

They scattered. Texts started to blow up Giulia's phone a minute later. Kord wasn't in the upstairs bedrooms or bathrooms. Nor the library or art room. Giulia started to panic but tamped it down. Panic was counter-productive. She ran downstairs, elbowing people aside without a single "Excuse me."

When the texts from every room came back negative, Giulia shoved her way to the downstairs bath. Yogi Bear came out. She almost screamed at him, then scrolled through the texts. No one had checked the kitchen. More shoving and elbowing. Only the caterers and the doll in state upon her throne. What had they missed? She pulled up the house blueprints and sent a final text.

KITCHEN.

Sixty

Ken Kanning and Pit Bull ran after Giulia.

"Where's my son?"

Giulia was trying to see detail on the blueprints. "Working on it."

Kanning's voice frayed. "Work faster, dammit."

The rest of DI reached the kitchen. Giulia spared half a thought for the oddity of a human Ken Kanning, then dismissed him.

"Zane, where exactly did we think the hidden room was located?"

Zane cursed. "I forgot about it."

"We all did. Find it for me."

They bent their heads over Zane's phone. "It's here. It's off the kitchen." They stared around the room. The doll stared back.

"Giulia," Dru Ann said in a hesitant voice, "That doll's eye opened when you looked at it."

"It can wait its turn."

Sidney turned her back on the doll.

Pit Bull brought up his camera. "Giulia, tell me what to look for."

"Shut up, Bull, she's concentrating." Ken Kanning raised his voice so it projected through the kitchen and into the hall. "Everyone shut up!"

It worked. Almost. A moment of silence followed by laughter and as many people as possible crowding into the kitchen to see *The Scoop*'s latest stunt.

Rainbow Dash: "What's the story?"

Twilight Sparkle: "Can we be in it?"

Papa Smurf: "I can act."

Giulia tuned them all out. "There." She tapped Zane's screen. "The pantry."

Everyone looked up. Giulia pushed past the dessert island and the caterers to the far side of the kitchen. The pantry door was built in the old-fashioned style: sixteen small panes of glass with painted wood dividers between them.

Sidney made a strangled noise. Zane said something in Estonian. Frank called after Giulia, "The doll moved."

"I'll deal with it later," she called back. The pantry door was locked. She crouched. The key was in the keyhole on the other side. She looked around for something heavy. Nothing. Desperate times: she wrapped an ornamental dish towel around her elbow and smashed the glass nearest the doorknob.

The room fell silent.

She pushed out the shards and reached inside to turn the key. The door opened. She unwound the towel and dropped it.

The shelves and drawers were packed full. Party supplies, table cloths, napkins, glassware, china, teacups, champagne flutes, saki sets, coffee urns, cow creamers—it was a microcosm of the rest of the house. There had to be a hidden switch. She opened drawers. Pressed knobs. Turned knobs. Felt underneath shelves. Pushed dishes and glasses aside to reach the backs of the shelves. At the edges of her attention she could hear party guests discussing her actions in shocked voices.

The shelf closest to the wall was stacked with two rows of ornamental serving platters. She lifted one after the other out of their grooves. She moved aside the last plate. Nothing. Panic tried to take her. She forced it back and turned her phone's flashlight into the corner. Up at the top, slightly higher than the tallest platter's dust outline, she saw a slightly darker one-by-three piece of wood. Holding her breath, she pushed in its top. The bottom tipped up. She hooked her finger in it and raised it parallel to the floor.

The platter shelves and the drawers beneath them swung inward with a low *creeeeeeak*.

Sixty-one

The hidden door opened to reveal an LED camping lantern on a dusty linoleum floor in an alcove the size of a walk-in closet. Unfinished plywood had been nailed to the walls.

The Whiteboard lay face up on the linoleum. Kord Kanning, on his knees, looked up at a red-faced RJ with a vein throbbing in his forehead.

"Make it talk! Stop screwing around!"

Kord was white and shaking, but he tried to sneer at the Great and Powerful Wizard of Oz. "I guess Shi's dad doesn't like you either."

RJ cuffed Kord across the mouth. Kord's lip split.

Shiloh reached the pantry. "Give me my daddy!"

The pantry drama became a tableau.

Without taking her eyes from Kord and RJ, Giulia snapped at Shiloh: "Explain about the Whiteboard. Now."

Shiloh clutched Giulia's hand. "I wanted to make sure the spell worked. The spell to bring Daddy's ghost into the Whiteboard. I couldn't take any chances," she gabbled. "So when I took it home to add the powdered aluminum and seal it up before the science fair, I went to the cemetery and brought home a scoop of Daddy's ashes. I added the ashes to the aluminum and it worked. Daddy's in the Whiteboard now."

Someone in the kitchen gave out a high, hysterical laugh. Clytemnestra wrenched Shiloh away from Giulia and slapped her across the face, audience or no audience.

"You desecrated your father's grave? What is wrong with you?"

Kord spoke before Shiloh recovered. "Really, Shi? That's messed up."

Back in the family room, the Zydeco band began playing an accordion arrangement of "In the Mood." The music, amplified to be heard over the increasing numbers of party guests, reached the kitchen now.

Giulia made a note to tell Rowan she'd been right: no spell alone was powerful enough. Whether she remembered after all this was another story.

RJ grabbed the Whiteboard with one hand and the back of Kord's head with the other. "Make the daddy ghost talk, kid. You want to be the star of your father's TV show? Here's your chance."

Kord touched his tongue to his bleeding lip. "Drop dead."

RJ yanked Kord up by his hair. Kord jerked the Whiteboard out of RJ's grip and RJ wrapped his free arm around Kord's neck.

"Back off, Miss Detective, or I'll snap his skinny little neck. Nobody moves until the ghost in here tells me where Vernon hid the rest of our family fortune."

Giulia said, "We've already found it."

A moment of silence in the pantry against the Zydeco/Glenn Miller background.

"You're lying," RJ said.

"Your grandfather bought a large number of jewels. He painted them black and used them as the glass eyes in the specimens around the house. Your uncle paid one of the guests to acquire them and turn them over to him."

"That's bullshit. That's—it has to be bullshit." RJ's voice quavered but his grip tightened on Kord's neck. "We were in this together. Owen and Blossom and me."

Giulia didn't move yet. The tension between them was too volatile. "We caught the guest, who revealed Owen's part in the plot. Owen and the guest were accusing each other as the police took them away. Apparently Owen saw a delivery of jewels to Vernon and followed up on it without telling either of you."

"You're lying," RJ blustered.

"*The Scoop* has it all on video." Giulia threw her voice over her shoulder. "Isn't that right, Mr Kanning?"

Kanning and Pit Bull squeezed in on either side of Giulia. Pit

Bull's camera was running.

"Got it right here." Kanning's voice was as smooth as ever. "You've been stabbed in the back, RJ. Too bad Vernon didn't like you as well as he liked *The Scoop*."

Giulia sent *Shut Up, Don't Provoke Him* thoughts at Kanning.

RJ forced a laugh. "I'm not falling for it. I know what you do. You peddle lies and sensationalist trash."

Kord's voice was thin but still held bravado. "Don't say that about my dad. He films the news everybody really wants to see."

Giulia tensed at the expression in RJ's eyes.

"Really?" he said. "Then film this, Mr. Scoop."

Sixty-two

The air around the Whiteboard was pulsing. As the tension built, it beat stronger. The vibration was different than the way it had acted when Kord brought it into DI's office.

Giulia eased her hand into her pocket and unscrewed the flask's cap.

Frank shouted from behind her, "Hey, here's Channel Seven. Come into the kitchen, guys. The real show's in here."

RJ's concentration snapped. Giulia flung Holy Water into his eyes. He spluttered and shook his head.

Giulia grabbed Kord. Shiloh grabbed the Whiteboard. Kanning leaped into the alcove and decked RJ.

Shiloh dropped the Whiteboard. "It jumped out of my arms." Her voice became plaintive. "Daddy? What's wrong?"

Pit Bull said to Giulia, "Nice work."

Kanning shook out his fist. "Driscoll? Not you, Giulia. Your husband. You have authority to arrest him on kidnapping charges?"

Giulia ignored Kanning and knelt by the Whiteboard. She saw it now: the weaker emanations of the original ghost were being overpowered by something darker and stronger.

Out in the kitchen, a woman screamed. "The doll turned its head!"

A man replied, "They didn't tell us we'd get a live ghost hunt."

Another woman said, "It's on wires. Can't you see them?"

A second man joined in: "These actors are great. Anyone getting this on their phone?"

"Frank. Zane." Giulia raised her head. "I need a hammer. A big one."

The men looked at each other. "Shed in the backyard," Zane said. They toppled a dwindling stack of paper plates as they barged to the back door through a roomful of people recording it all.

Kord reached for the Whiteboard. Shiloh picked it up but dropped it again. "It tried to shock me." Her eyes teared up. "What's wrong with Daddy?"

"Did you stop to think how dangerous it is to cast a spell when you don't know what you're doing?" Giulia needed all her energy. She didn't dare waste it on anger. She hadn't forgotten the possibility of angering the ghost if she tried to destroy the Whiteboard, but it was too dangerous already. She'd have to control it somehow.

Shiloh wrote on the Whiteboard, "Talk to me."

Kord said, "Shi, maybe he's scared."

Mary Maclay was trying to push through to Shiloh and failing. People with phones hissed at her and wouldn't let her pass. Kelly Kanning was having similar luck. The Whiteboard wrote "Shi—" but straggled off into jerky angles until the line reached the lower corner.

Shiloh hugged it to her chest. The pulses ballooned around her. Her eyes rolled back in her head and she jerked and shook as though she was having a seizure. Kord tried to hold her but the violence of her shudders threw him off.

Frank and Zane threw people aside and ran up to them, panting. Giulia ripped the Whiteboard away from Shiloh and threw it face up on the floor.

"Here," Frank and Zane said.

She assessed the tools they offered. Zane held a mallet. Frank held a small sledgehammer.

Giulia hefted the sledgehammer. "Move back."

Frank pushed the onlookers away. Zane dragged Shiloh by the armpits, but she recovered and tried to crawl back to the Whiteboard.

"Move," Giulia said.

"It's mine!"

"Back off."

Shiloh retreated a few inches. Giulia didn't dare waste any more time. She raised the sledgehammer and brought it down on the Whiteboard. SMASH. It bounced. Again. SMASH. The plastic cracked. A third time.

SMASH.

The Whiteboard shattered into lethal plastic shrapnel. Powdered aluminum and cremains exploded. The dust coated Giulia, Shiloh, Kord, *The Scoop*, RJ, and the pantry.

The world stopped.

The only noise in the kitchen was the whirring of Pit Bull's camera. Back in the family room, "In the Mood" changed to "Tuxedo Junction."

Two long, thin, desiccated arms reached up from the wreckage of the Whiteboard. Their skin appeared greenish-black, like mold behind old wallpaper. The hands curled in and ten cracked fingernails clutched Giulia's throat.

Sixty-three

This ghost had strength. She grabbed the spectral wrists and tried to ease them off her windpipe. Frank's voice shouting her name penetrated the ringing in her ears.

Giulia shut everything else out, including Frank's panicked voice. Rowan had advised her to find her strength for these situations. When Florence the Gibson Girl ghost had invaded her pregnant body last fall, Giulia's strength had been family: Frank and still-growing Finn. Finn was safe at his grandparent's house. Frank was in the main kitchen here, out of danger.

That knowledge gave her strength. They were safe. She had a loving home to return to.

No ghost was going to take her home from her.

As the world darkened around her, she pictured a bright yellow legal pad and thought in bullet points:

—Act fast before you pass out.

—How to break hold?

—It's not inside you. You have the advantage.

—Ghosts don't always know their own rules.

—That's it.

She fumbled for the flask with numb fingers. It was still uncapped. She dumped the rest of the Holy Water into the shattered Whiteboard and rasped, *"Exorcizámos te, ómnis immúnde spíritus in nómine et virtúte Dómini nóstri Jésu Chrísti."*

The dead flesh sizzled. Foul green-black smoke choked the air.

Giulia pushed her arms up between the ghost's and broke its hold. Giulia fell to hands and knees, coughing and gagging.

A man-shaped figure rose from within the smoke. She raised her head. Its eyes shone black as real glass beads. It loomed over her, still-sizzling arms reaching for her, nails poised to claw her eyes out.

Her ears began to work again, Frank's furious, frightened voice closer now.

She cleared her throat to continue the exorcism rite.

A different, pale shape formed behind the dark one. It grabbed the dark shape in a rugby hold. Giulia reached into the remains of the Whiteboard and touched the crossed metal arms that had formed the grid for the knobs. She snatched them up and impaled the clawing ghost through the forehead.

It screeched in a high voice like RJ's giggle, but with a gravelly undertone. Its body exploded in black and rotted-lettuce green.

Giulia waved the air in front of her face until it cleared. The other ghost gave Giulia a thumbs-up, then with a finger wrote "Help us" in the powdered aluminum and cremains. The writing mimicked the script from the answers on the Whiteboard.

Frank was still yelling Giulia's name. She gave him her own thumbs-up to him before raising Shiloh to a sitting position.

"You broke the Whiteboard," Shiloh sobbed. "I can't talk to Daddy anymore."

Giulia found a scrap of patience. "Can you see?"

Shiloh followed Giulia's pointing finger. "See what?"

Giulia tried what was starting to work on Pit Bull: seeing via a connection with her. She took Shiloh's head in her hands and turned her face to the ghost. "Look."

The teenager gasped. "Daddy!"

The ghost smiled with affection.

"Daddy, you're still here. I can still talk to you. I'll make a new Whiteboard and everything will be good again." Tears flowed down her face, ruining the remains of her makeup.

The ghost's eyes pleaded with Giulia.

"Shiloh, you have to let him go. He needs to move on."

She shook her head *No, no, no.*

"Shiloh, he stayed here because you needed him, but if he stays too long he'll be trapped here forever. Do you want him to be lingering on after you grow old and die yourself? You've been lonely without him, but think of how alone he'll be forever—not seventy or eighty years, but always and forever—after you die and pass on and he can't." She paused to give her last sentence extra weight. "Would you want someone you love to suffer like that?"

Not a sound besides Pit Bull's camera broke into Shiloh's endless sobs after Giulia's speech. The band must have gone on break.

After an endless, stretched-out minute, Shiloh gulped. "I love you, Daddy."

The ghost wrote, "I love you, Pumpkin."

Shiloh reached toward him. He blew her a kiss. Giulia took the ghost's hand. The sensation on her fingers was like fog trying to turn into a snow cone. Ever since Florence, a few talkative ghosts had told her it was easy for her to touch them because they knew she was there to help.

With her free hand she mimed opening a door. A shimmering doorway appeared. Pit Bull gasped.

The ghost floated through the doorway and the light *poofed* into glowing dandelion seeds and vanished.

Sixty-four

Frank pushed Kanning out of the way and almost cracked Giulia's ribs in his embrace. In between murmurs of *muirnín* and *Thank God,* he cursed in Irish and English and berated her in broken phrases.

"I couldn't get to you. Saw something...dark, ugly...choked you..." More cursing. "Don't tell me you're capable...doesn't matter..."

"The Neanderthal in you reared its head?" Her voice was ragged.

He squeezed harder. "Woman, I have never wanted to club you over the head and drag you to my cave more than tonight." He buried his face in her ash-filled wig.

"I love you for the impulse. May I have my ribs back?"

"No." He sneezed and released her. "Did I just breathe in somebody's cremains?"

"Probably."

"I may puke."

"Arrest RJ first, please?"

He straightened his ascot. "With great pleasure."

As though the ascot was a signal, the entire kitchen burst into applause and cheers. Blossom was brought forward from wherever she'd been hiding along with the Children with Cancer staff. Their hands were shaken by everyone who could reach them. Three Fortnite characters pushed beers into their hands.

"This is the best party show we've ever seen."

"A thousand times better than last year's gala."

"How did you manage the special effects? Flash paper? Sparklers?"

Marcia and Angie, bewildered, accepted the drinks and gave non-answers. Blossom pretended she'd known it all along. Giulia turned back to the important actors.

Pit Bull had zoomed in on the messages in the aluminum powder. Kord said, "Ms. Driscoll, that was awesomely cool," before Mary Maclay cleared her throat behind Giulia.

"Do you mean to say it was real? All of it? My husband's ghost was in that toy all this time? What kind of insanity is this?"

"Mary, I explained the situation as I understood it at the time."

"Don't try to squirm your way out of this. You promised you'd protect my daughter."

Giulia lost her temper. "I did and I have. RJ is neutralized and Vernon's corrupt ghost attacked me and not her. Do you have a problem with this outcome?"

Clytemnestra shrank into herself. "I—no. No, I don't. Thank you." She sat next to her still weeping daughter and rocked her like she was a little girl.

Frank hauled RJ to his feet. The Wizard of Oz's glossy hair was matted with ash, his emerald-topped cane had vanished, and his dapper suit was filthy.

"What happened? Who are you?" He shook his head like a wet dog's. "How'd you find the secret room?"

"I didn't. She did." Frank indicated Giulia.

RJ squinted. "There's the little Goth chick. Her head was so easy to play with. Best fun I've had in months." He raised his voice. "Hey, Daddys_Girl, come over here and let me tell you how easy it was to send you out into the cemetery and then ruin your hopes."

Shiloh sat up, her eyes wide. "You're Friendly_Casper?"

"You bet. Your pain and angst was the best show I've orchestrated in years. The obsessive ones make the best toys."

Clytemnestra stood with the ease of an athlete and smashed her fist into RJ's face.

A second wave of applause ran through the room. Several more loud whistles followed.

"Great prosthetics."

"The blood looks real."

RJ said through a mouthful of blood, "It is real."

Laughter. "Sure it is. We'll play along."

More police arrived.

"Look, Detective," he said to Giulia, "get me out of this and I'll make it worth your while." He paused to snort blood and clear his throat. "I didn't hurt the kid. I only meant to scare him. The cute little Goth will get over herself. Come on."

Giulia turned her back on him.

As Frank turned RJ over to the police, Blossom intercepted the perp walk. "RJ, sweetheart, let me show you something." She took the winking doll from the island and pried out one eye. "Watch." She scraped off the black paint and held it up. The surface reflected the white overhead light.

RJ stared. "It can't be. I had a medium contact Vernon right after he died. I knew she channeled Vernon when he was his usual nasty self. He refused to tell me where he hid the rest of the money. He only hinted it was flat."

Blossom's smile was hard and cold. "You think you're the only one who listens in on phone calls? I hired that medium to create a red herring to keep you occupied. Then I told Owen's thief only certain dolls and animals had real jewels so Owen would think he got them all." She tossed the doll at RJ's feet.

RJ smashed the one-eyed china head with his patent-leather boot. "You lying, thieving hag! You dried-up sack of bile and shit! You stole my inheritance from me! I wasted fifteen years of my life waiting on your withered ass!"

The police pushed him toward the doorway.

"I demand to talk to the family lawyer." Blood flew around the room as RJ struggled. "You can't pin any of this on me. I'll be out by tomorrow night and then I'll give you amateur detectives what you deserve."

When the front door closed after him, DI and partners looked at each other.

"If he'd known his lines," Giulia began, "he would've said—"

Twenty voices finished: "I would've gotten away with it if it weren't for you meddling kids!"

Sixty-five

Blossom came over to Giulia with a satisfied smile. "You and your staff more than earned your fee. Unlike some members of the family, I believe in paying people what they're worth. Follow me."

She led Giulia past Olivier, who was discussing a counseling appointment for Shiloh with Mary Maclay.

"Thank you. I'll call you tomorrow." Mary got a firm grip on Shiloh. "We're going home because you're too young to be at an event where alcohol is sold."

She herded her daughter out without a word to anyone else.

"One down," Giulia murmured as she followed Blossom into the hidden room in the pantry.

"My nephew thinks he's clever, but he has a lot to learn." Blossom opened the bottom drawer and reached under a pile of tablecloths. She came out with a bulky table runner. "Men who never set the table don't think to search what they consider women's territory. It helped that my nephew and brother-in-law thought I was getting senile." Her smile became harder. "Owen saw a jewel delivery, and I spied on Owen. As soon as he told his clown thief which pieces to target, I removed every other jewel in the house and replaced them with painted wood." She unrolled the table runner. In its center lay a drawstring bag. From the bag, Blossom extracted two dozen oversized seed packets. She handed Giulia a thick one labeled "Vanilla Bean Seeds."

"This contains the cash value of ten diamonds, four emeralds, and two rubies. Also inside is a certificate, signed by myself, a lawyer, and a jewelry appraiser that the cash is fair value for the jewels. You own this money free and clear. There's probably going to be trouble about the bank accounts with my relatives in jail." She patted Giulia's hands. "Life doesn't have enough instant gratification, don't you agree?"

"Thank you." Giulia gathered herself together. "We'll send you an itemized bill tomorrow marked Paid in Full."

"Good. I like things tidy." Blossom tucked the rest of the seed packets back into the table runner and returned it to its place under the tablecloths. "Now I believe I'll have the handsome young bartender make me a Cosmopolitan."

Sixty-six

Kord left his father's side and bounced up and down in front of Giulia as soon as she reentered the kitchen. "Ms. Driscoll, wasn't that awesome? Wasn't it cool? I'm building a new Whiteboard and I'll get Shi to teach me the spell and I'll see who's buried in the cemetery and my new Whiteboard will have its very own ghost, too." He dragged on his father's sleeve. "Dad, maybe I'll make it a fran—a franchise. I'll be able to pay Shady Side's tuition all by myself. Hey Mom! Listen to this." He began explaining his idea to Kelly. "Hey, Ms. Driscoll, we can work together! You can help me convince the ghosts what a great idea it'll be to live in my Whiteboards. Well, not live, exactly. You know what I mean. Isn't it a great idea? Dad, tell Ms. Driscoll what a great idea it is."

Agamemnon's helmet looked like it was about to hit the ceiling under its own power, but she turned to Giulia. "Ms. Driscoll, in all seriousness, thank you for saving my son. How did you manage all those special effects to throw that evil man off guard? Of course," she raised her voice, "he wouldn't have been in danger if his father wasn't the world's prime idiot."

Giulia was too tired to try and explain. For once Ken Kanning came to her rescue.

"Kelly, Giulia, Kord, come here and see this."

"I don't care about your show, Ken."

"Kelly, don't be pig-headed."

Kanning's ex-wife visibly got herself under control. "Fine. Show us what?"

Frank was hovering at the edge of Giulia's peripheral vision. She gave him an "okay" gesture and he subsided.

Pit Bull replayed the footage from the shattered Whiteboard on. The aluminum-and-cremains cloud was visible, but at first Giulia looked like she was part of a Method Acting workshop. Pit Bull fast-forwarded to the moment when the Maclay ghost vanished in the equivalent of fireflies and sparklers.

Kelly looked from the screen to Kanning. "I don't see your point."

Pit Bull said, "Watch what happens when I adjust the contrast by 10 percent and increase the brightness by five."

He replayed the footage. This time the hands and the ghost were both visible as shifting but recognizable shapes. The outline of light and its vanishing like a fading firework showed up in the manner of the sun shining around the edge of a window with its shade drawn.

Kelly said in a tremulous voice, "Bull, did you doctor this? Be honest."

"Kelly, you know I don't doctor. I only edit." Pit Bull was too excited over the footage to take umbrage at the implied slur on his integrity.

"You've never lied to me." Kelly backed up to the nearest wall. "My legs don't seem to be steady. Give me a minute."

Kord had no such issues. "I knew it! I knew it! Pit Bull, you totally have to edit this for my Shady Side presentation. It'll knock their socks off!" He danced around them in the little space. "Oh, yeah. Oh, yeah, Kord has proof of a Whiteboard ghost. Dad, can we get into the big time with this? Can we?"

Kelly reined in her son. "Kord, regardless of what you want to present to Shady Side Academy, it is past ten o'clock and you have school tomorrow."

"Aw, Mom, can't I skip? I've experienced severe personal trauma tonight. I need time to recover." He turned the Kanning Smile on her.

"You, young man, are a weasel. Get in the car now without arguing and we can discuss it on the way home."

"Cool! I'll get my coat." He ran off.

Kelly looked around. "Ms. Driscoll, where's the psychologist Mary was talking with?"

Giulia pointed out Olivier, back in his complete costume.

"Right. Vegeta. Thank you. One of Kord's parents needs to take care of his mental and physical health."

Giulia shut everyone out and unfocused her eyes on the crushed doll. Nothing appeared above it. She turned her unfocused gaze on the kitchen as a whole and saw it: a Marie Antoinette doll with moving eyes, in the midst of a hanging basket with artificial fruit. She'd have to tell Haley Comette.

"Giulia," Ken Kanning said, "now do you see how well we work together? We could..." He trailed off and held out his hand. "Thank you. You saved my son's life tonight."

Giulia took it. "I was happy to do it."

Kanning nodded. "I'll be by tomorrow to pay your bill."

"Thursday. We're closed tomorrow."

"I may sleep in myself. Thursday then." He straightened his shoulders. "Come on, Bull. Let's finish up here." He said to the guests still in the kitchen, "*The Scoop* would love to hear your reactions to tonight's amazing entertainment. Who'd like a chance to be on our show?"

Fifteen hands shot into the air.

Pit Bull said to Giulia as he passed her, "I saw it with my own eyes this time. You've got to teach me how to do it for myself. I'll call you."

Frank took possession of her. "Did I see Ken Kanning without his mask?"

"You did. It was unnerving."

"He should kiss your feet."

Giulia pecked him on the nose. "That would be even more unnerving. It was almost worth getting strangled by a ghost to shut Ken Kanning up." She saw Kelly walk out of the kitchen. "Sidney, Zane, Olivier, Dru Ann?"

Frank stopped her. "No, it was not worth it."

"Your inner Neanderthal is showing again."

They gathered in the pantry. Giulia opened the seed packet in front of them all.

Frank's voice thinned. *"Cac naofa."*

"Dear, you are sometimes predictable."

Zane said something in Estonian. Frank said, "Please tell me that was 'holy shit.'"

"It was." In a small voice.

Sidney said, "Count it? Please?"

Zane said, "We don't have to. Brown is five thousand dollars. Yellow is one thousand."

"Six grand." Awe filled Sidney's voice. "Can I touch it?"

"Fondle away." Giulia passed it around. "We haven't used up all of the retainer, so there will be bonuses this month." Giulia grinned. "Especially since we had extraordinary assistance from the Driscoll Investigation Emergency Squad."

Zane hooked his arm into Dru Ann's. "Darn right she's extraordinary. We are now going to celebrate our engagement by dancing."

"It was nice to meet you," Dru Ann said. "Helping solve a mystery is more fun than reading them."

Sidney pulled Olivier toward the music as well. "We're staying awhile, too. Why waste a night of babysitting?"

Giulia and Frank maneuvered through the hall. Frank snagged their coats. They ran to the car and turned the heater on full blast.

Frank grasped Giulia's hand.

"Let's go home," she said in a contented voice. "I'll call Rowan in the morning to have her teach me how to cast a protective circle. No ghost is going to contact me before noon on Thursday."

Frank said, "Did you forget we have a Finn-free night?"

Giulia snuggled down into the seat. "Sleep."

"Wait a minute..."

Alice Loweecey

Baker of brownies and tormenter of characters, Alice Loweecey recently celebrated her thirtieth year outside the convent. She grew up watching Hammer horror films and Scooby-Doo mysteries, which explains a whole lot. When she's not creating trouble for Giulia Driscoll, she can be found growing her own vegetables (in summer) and cooking with them (the rest of the year).

The Giulia Driscoll Mystery Series
by Alice Loweecey

Novels

NUN TOO SOON (#1)
SECOND TO NUN (#2)
NUN BUT THE BRAVE (#3)
THE CLOCK STRIKES NUN (#4)
NUN AFTER THE OTHER (#5)
BETTER THAN NUN (#6)

Short Stories

CHANGING HABITS
(prequel to NUN TOO SOON)

Henery Press Mystery Books

And finally, before you go...
Here are a few other mysteries
you might enjoy:

BOARD STIFF

Kendel Lynn

An Elliott Lisbon Mystery (#1)

As director of the Ballantyne Foundation on Sea Pine Island, SC, Elliott Lisbon scratches her detective itch by performing discreet inquiries for Foundation donors. Usually nothing more serious than retrieving a pilfered Pomeranian. Until Jane Hatting, Ballantyne board chair, is accused of murder. The Ballantyne's reputation tanks, Jane's headed to a jail cell, and Elliott's sexy ex is the new lieutenant in town.

Armed with moxie and her Mini Coop, Elliott uncovers a trail of blackmail schemes, gambling debts, illicit affairs, and investment scams. But the deeper she digs to clear Jane's name, the guiltier Jane looks. The closer she gets to the truth, the more treacherous her investigation becomes. With victims piling up faster than shells at a clambake, Elliott realizes she's next on the killer's list.

Available at booksellers nationwide and online

Visit www.henerypress.com for details

LIVING THE VIDA LOLA

Melissa Bourbon

A Lola Cruz Mystery (#1)

Meet Lola Cruz, a fiery full-fledged PI at Camacho and Associates. Her first big case? A missing mother who may not want to be found. And to make her already busy life even more complicated, Lola's helping plan her cousin's quinceañera and battling her family and their old-fashioned views on women and careers. She's also reunited with the gorgeous Jack Callaghan, her high school crush whom she shamelessly tailed years ago and photographed doing the horizontal salsa with some other lucky girl.

Lola takes it all in stride, but when the subject of her search ends up dead, she has a lot more to worry about. Soon she finds herself wrapped up in the possibly shady practices of a tattoo parlor, local politics, and someone with serious—maybe deadly—road rage. But Lola is well-equipped to handle these challenges. She's a black-belt in kung fu, and her body isn't her only weapon. She's got smarts, sass, and more tenacity than her Mexican mafioso-wannabe grandfather. A few of her famous margaritas don't hurt, either.

Available at booksellers nationwide and online

Visit www.henerypress.com for details

MURDER AT THE PALACE

Margaret Dumas

A Movie Palace Mystery (#1)

Welcome to the Palace movie theater! Now Showing: Philandering husbands, ghostly sidekicks, and a murder or two.

When Nora Paige's movie-star husband leaves her for his latest co-star, she flees Hollywood to take refuge in San Francisco at the Palace, a historic movie theater that shows the classic films she loves. There she finds a band of misfit film buffs who care about movies (almost) as much as she does.

She also finds some shady financial dealings and the body of a murdered stranger. Oh, and then there's Trixie, the lively ghost of a 1930's usherette who appears only to Nora and has a lot to catch up on. With the help of her new ghostly friend, can Nora catch the killer before there's another murder at the Palace?

Available at booksellers nationwide and online

Visit www.henerypress.com for details

FIXIN' TO DIE

Tonya Kappes

A Kenni Lowry Mystery (#1)

Kenni Lowry likes to think the zero crime rate in Cottonwood, Kentucky is due to her being sheriff, but she quickly discovers the ghost of her grandfather, the town's previous sheriff, has been scaring off any would-be criminals since she was elected. When the town's most beloved doctor is found murdered on the very same day as a jewelry store robbery, and a mysterious symbol ties the crime scenes together, Kenni must satisfy her hankerin' for justice by nabbing the culprits.

With the help of her Poppa, a lone deputy, and an annoyingly cute, too-big-for-his-britches State Reserve officer, Kenni must solve both cases and prove to the whole town, and herself, that she's worth her salt before time runs out.

Available at booksellers nationwide and online

Visit www.henerypress.com for details